Irene González Frei is a pseudonym. The author is from Latin America. At the time she wrote this novel she was a student, resident in Rome. She works as a translator.

'[*Your Name Written on Water*] sheds plenty of light on the nature of narcissism and desire' *The Times*

'In its scenes beats the heart of Miller and Nin, but also, closer to the surface, there are echoes of Sade' *El Nais*

'A taut and agile novel . . . through the dual and singular love of Sofía and Marina, the author shows us that love, tenderness (and also its opposite) are the best erotic catalysts' *Cordoba*

Your Name Written On Water

An Erotic Novel

IRENE GONZÁLEZ FREI

Translated from the Spanish by Kristina Cordero

An *Abacus* Book

Originally published in the Spanish language as *Tu nombre escrito en el agua*
by Tusquets Editores, Barcelona, 1995
First published in Great Britain by Abacus in 2000
This edition published by Abacus in 2001

A CIP catalogue record for this book
is available from the British Library.

ISBN 0 349 11373 4

Printed and bound in Great Britain by
Clays Ltd, St Ives plc

Design by Laura Hammond Hough

Abacus
An imprint of
Time Warner Books UK
Brettenham House
Lancaster Place
London WC2E 7EN

www.TimeWarnerBooks.co.uk

For Marina who,

of all the people in this story,

is the only one whose name

I did not have the courage to change.

Your Name Written on Water

Part One

*W*herever you are now, Marina, don't ever think I've forgotten you. I still hold on to fragments, the vertigo of our love, in between the fissures of pain and grief. My body still trembles with the memory of your gentle hands, and the silence holds the sound of your voice. Every image that my memory rescues is a remnant of life for my eyes, eyes that are nothing without yours.

We were more than Sofía and Marina; I was you, and I will be you, once again.

At night, you visit me in my dreams, and I hate the sun because it separates us, it pulls you away from me. I lost you once, and I lose you every morning the sunlight reminds me of your gaping absence. And now, too late to experience it, I search for your name and your face in empty mirrors. I search for your features, which were so like my own, more identical even than those of a twin, and I want to seize again the watery reflection that one sees in Narcissus. But I find only secret voices, memories, shadows. I find the scent of Paradise and the ashes of glory.

He had two women, all to himself: Marina and I, tied to one another, face to face, naked. At his disposal. How could he not take advantage of the opportunity? He crossed the room in long strides, and then I lost sight of him.

We didn't care about what happened. I was underneath, my back against the bed, and Marina was on top of me. I could feel her pulse beating in mine. A double handcuff of thin leather straps held my left wrist to her right and her left wrist to my right. He had also tied us up at the ankles, so we were positioned like two people ready to be torn apart, or ready to make love. Our legs wide open and arms raised high, every part of my body corresponded with its exact opposite in hers, Marina's body, from our legs up to our hands.

I tried to sit up, but the weight of her body pressed me against the mattress, and I realized that I couldn't move more than a few centimeters. The clasp of the handcuffs tied our ankles and wrists to the bedpost. There was no way out; we would remain in that position for as long as he wanted. Yet again, I thought, yet again. But at least I'm not alone.

I looked for Marina's lips, and found them behind a light, short breath. I placed mine against them. At first, I didn't notice the hot dampness of her mouth — first I felt the arousing, unmistakable taste of her lipstick. I tasted it, traveling with my tongue through the soft surface of her upper lip, through the juncture into the middle, and then to the other side, and the lower lip. My tongue made its way and felt the small vertical cracks that the makeup had passed over. Her mouth, then, was as warm as my own and we slid into our kiss, which tasted of blood. She looked at me, her black eyes locked into mine, and the look we shared held the message that our love united us beyond all circumstance.

I opened my mouth to receive her tongue, the first woman's tongue that had ever been introduced into my woman's mouth. It was the first and only to cross the boundary that separated me from the most intense passion of my life, to caress the irregular lines of my palate and play in the peaks and narrow passes of my teeth before returning to the curve of my gums. She drove her pubis so I could feel the now unreachable heat of her sex against mine, and I filled my lungs with air so my breasts could transmit to hers the pleasure I would feel with her on top of me, despite everything. We entwined our fingers, and the contact we made was perfect, just like our love, like a mirror reflection of one another. We had managed to abstract ourselves from the world around us, to rise up onto the island of our union in the middle of all the storms of that uncertain ocean that was waiting for us. We were nothing but our embrace and her sex and our intertwined hands and my breasts.

'Sofía,' she murmured, and I had trouble recognizing her voice; it was nothing but a whisper, with no ring to it, no strength. 'Sofía, I love you.' And then the sweet tone of her voice opened up and made its way to my ears.

'And I love you,' I said, kissing her again. The water in our mouth said more than our voices could.

Her pulse accelerated, and I raised my pelvis in an effort to bridge the distance that separated us.

Right at that moment, he returned. He was naked now. His penis was hanging, limp and inert, like some kind of atrophied appendage. He'd gone out for a drink, which I realized afterward, when his breath assaulted me. His ribs protruded from under his skin. I couldn't quite understand the expression on his face. Kneeling against the bed, he contemplated us for a while, almost as if he didn't know what was going to happen in the next few moments, either. Then he opened his hand and wrapped it around the back of Marina's neck. I thought he was going to hang her, but instead, he caressed her, a long, slow ecstatic caress down her back. I tilted my head to observe him through the little window created between Marina's arm and mine, beneath our armpits. Now he was caressing her ass, but his hand quickly lowered to the outside of her thighs, the backs of her knees, her calves, and that smooth, curved ridge that I've touched so many times.

Then I felt the tips of his fingers touch my body, gripping my ankle and the leather strip that rendered me immobile. The three of us remained there, in the confusion created by gasps of desire and fear. Then, his hand resumed action, but in the opposite direction. It now moved up, touching both of us at the same time: calves, the backs of our knees, continuing (he wasn't going to stop) to the inside of our thighs. And then, naturally, he reached our sexes, my own and Marina's. They were damp from our earlier contact and our kisses, hot like his fingers. Two sexes all for him, one on top of the other, for his hand only, his hand that climbed and descended like music, and made its way between lips before finally reaching the most delicate, smooth flesh within.

He introduced a finger inside me, very slowly. It was his index finger, and once it reached as far as it would go, he pressed it upward. I realized he was doing the same thing to Marina with his ring finger, because I felt the resistance of her abdomen, which fell as mine rose, and his two fingers tried to find each other through the obstacle of our two bodies.

Marina unfurled her tongue and licked me behind the ear. I turned to look at her, so she might kiss me again. Our lips had barely brushed against each other when he grabbed Marina by the hair and jerked her head up. This time, he wasn't violent with her.

'No,' he said. 'No kissing for you two. I'm the one who makes the rules today.'

He stood up. I could see his prick was stiff now. He rummaged in the closet, came up with two handkerchiefs, and then gagged us. He tied them firmly, around our open mouths, and that was when I smelled the alcohol on his breath. He had been able to rob us of the comfort of kissing, but the penetrating looks we shared were ours, and he couldn't take that away. And even if he'd blindfolded us, I still would have been able to communicate with Marina. I could feel the rhythm of her heartbeat on the right side of my chest, her breaths that seemed to be in search of air, the sweat of her palm against mine, the light fuzz that brushed against my skin. We were tied up as if we were one person, and we were. I bit into the handkerchief, but my incisors weren't able to find each other and close completely.

He stood there for a few moments. With the five fingers of his right hand he encircled his penis and started to masturbate, while controlling the resistance of our ties with his left hand. Then, continuing to caress himself, he knelt down on the bed again, between my open legs, between Marina's open legs. He separated the cheeks of her behind and leaned on top of her. I knew he was looking straight into the thin orifice that was her anus. He licked it, covering it with saliva. I could tell because I felt it drip onto my sex in thick, warm droplets. Then he raised his prick and put both hands on Marina, one on each cheek, and separated them. He nestled his prick in between them, and I thought he would penetrate her, but he didn't. He simply closed her ass around his penis and swayed back and forth, up and down.

But that wasn't enough for him. He pulled out from Marina's ass and began to lick it again. Then he wet his fingers in his mouth and brushed them against my ass, dampening me, moving up toward my sex. I felt the tickle of the hairs that stuck to my skin. He wet his fingers again and instead of touching me on the outside, he introduced a finger in my anus, undeterred by my grimace of pain, as far as it would go. Then he removed it and prepared to fuck us.

I saw Marina's eyes shut for a moment and then open again to look at me. It was about to be the first time a man would ever penetrate her. We had discussed this topic many times before — we'd even planned it — and now it was about to happen.

He placed his hands high up underneath my thighs, almost on my ass, and raised me up about twenty centimeters. With that movement, my clitoris met Marina's sex and remained there in the air, for one sudden, unexpected moment of pleasure. Then the hot flesh of his prick penetrated me from behind, surging forward slowly, breaking the resistance of my contracted muscles. The pain was intolerable, and I had to bend my knees as much as I could (which wasn't much) and let Marina's legs fall in between my own; otherwise his prick might have destroyed my rectum. The pain was intolerable, in the beginning. But then, when it was completely inside, I felt a sense of relief. I begged him not to take it out, not to ever take it out because I knew I would suffer again when he removed it. It would be like taking off a tight glove; he would rub his penis against my dry, irritated skin. Nevertheless, he did it. After two or three attacks which bore into my bowels, he removed his prick with a flourish and went looking for Marina. He pushed my thighs downward, to get Marina and me on the exact same level. She pressed her hand against mine, and through her straining fingertips I could sense the exact moment he penetrated her. It had happened, finally.

Without freeing my thighs, he shook us up, so we would wiggle and tremble around his prick. I stretched my legs again. The ties had begun to chafe against the skin of my ankles. But he didn't realize, or else he didn't care. He just wanted to continue with his game: two women all for him and four orifices waiting for his next move. He exited Marina's vagina, stretched out over her body, covering her like a shadow, and then fucked her up the ass. She let out a wail, but it was drowned out by the gag in her mouth, and right then the pressure from her hand hurt me more than the straps and ties all over my body. But I didn't say a thing, because I loved being able to console her, to be the last resort in her desperation, the shrub that she could cling to on the ledge of the precipice, before her inevitable fall. Her eyes, their gaze fixed on my face, filled with tears.

Now I had two bodies pressing against me and I couldn't breathe.

He found his way to my sex, then back to Marina's anus, Marina's sex, and my anus, one after the other. Each time he did it faster, without any particular order or rhythm to his movements. He tied and untied me, placing us where he wanted to, at whim, and he would occasionally fall to his knees or stand up in order to find just the right angle of penetration. He would hop from one orifice to the other as if he were jumping on stones in order to cross a river. It was as if he wanted to slow down, to hold back that moment when he'd finally reach the other side of the river, so he kept going back over the same stones, he went forward and backward – an anus, Marina, a vagina, me – until he couldn't contain himself any longer and finally reached the other side. He was with me when he began to tremble, inside my anus, and I could feel the hot whirlpool rising within me, his spasms, the final charge through the tip of his prick and the very bottom of my rectum. And then he released his hold on my ass, and fell on top of me and Marina as he came, his penis still inside me as he reveled in the last quivers of his orgasm. He extinguished it slowly, and with the satisfied smile on his humid lips he offered Marina and me first an insult and then a curse.

The day I saw Marina for the very first time, a series of premonitions indicated to me that my life was about to change. They seemed like coincidences, but they created this dark intuition inside me that something extraordinary was going to happen. The first sign came to me in a dream. I was standing at the entrance of a deserted cathedral, from which I heard an unknown voice urgently calling my name. I went inside. Two rows of identical columns led to a blinding light. With that peculiar logic that exists in the realm of dreams, I knew for certain that the light and the voice calling after me were one and the same thing. As I walked toward it, the light slowly ebbed and transformed into a mirror, which returned my gaze with a perfect replica of myself. I was walking through the mirror as if it were a door when I woke up, filled with an inexplicable kind of happiness. How could I know that just then I had received the announcement of my imminent encounter with Marina? Like most people, I was vain enough to think myself unique. The idea seemed unthinkable – that somewhere, there was someone who was my exact double. Not to mention that I would actually meet her, kiss her, and then finally fall in love with her. Still drowsy, I lifted my hands to touch my image, the image I still thought was before my eyes. But in reality all I touched was the sleeping body of Santiago, who rolled over in the tangle of sheets to hug me. My breath quickened; that must have alarmed him.

'What's wrong, Sofía?' he said in a thick voice. 'Did you have a nightmare?'

I didn't answer. I felt his penis, already stiff, pressing against my body. I jumped up from the bed and felt my way into the kitchen, taking slow, indecisive steps. I was afraid to look in the mirror, afraid that it would break the spell of the dream, that I would find a transparent pane of glass that didn't reflect my image back to me. It couldn't have been later than six. The night had begun to turn yellow in the dawning sky. I knew I wouldn't return to sleep.

I stood in front of the kitchen window for a while, looking out at the city, asleep during that uncertain hour when the eternal battle between light and darkness finds a moment of perfect equilibrium. Before I married Santiago, early morning was my favorite time of day, the most indiscreet hour, when people on their way to work cross paths with people who still haven't gone to bed, the 'already' awake and the 'still' awake. It's the hour when priests, bricklayers, doormen, and tailors walk shoulder to shoulder with hookers, drunks, transvestites, and gigolos. The moment when Madrid is at its most beautiful, as if no one had ever touched it before, it was able to make even a foreigner like me feel as if I belonged, by promising a different, better life than before. But the inevitable, downward passage of time strips away your illusions, one by one, with overwhelming force. And then you return to the environment of routine, the net of familiar, comforting habits. Until that moment arrives, morning feels full of things like adventure and risk, and the inexplicable sense of destiny in which anything is possible.

Although it hadn't been erotic, the dream of the cathedral left my whole body aching with an unidentifiable desire. I was practically naked, barefoot. The lightest contact – a hand on my thigh, an arm above my breasts, one lip against another – would be enough to provoke the warm trembling that ran up my spine and squeezed the deepest part of me. I wanted to separate myself from that urgent sensuality. The best thing to do, I knew, would be to go back to bed, wake up Santiago, plaster myself against him to feel once again those inevitable signs of his virility, suck him off, wait with open legs to feel the force of his sex inside of mine, and bury my uncertainty with the weight of his body and forget about my dream forever. But I didn't move. Mysterious as the luminous voice of the dream, something inside of me asked me not to. So I stood there contemplating the city through the windowpane.

Without realizing it, I began to caress myself. At first my movements were slow and involuntary, mere brushes that little by little increased my desire, just the way the dawn slowly looms over the night. My stroking gained momentum until it became a deliberate frenzy, and the sound of my breathing excited me even more, as did my hands: on my breasts, on my stomach, taking off my bikinis and stirring up my pubis, warm and expectant. All of a sudden, I interrupted myself. An unexpected wave of scruples stopped me from fully releasing my pleasure. I then asked myself: Is it possible that no one but myself is capable of fully satisfying me? That only my own body understands the size and shape of my desires?

But at that precise moment, the sun appeared in between the roofs of the houses outside, opening a resplendent crack through the space outside, illuminating me with its still-immaculate light. And then my face appeared before me just like in the dream, reflected in the window glass, slightly obscured by my dark hair but otherwise awash with clarity, and I saw my calm smile in the glass. My desires discovered themselves free of impediments and once again I found myself in my dream.

I was standing with my legs open, on tiptoe, almost in the air, as if trying to rise above and beyond myself and my ferocious pleasure. I put my hand on my organ, now free, and my fingers worked their way through the warm down resting against my panties. They paused at the clitoris, the labia, looking for a shortcut through the abyss of my organ, going deeper, deeper, deeper, skidding off either wall and at the same time advancing forward between two rows of identical columns, searching for the calm pools of water that Narcissus peered into, in search of the core of the core of my being, beaten by the debilitating storms of desire and premonition. Just as I did in my dream, I sensed that my fingers were my fingers and something else besides, something much deeper and happier and truer, and in my sex, the storms were in fact my reflection in the glass, broken in pieces. And my own naked body was feverish, both in the flesh and in my reflection, the reflection that levitated me against my will and carried me to the highest kind of pleasure where all things are possible: dawns and tempests, my own hands and those of others, prostitutes and priests, my kiss meeting my kiss on the windowpane, light and darkness, the breath from my silent moans, my adored and adoring organ, the dawn, the core of the core, the premonitions, my breasts in the fire of my own breasts and the mirrors, and the love between two identical bodies that, together, reach a single orgasm.

That day, little omens nagged at me all day long. I threw on a
light dress and a pair of low-heeled shoes and then went down
to the street, without saying anything to Santiago. At a café
downstairs, I ate breakfast: café con leche and hot churros. I had
almost an hour before I had to be at work, so I decided to wait,
like a criminal waiting for his next victim. I felt as if the morning were mine, all mine, and I wanted to feel it on my skin, still
tight from the memory of my solitary, double pleasure earlier
that morning. My body retained the memory, in a way much
more intense and deep than any figurative image my mind's eye
was able to produce.

The day's first sunlight sparkled on the pavement, where a
woman, slow and drowsy, washed the entranceway to a building.
Her movements possessed something of the sublime: it seemed
that behind them, and behind the brilliance of the water, and
behind the anxieties within my own body, a signal was hidden,
a fugitive sign that was the key that would somehow help me to
figure out what the hell was happening to me. I felt as if someone had put me under a spell, as if I were just one step away
from making that leap which would give me that key and explain
all this. It was a leap that I had to make with my trembling body,
now free of all thoughts and ideas, with nothing else inside.

The premonition was then interrupted.

'Señorita, Señorita!' A man was at my side.

I waited a while before looking at him. I blinked a few times,
and unwillingly returned to the real world. He looked a good
fifty years old, with limp strands of oily, dirty black hair. He
wore a tight gray suit, as if he wanted to give the impression that
there just didn't exist clothing capable of hiding his kind of

muscles. He wasn't unattractive, exactly, but on top of his high cheekbones and sharp nose, he had the kind of glassy eyes that warned you not to trust him with too much.

'You should be careful,' he added, mawkishly, and then he lowered his voice. 'There are too many dangerous individuals roaming around these days.'

He pointed to an old man, visibly disoriented in a corner of the café. His head nodded about in a dream state, and it was clear that the sun had caught him right in the middle of a drunken stupor. He wasn't even aware that someone had just targeted him as a potential aggressor, a savage criminal. His only activity was to hiccup, with short, adolescent spasms.

'If you'll allow me to accompany you . . .' the man said.

'No, I won't. I don't allow it,' I answered, and walked toward the exit, but he grabbed my arm.

'Let go of me!'

'Don't forget what I said to you.'

'Let go of me,' I repeated.

'All right, as you wish.' He released me. 'But be careful.'

I left the bar and wandered through the streets, trying to recover that moment of imminent revelation, but I couldn't. My mental effort was taking me further and further away from my emotions. A cool breeze blew, in slow gusts. It was the beginning of May and had just recently begun to get hot. At that hour, however, the sun wasn't at its full strength.

For Holy Week, Santiago and I had gone up to Santander. No sooner had we arrived than it began to rain, in buckets, and it continued for practically the entire time we were there. Of course, that didn't prevent Santiago from stubbornly clinging to his habit of taking photos like a maniac, even though the results would obviously be utterly awful. His photographs were always blurry, poorly focused, always catching things in mid-motion.

I decided to pick up our pictures from the trip; the girl at the photo shop had promised them for that morning. Each image bore the mark of Santiago's unmistakable photographic style: either the camera was tilted at an angle, or he'd cut off my head and legs, or he'd snapped a photo of my back, from far away. This time, his typical incompetence had reached new heights, almost miraculous proportions. How could it be that even with something as basic and majestic as the sea, he could manage to make it look blurry and unfocused? As I looked closer, I noticed there was another problem with the photos that couldn't be blamed on Santiago, but rather on the person who developed them, or perhaps on chance, or fate. For the two photographs in which I appeared alone, in the foreground, there was an identical copy. Among the grainy vistas of the empty beach, the cloudy sky, and the crashing surf was an image of me superimposed on top. I studied the negatives, but the phenomenon only manifested itself in the prints and not in the film. The girl behind the counter wasn't able to offer any explanation.

At five to nine, I reached the gallery. I flicked on the light and sat down at my desk. The paintings spied on me from the walls like imperfect ghosts, imprisoned in the jail cells of their wooden frames. The artist on exhibition was Manolo Díaz Mendoza, a young abstract painter whose vague images began to take shape as my imagination sketched outlines for them. I contemplated the two double-exposed photos in front of me. I began to think that maybe they didn't reveal the dark but rather the visible side of my life, the one side that really exists. It was as if they proved me to be a basically incomplete person, nothing more than a façade.

The phone rang. It was Santiago.

'Are you all right?' he asked.

'Fine.' What else was I supposed to say? 'Why do you ask?'

'Because you left without waking me. I've been waiting around for you all morning. I thought you were coming back.' From his tone of voice, I could tell that he was trying not to reproach me. Ever since Laura's death, Santiago had had to shrug off my little acts of defiance and resign himself to my taciturn, cool attitude toward him. It wasn't easy for him.

'Well, nothing's wrong. I'm fine,' I said.

'Sofía,' he added. 'I love you.'

I remained silent.

'Did you hear me?' he asked.

'Yes.'

He hesitated a moment, and I could hear his breathing at the other end of the line, and then, with forced enthusiasm, he suggested to me:

'If you want, we could go to the movies this evening.'

'I don't know.'

'Think about it. I'll see you later on tonight. Okay?' he asked, at last.

'Okay.' I hung up.

I washed my face, made myself a cup of coffee, and put the photos away. I called the gallery owner, as I did every day, and told her that there was nothing new to report, and I spoke with people who stopped in. I was attempting to re-create the regular rhythm of my life, with all the certainties and tedium that normally went with it, when Manolo, the painter, walked in, and brought with him the premonition which was the crowning moment of that most disturbing morning.

'Do you remember the story of Orbaneja, the painter from Ubeda?'

'No.'

'Where did you go to school, lady? It's one of the stories by Cervantes, in *Don Quixote*.'

'I don't remember it,' I said. 'If you want to tell me, fine. If not, leave my memory and my education out of it.'

'Sofía, come on,' Manolo said. He carried a package, wrapped up in pages from the newspaper. It looked like a piece of artwork. 'You woke up in a bad mood today, didn't you? Yesterday at the opening, you were radiant. But today . . .'

Manolo was about thirty-four, with a very white face and sunken eyes, ringed by a perpetual halo of dark circles. He tended to stay up all night, and rarely went to bed before nine in the morning. He didn't have a twirly, stylized mustache, and he didn't wear eccentric clothing, and he didn't create dramas of studiously orchestrated chaos, or do any of the things modern artists supposedly do. He lived for his art, and he was a sensitive, understanding kind of person. I think both of us felt we could have loved one another, maybe not in such a passionate way but certainly in a deep, lasting way – that is, if the circumstances in which we'd met had been different. And with that sadness caused by potential lives never lived, we also realized that we weren't in a time or place to become great friends, either. At that moment, though, I decided he was just the right person to listen to me. I wanted to relieve my anxiety with someone who didn't know me well; that way, I wouldn't have to give a blow-by-blow account of every detail that was happening with me. I didn't care that he was a man. I didn't have any women friends left, anyway.

'I had a bad night last night,' I said, to start my confession in a normal, typical way.

I recounted to him my dream about the cathedral. Manolo's face grew paler than I'd ever seen it, practically white, if that had been possible. He shook off the papers covering the painting he'd brought with him into the gallery, and showed me the piece. It was a portrait of me. It wasn't a figurative painting, no . . . the figure was shadowy, difficult to make out. Like in a dream. On either side were two converging groups of vertical lines, which gave the impression of a long series of columns.

'When did you do this?' I sputtered.

'Last night, when I went home.'

We were silent, shocked by the coincidence. I'm very super-stitious – when I accidentally brush against the dark world of the supernatural (that is, what I assume to be supernatural) I tend to overlook it and act like it didn't happen. I didn't want to talk about myself anymore, so I changed the subject.

'What are you doing awake at this hour? For you, noon is like the middle of the night.'

'Well, a reporter called me,' he said, with that arbitrary dis-dain that he always used when describing people of certain professions, like psychoanalysts, publicists, dentists, and, of course, reporters. 'She's always calling me, this one, always inviting me to such horrible places. Her house, this time. Last night she called me so many times that I figured there had to have been some disaster, so I actually picked up the phone. And you know how much I hate the telephone – with good reason!

Those things don't do anything but cause trouble . . . like that journalist.' I had to hold in my laughter at his agitation.

'She told me she wanted "to ask some questions" that were "left over" from last night at the opening. You tell me, what could possibly be "left over" from last night?'

'So what did you say, then?'

'The exact opposite of what I really think – on purpose, of course. As revenge. But I couldn't go to sleep after that, so here I am.'

'Well, I have a question left over from last night, too,' I said.

'God have mercy! Is this some kind of conspiracy?' He was only joking, but then he puffed out his chest, as protection against imaginary missiles to be fired at him, and said:

'All right. Give me the question. I'm ready for anything.'

'What does Cervantes have to do with the painting?' I pointed to the portrait.

'You're right! I almost forgot!' Manolo exclaimed.

'Of course you did. You're still asleep.'

'Well, this is the story. Orbaneja, the painter from Ubeda, was such a bad painter that if he painted a chicken, he'd have to write "This is a chicken" in big Gothic letters underneath it. And when they asked him what he was painting, he'd say, "Whatever comes out."'

We laughed. Manolo's presence always made me feel better.

'Well, all right,' he said, rubbing his black-ringed eyes. 'That's exactly what occurred to me with this portrait. I wanted to create something abstract, but what came out of me, instead, was you.'

I could lie, or exaggerate, that morning's coincidences, or invent more premonitions, but I'm writing for you, Marina,

for you to hear me from your silence, and you know that that
was the whole story, those were the signals that fortune, or
providence, or your love, still in its infancy, sent to me, with
the intention of announcing the revolution that was about to
demolish the last vestiges of my former life. 'There's no such
thing as coincidence,' you once said, with a smile to soften the
impact of your statement. 'The happiness of two souls can't be
set free simply by chance.' And I believed you. Why shouldn't
I have? We were at the height of our intimacy, and the wind
coming off the sea cooled our intertwined bodies. That same
night, a balmy summer night on the Gulf of Naples, we made
the pact. The hotel had aristocratic illusions about itself, and
was called the Hotel Royal. The bathroom was almost as big as
the bedroom, the furniture was gilt-edged, and the walls were
papered with magnolias, pheasants, temples, and willows. You
and I were stretched out on a bed under a canopy, but none of
it mattered much to us. I was sketching the humid strokes of
my tongue across your naked belly, moving up toward the tip of
your breasts. I stopped at your trembling nipples and then fell
back down to your navel, wandering slowly, occasionally stopping, to lick the curve of your hips, to kiss the lips of your sex
with my own burning lips, to slip my tongue into that inviting
cavity. My tongue, which seemed to have been made just for
that purpose, still held the taste of your skin on its surface. I
could feel your heartbeat in the abyss of your sex as I rubbed
my face against it, filled my mouth with its humid wetness,
breathed in its air to draw deep inside my lungs. With those
warm drops I could fill the space in my eyes that once held
tears, and then hear your whispered words of love as you came
on my tongue and then hear my own as I dissolved in your

hands. But those words were not enough and we made the pact, the pact that I will never dare to break. These are our truths and we can't change them. And now that both you and I have been expelled from the paradise of our happiness, I refuse to lie: I don't want to lose you again. You no longer live in anything but the reality of my memory, and it's so painful, so Clara, and so very little.

The moment Manolo finished his sentence, the man in the gray suit, the one who had been bothering me at the café, walked into the gallery. Manolo assumed he was a visitor like any other, and whispered to me under his breath:

'Don't tell him I'm the painter.'

Right away, Manolo planted himself in front of his paintings, pretending to look at them with mild disinterest. That was the way he was: incorrigibly timid and humble. That particular idiosyncrasy of his was amusing, even though it required me to work wonders at all of his shows in order to sell his pieces.

But the man in the gray suit had no interest in paintings, which he made obvious a moment later. Without even looking at the artwork on display, he turned to me.

'How are you?' he asked, nailing me with his glassy eyes. 'I hope you haven't ignored my advice.'

'You followed me.'

'No, miss. What makes you think that?' asked the man in gray, stroking his greasy hair. 'I work two doors down from here. I went out for lunch and I saw you from outside—'

'What do you want?' I interrupted him. This guy was irritating, with his almost professional air and that good-Samaritan, concerned-for-my-fellow-man ploy.

'Well, now that you've put it that way.' He rubbed his hands together. 'And seeing as how it's such a lovely day outside . . .'

Manolo had stopped playing his game of studying his paintings, and was now looking at us.

'I . . . I wanted to invite you, miss, to go swimming with me,' said the man in gray.

'Swimming?' Manolo and I had to control ourselves not to start laughing out loud.

'I know of a public pool, outdoors, only about fifteen minutes from Madrid,' said the man, shrugging his shoulders. Nothing seemed to shake his obstinate insistence. 'We could have lunch there, take in some sun, then come back . . .'

Like an agent of destiny, the man had just finished saying the words that would bring me to you for the first time, Marina. But how was I to know that, then?

'I'm married,' I answered, 'And—'

'Don't misinterpret my intentions!' he exclaimed hurriedly.

'I don't care what your intentions are. I'm just asking you to leave me alone.'

The man looked at Manolo, hoping for some fraternal support.

'You're the witness, sir,' he said. 'Not once have I shown disrespect to this young lady.'

But Manolo wasn't on his side.

'You heard what she said.' He limited himself to that observation. 'It's best if you leave.'

The man in the gray suit garbled out a ceremonious farewell and then walked out. Before leaving, however, he stopped at the front door. Without either of us asking him, almost as a threat, he informed us:

'My name is Carranza.' And he disappeared in the crowds on the street.

In spite of it all, the man in the gray suit had a point. It was far too sunny to go to some dank, crowded restaurant where I'd have to eat standing up with people ready to rub up against me, push and spill beer all over my dress, and with waiters eyeing me, silently urging me to finish my meal and get out of their way.

'What do you think of going to a pool for lunch?' I asked Manolo. 'I have a couple of hours free. We could go, just the two of us, alone.'

'That sounds like a terrible plan.' He dropped his hand as if he were swatting a fly. 'Doesn't grab me at all.'

'Well, don't think I'm trying to seduce you,' I responded, stupidly.

'I hope not. I've known your husband much longer than I've known you.'

It was true. They had met when they were in school, study-ing advertising. Manolo had been looking for a job that would earn him some money. He'd been coerced into it by his parents, who didn't want to see him fall prey to the typical artist's poverty. He soon realized that advertising didn't suit him and stopped going. Luckily, things didn't work out so badly for him as an artist. Santiago, on the other hand, finished the program and now was working as a commercial artist at a second-rate advertising agency. Manolo had been one of the witnesses at our wedding.

'No, you're not the problem. It's the sun,' Manolo added. 'I hate it; it makes me drowsy, stupid. Like I'm wasting time.

And pools: they're just like all those other places where you have to pay a fee in order to have fun. They're filled with people who can only have fun by paying for it. You know: pedicurists, dentists, lawyers, travel agents——'

'Oh, please! Don't start again with that speech of yours,' I interrupted him. 'I'll go myself.'

'I'm telling you, you're going to hate it. You'll end up sick from the experience. But go ahead, do what you want,' he said.

I placed Manolo's portrait of me behind the desk. I said good-bye to him, closed the gallery, and walked back home. I found the bathing suit I'd taken to Santander for Easter vacation, and put it in my bag. I'd never even used it, on account of the rainy weather, and it still smelled like gasoline. I got into my car, an old Seat Marbella, headed up the Paseo de la Castellana, and left the city behind.

I remembered having seen a sign advertising a swimming pool along the Madrid-Burgos highway, when we were stuck in the tourist traffic and Santiago had taken advantage of the time to take photographs of some gypsy shanties along the side of the road. For some ridiculous reason, the name of the pool stuck in my head: the Torrid Tropics. I stopped at a gas station, filled the tank, and continued driving.

On the radio they were playing old boleros, the same ones that always reminded my mother of my father, and allowed her to cry, long and hard. Songs like 'Ojos negros,' 'Perfidia,' 'Obsesión,' and another whose name I didn't know, but which always fascinated me: 'Fuse your voice with mine/to call out our victory/and if love is a sin/then the Heavens can explain/because the feeling is divine.' At the time, I didn't think of it as an omen of what was to come, because it didn't make me think of my father, but of Santiago. He used to sing it to me, with huge gestures, one hand on his chest and the other raised up high, like someone begging for change, exaggerating the South American pronunciation, and looking off into the distance. He sang it a lot before we were married. It was his way of dealing with the remorse we both felt as a result of our own love story. It was a classic episode of youthful betrayal, with a drama and complexity that in retrospect are kind of amusing, although at the time it was pretty traumatic.

It all started because of punctuality. Or the lack of it. I wasn't even twenty-one years old, and I'd been living in Madrid for two years, dating a man considerably older than myself, with a name of biblical proportions, a theological statement in and of itself: Juan Marcos Lucas Mateo. Mateo, in fact, was his last name. To make things easier, his friends called him Pulga, 'the Flea,' a nickname that stuck. He was the kind of man who was comfortable living in the midst of decadent neglect. He had a perpetual scruffiness about him, although he was never grimy. His clothes were disgusting, his hair was a mess, and his beard was usually at least a couple of days old. His eyeglasses were held together by a tiny piece of electrician's tape wrapped around the bridge. He definitely had lice. His apartment was a dump, littered with empty beer bottles, dirty clothing, and pornographic magazines. The utter indolence with which he lived was exactly what prevented him from ever doing anything to arrest the spiraling growth of the clutter, which almost seemed like a force of its own, controlled not by Pulga but rather by destiny. He was such a lazy slob that many times when we fucked, I had to get on top of him because he just couldn't be bothered.

'You do the work, toots,' he would say. 'You're still young.'

And he would tumble back into his chair, with his feet propped up on a teetering pile of magazines. I'd have to undress him, taking his clothing off bit by bit, like you would a drunk, or a sleeping child. I'd leave his eyeglasses on, deliberately, and place the plants on the floor. And then, I'd slowly awaken his penis, always as tired as he was. I'd stroke it, then suck it until he would grace me with an acceptable erection. Then I would climb on top of him, balancing him between my legs so his penis wouldn't slide out – he couldn't even do that for himself. And I would rock and wiggle at just the right velocity so that he would begin to get excited, although not too excited – after all, I didn't want him to come too soon. Pulga masturbated, just like I did, but he was even lazy about that; he only exerted the very minimum effort required – puff, puff, and that was about it for him. Nevertheless, I liked exactly what he liked: watching me. He left me to my devices, and that aroused him more than anything. 'Touch yourself,' he would ask me, and then I, mounted on his prick, would have to touch myself I would brush one hand lightly over my breasts, and the other over my clitoris, and little by little Pulga's eyeglasses would slide off his face. It was kind of amusing, actually. I always enjoyed watching those little beads of drool falling from his lips. By that time, I would stop watching him as I continued touching myself, my hands sweeping across my body again and again until I reached orgasm. I would start shaking, harder now, and then two efficient little throbs was all it took for him to come, right along with me.

Pulga had a two-floor attic flat, which was actually two separate rooms connected by a small set of stairs, like the kind in a submarine. At one time, the top floor had been a bedroom, but living in the style that he did, the room inevitably reached the point in which one couldn't even enter it, and that was when Pulga made a truly inspired decision: he threw his mattress down the stairs and never went back up there. He assured me that when the bottom floor got the same way, he would leave everything as it was and pay for another place. I don't know why, but Pulga seemed to hope that I would wash the dishes and clean up his pigsty, at least a little, I suppose so he wouldn't have to actually fulfill that macho dare he'd put himself up to, of abandoning the place and finding another.

One afternoon, as we were watching television, he said to me:

'Sofía, in every relationship, there comes a moment when a true bond forms between the two people in question.' It's no great revelation that men who get involved with younger women – younger by a few days, even – fancy themselves responsible for the edification and intellectual formation of their mate, and to that end, tend to deliver lectures, usually academic and didactic in tone. I didn't listen to his lectures.

'Shut up,' I said. 'I want to see the movie.' A Wertmüller film was on TV.

'Sofía, this is important,' he insisted. 'Today I've taken the trouble – actually the pleasure, naturally – of making a copy of my house keys. They're for you.' And he added, solemnly, as if he were decorating me with a medal, 'Here you go. They're yours.'

I knew that the gesture didn't amount to much for him. All his friends had the keys to his little hovel. He gave them out left and right so he wouldn't have to get up and open the door when they came by. Moreover, I knew he was lying about the 'trouble' he'd gone to in copying the keys. Several months earlier he'd ordered a dozen copies, precisely to save himself the hassle of having to do it over and over again in the future. He barely even left the house to get take-out Chinese food or a videotape, or to scrounge money from his father, a printer who became rich when Franco died: he went from making lithographs of saints in ecstasy to making stickers of women, dressed in black leather, in ecstasy. To top it off, Pulga added:

'From now on, my home is your home.'

'Thank you,' I said. 'But I will never consider this pigsty any home of mine.'

'And seeing as how this is now your home,' he continued, pretending not to hear me, mainly because talking tended to tire him out, 'you can do whatever you'd like here. If you want to organize things a little, feel free to do it. If you want to clean things, go ahead and clean.'

I averted my gaze from the television screen, incredulous.

'Even if you want to . . . I don't know, hang a poster you like, feel free,' he finished, magnanimously.

'You know, in the life of every relationship,' I began, imitating his pomposity, 'there comes a moment in which it becomes time to hire a cleaning lady. If you were hoping I would be the one to fill that position, go fuck yourself.'

Before I could begin to regret what I had just said, I grabbed the cluster of keys dangling from his hands and resumed watching the movie.

When I was a child, my family led a rather nomadic life, moving from city to city, effectively 'insuring that I would never meet so-called nice people.' Despite this fact, my mother, the granddaughter of very strict Germans, never got used to seeing me in the company of men she never cared for – men of low caliber, as she would say. Sofi, the same thing that happened to me will happen to you . . . Don't trust them, she would warn me. She didn't leave me many options, though. Her experience had taught her to despise men who were dreamers, and also men who were exceedingly proper. That was why, I suppose, Pulga was the first boyfriend of mine that she could accept: he wasn't overly circumspect, and he came from a wealthy family. He was a balanced combination between the two extremes she hated so fiercely. Right in the middle. My poor mother. Before she died she made me promise I'd marry Pulga, and I agreed because she was sick and I wanted to make her happy, but I never had even the slightest intention of marrying at such a young age, much less with someone like Pulga.

It wasn't that I was opposed to the institution of marriage, either – exactly the opposite, in fact. In those days, I saw marriage as a rigorous, binding commitment, to be carried out only in the event of true, profound love. And at the time I was still on the lookout for the man of my dreams. With that feverish anxiety of illusions destined for frustration, I had long been searching for him: down the streets of countless cities, in high school, in casual flings, in sordid, exultant screws, in close friends, in the eyes of some stranger who caught my eye on a crowded street. Mine was a passion with no object, an absurd, obviously conceited pursuit. The idealized outer shell of what passion should be. It was an idea of love that I had created, and was focused entirely on myself. It took the shape of all my desires and the oscillation of all my uncertainties.

For that very reason, I finally and painfully realized that, until this point in my life, I was the only person capable of satisfying myself. And Pulga, of course, wasn't what I was looking for. His personality, his manner entertained me, but I wasn't in love with him, and I couldn't ever imagine sharing my life with him. On the other hand, I guess I wasn't much more than a diversion for him, either: the classic helpless, provincial young girl, lost in Madrid, who pretends to be carefree and with whom a man can amuse himself – that is, until she begins to become a bore. After all, Pulga's friends meant much more to him than I ever did.

Santiago was among those friends. I found him good-looking, but also a bit priggish. He hadn't really known very many women, which he liked to attribute to the high standards he set for himself. Of course, that didn't stop him from nagging me to set him up with my friends, which he either did in the most brusque, nonchalant way or else as if he were doing it to satisfy my own (nonexistent) pleas. I didn't think it was such a good idea, so I refused at first, but then gave in, realizing that another feminine presence in Pulga's house would be a great advantage. Pulga's friends basically ignored me; they treated me as if I weren't there at all – it must have been the musty atmosphere up there in the attic. They said disgusting things, farted, peed with the bathroom door open, and even picked at their balls when I was around. Nevertheless, I sent the word out about Santiago to all my single girlfriends, though I have to say that my reports turned every one of them off.

Only one agreed to enter into pursuit, because she couldn't afford to turn down the opportunity. Francisca, a sociology student, had recently arrived in Madrid from Andalusia. She was tall, thin, and nervous, always high-strung, and worried about a thousand unavoidable obligations: political meetings, Spanish classes for illegal African immigrants, and other similar activities ate up all her free time. She was a red, from head to toe, the kind that's practically extinct these days – the kind that, if you aren't on your guard, will launch into a speech about how Stalin's only downfall was his penchant for excess. Impossible, to imagine two people as dissimilar as Francisca and Santiago. Nevertheless – and I'll never understand how or why – they began seeing each other, sharing their rare free moments, melancholy and without great expectations, their time together punctuated only by the most sterile of discussions.

Naturally, it was inevitable that the four of us would get together frequently. If we managed to drag Pulga out of the house, or find a hole in Francisca's busy schedule, we would go to the movies or to a bar for a drink. Otherwise we'd find ourselves in the filthy attic, smoking joints and watching TV or a video, killing time with board games like Doblaje or Nostalgy. With the same wistfulness one feels for a misspent youth, I remember that time of my life as a period of infinite monotony, of discontent, of long solitary walks down the streets of a city at the height of its splendor. Madrilenos are able to notice intangible little nuances in every corner of their city, and maybe because they look down their noses at Barcelona with a bit of secret envy, they tend to call their city a great big village, or mosaic of so many disparate elements. For those of us who come to know the city all at once, it's different. To me Madrid is like a car hurtling at full speed, that you can't climb into without getting knocked in the head. The inhabitants of all great cities never seem to realize exactly to what extent they segregate themselves, unintentionally, from foreigners, who end up leaving for some other city, for a place they can become fanatical about all over again, with that brand of intensity found only in the soul of the recent convert. It's an intensity that authentic inhabitants naturally lack; they don't need it. The other option for foreigners, of course, is to socialize together in pathetic, folkloric ghettos where they can cry about missing their homeland. The last alternative is simply to vegetate amid the indifference, which is what we did.

Of the four of us, none was from Madrid, except Pulga, who actually bragged about not knowing where the Metro was. So, of course, we always arrived late to events, made fools of ourselves when trying to speak in local slang, and felt excluded from the traditions and customs. We knew we fell into a certain category, or class of people, and we felt it: nobody would ever welcome us into their circle with a friendly slap on the shoulder, for example. We could see it in their eyes: peasants, they said. That was what we were, and that's what united us.

And this is the part of the story that has to do with punctuality. Or the lack of it.

Pulga (because of his slovenliness) and Francisca (because of her overwhelmingly hectic schedule) were always making Santiago and me wait around. Endless stretches of time. At first, we would try out little tricks to circumvent the problem. We would say, for example, that a movie began half an hour before it actually did. But the strategy ended up backfiring on us: when they realized what we were doing, they wouldn't believe anything we said, and from then on they'd arrive even later than they had before.

During those long hours of waiting around, Santiago and I got to know each other, and we even became friends, and I discovered that Santiago's arrogance was nothing more than a cover-up for his shyness. He was like a little boy, the way he masked his insecurity with a facade of attitude and aplomb. It explained as well why he was prone to occasional sudden flashes of violence. Yet this inspired in me — contrary to all logic — a deep desire to protect him. I wanted to take care of him, to protect him from more suffering. Because he'd certainly suffered enough already; it hadn't been without a few misgivings that he'd told me the painful story of his life.

He was born in one of those little villages lost in the Sierra Morena, the eighth and youngest son of an unhappily married couple. His father was a tax collector who had willingly resigned himself to his destiny as an exile, an imbecile who never had a single opinion of his own, but submitted himself entirely to the whims of his wife. As a mother, she never took much interest in her children, and she was forever reproaching her husband for the oppressive, provincial life they led. Santiago still couldn't read when he was eight years old, and at fifteen he got involved with a woman much older than him, married to an army general who had recently been stationed in the area. When his lover was widowed and returned to Madrid, Santiago ran away from home and went in search of her, but she rejected him when he arrived in the city. She, of course, had merely been using him to escape the tedium of life in the provinces, the same tedium his mother complained of so bitterly. Santiago decided not to return home, and his parents didn't make much of an effort to find him. In fact, from then on he never saw them again. In Madrid, he held the kind of jobs you'd expect from a teenager with no family. In the beginning (I later learned), he'd even been reduced to prostituting himself. For a roof over his head and a hot meal, he'd fuck gay men on the hunt for fresh young bodies. Slowly things got better, and he eventually finished school. That was the reason he aspired to live a quiet, peaceful life, just as I did. It wasn't just to satisfy some bourgeois ideal: both of us had a desperate desire to find some modicum of peace and happiness. Compared with Santiago, Pulga all of a sudden seemed immature, and insignificant somehow.

One afternoon around the end of August, it was hot as hell, and the four of us had planned to meet in Pulga's flat. When I got there I found Santiago alone, washing his friend's dinner plates, that titanic labor to which I was so fiercely opposed.

'My goodness!' I exclaimed. 'You're some hero.'

'Well, it's been about three months since the last housecleaning,' he joked. 'And anyway, I wanted to cook today. I'm sick of Chinese food.'

I was bathed in perspiration, even though I was wearing a loose cotton dress, the only way I knew how to survive the asphyxiating summers in Madrid. I went into the bathroom, undressed, entered the shower stall, and situated myself directly under the stream of icy water. I used the opportunity to wash my hair with anti-lice shampoo; I still couldn't seem to get rid of the things. The last thing I wanted was to get back into my sweaty dress, so I rummaged through Pulga's things until I found a shirt that didn't stink. When I emerged, Santiago had finished tidying up. I was barefoot, and as I crossed the room, I could feel the soles of my feet getting dirty again. Then he asked me a question:

'Do you think there are more plates to clean upstairs?'

Nobody had dared to go up to the attic in months; we all knew how disgusting it was, and we collectively pretended it didn't exist. Pulga had gone to scrounge more money from his father that afternoon; it would be a while before he returned. It was getting more and more difficult each time for him: a few duros took hours of cajoling on Pulga's part.

'I'll go take a look,' I announced as I began to climb the first few steps leading up to the attic.

'I'll come with you. That's no place for a girl to be alone, even with dirty feet,' said Santiago with a laugh.

He followed me upstairs. I could feel the noxious fumes from the anti-lice shampoo trailing behind me.

'Sofía, what a smell!' he exclaimed.

'That's the Nopioj,' I informed him when we reached the attic.

'What the hell is that?'

I explained that Nopioj was not a joke, nor was it some vulgar insult, but that it was an anti-lice shampoo. At that moment, Santiago abandoned his search for dirty plates and said to me:

'Well, for me, I don't have much faith in those "modern" products. The best remedies are the ones that have been used since the beginning of time. The method that the monkeys still practice, in fact.'

Garbage was strewn across the floor, and we found more of the same on the wire mesh under the mattress. Santiago tilted the bed to one side and lifted the mattress so that all the bits of clutter tumbled down, forming a new heap atop the already-existing heaps of garbage. Then he grabbed a woolen blanket and spread it across the mattress.

'Come here,' he said as he sat down on a corner of the bed.

I fell down onto the blanket, face-up, and rested my head against Santiago's legs. Gently he ran his fingers through my brown hair. It was the first time he'd ever touched me, outside of the conventional greetings and friendly exchanges.

'Here's one,' he murmured.

'How can you see it?' I asked.

The light from downstairs barely reached us, and we were sitting in a shadowy darkness through which I could barely discern the outline of his features. I was having difficulty remembering them. He continued stroking my hair, and I felt a confused mingling of sensations, the sum total of all the stimuli reaching out to me that afternoon: the stifling heat, the cold shower, the darkness, Santiago's hands, the scratchy blanket against my skin. They conspired to offer me the hope that I might be able to escape the disenchantment of life with Pulga, and the dream that perhaps I'd finally found the man I had been searching for, after so much time. It all sank into me, into a bottomless fatigue. Suddenly, I heard Santiago's voice, in the same way you hear a voice the moment right before falling asleep. He said:

'There's another place lice like to hide.'

He didn't need to explain what place he was referring to. I opened the buttons of Pulga's shirt and brushed my hands across my pubic hair. Santiago caressed me once again, and my languor had now become urgency. I wanted him, I wanted him like I'd never wanted anyone before. I opened my legs, so he could feel the contours of my vagina, and my vagina itself. He spread out his fingers like a fan: his thumb and index finger circled round and round my pubis, and with his middle and ring fingers he found his way through the rough hair before reaching the incipient softness of the lips, and with his pinky he completed the task by placing pressure on that provocative stretch of skin between the vagina and the anus – a place that serves as an end and also as a beginning, a line not of separation but of unity. I felt his fingers, mute but resounding, as they rubbed up and down the length of my pelvis, almost inside me, the same feeling as eating turrón with your eyes closed, when it feels as if your teeth might fall out from the pleasure. Then I noticed that his fingers no longer wanted my pubic hair; they now went in search of something better, inside my cunt. With his thumbs now resting on my clitoris, one index finger slowly advanced, calling out to the other index finger, and together they filled and penetrated me, only to separate once they reached inside of me, and the other three fingers unglued my lips in order to facilitate their progress. I, on the other hand, didn't have any use for my fingers – all I needed were two, to grab the nape of his neck and force his head down over me. I wanted to break the symmetry of the ten matching fingers by adding something else: a tongue, so I could experience the eccentric pleasure of eleven rigid, damp, tender fingers moving in unison on my clitoris, on my vagina, on my opened lips. Santiago's maneuvering was a bit brusque, but it turned me on to think that his final destination was my cunt. I felt my body acquire a heightened sensitivity: in the darkness of the room, a long row of smells seemed to parade before my eyes. The soap and the shampoo on my body, the scent of Pulga on the shirt I wore, the humid and fetid scraps piled up around us in the attic, the washing detergent on Santiago's hands, and the bitter sweat of his chest mixed in with the waning smell of the cologne which he'd applied earlier in the day. His hot, wet tongue rose and fell upon me, it surrounded me, blanketing me with anxiety, and returned to satisfy me once again. It's funny, that it was then that I noticed how

Santiago's cheeks didn't have that half-shaven beard that Pulga always wore. I liked it.

The warmth of the moment was concentrated in my belly and in my thighs and, like water escaping from a drain, was about to spill over into the basin of my cunt. The metal springs under the bed creaked. And Santiago interrupted himself, turning his face and his hands away from my vagina.

I was almost at the point of orgasm, at the point of falling into that abyss of unstable, uncontrolled happiness, but he made me stop just a moment before the fall, a moment before throwing myself into all that pleasure. And I was yanked back into the realm of reason and common sense. Thinking about it now, in some way I can see that first unrealized orgasm as symbolic of the nature of our love, always a hair short of being more than it turned out to be. An eternally renewed promise that was never truly fulfilled, a great spectacle that had to be pushed down because of its own frightening threat to itself . . . like a dead person who kills because he can't resign himself to death, a painful reflection in the mirror. But I didn't see it that way back then. I insisted on seeing my illusions become reality.

'What's the matter?' I asked after a moment.

'We can't –' he said, straightening up.

'Santiago,' I tried to interrupt.

'I said no. Pulga and Francisca don't deserve this.'

Despite his response, I removed his belt, unbuttoned his pants, and unzipped the zipper. I took my time, plenty of time, to do it. My position, combined with the darkness, didn't exactly facilitate movement, either, but he didn't reject my advances. I could feel his nervous breathing through the afternoon silence. I searched for his cock under the many layers of material: the pants, his shirt, his shorts. Then, I found it. It was large already, and standing up tall. I needed both hands to hold it. I turned around until I was facing him and then I began to suck it.

'No,' he said, without moving away. 'No.'

I've always felt that one's first romantic embrace with someone reveals a great deal. In the beginning there is a brief moment of surprise, in which your memory – almost instantaneously – reviews all the bodies you've ever lain with in the past, and compares them against this new one, classifies it, and unconsciously evaluates it, rates it, and gives it a mark. The first part of Santiago's body that I felt in my hands was not his body stretched out in an embrace, but rather his rigid, trembling cock.

'No,' he said over and over again, until at last his convictions tumbled down with him and he babbled a final 'Yes . . .'

At that point I accelerated my hand movements and began to softly bite him, running my teeth over the back of his glans, saving for my tongue and palate that hot, smooth sphere, a bubble which I sensed was filled with semen and which I would allow to explode in order to satisfy him. The sphere was bisected by a small ridge into which I would introduce the tip of my tongue, and then apply pressure. It was a hard protuberance, now supported by a shaft, down which he could release his pleasure. I grazed my teeth farther, sinking them into the bubble, which then popped, and he came, spilling his fiery, bitter load into my mouth. I was still for a moment or two as he collected himself, and held the semen on my tongue without swallowing it. I turned, so as to spit, and he realized what I was about to do.

'Wait,' he stopped me. He pulled me up, yanking me by the hair he had so recently caressed. 'Don't spit it out,' he said. 'Give it to me.'

He kissed me, and opened his mouth for me to deposit all of his semen. I unfurled my tongue and released the liquid, just as he had done to me. He swallowed it. And that was our very first kiss.

'Now you come here,' I commanded, without giving him time to refuse. He pushed me onto the mattress.

I took him by the hand and made him kneel down between my legs, and guided his face back to my vagina. I made him kiss me over and over again, without allowing him to stop for breath. I held him by the hair, and I raised and lowered his head so it would rise and fall at exactly the right rhythm and direction according to the compass of my desire, in which his tongue was both an aid and a nuisance. I pulled him, as if he were a doll, and I drove my fingernails into the nape of his neck until it bled. I used his face as a way of giving back to me what he had taken away with his fingers. I held his nose on my clitoris, his lips and his tongue in my vagina, his beard crossing the line between my anus and my cunt, and when the moment arrived, I buried his face farther into my cunt as if his whole body was a penis thrusting against my inflamed clitoris and feverish vagina. And the heat of that hellish day licked its way in between my legs, like a bonfire whose flames had the shape of my organs and the appearance of my own image, exactly as it is reflected in front of a mirror. I used him for myself and my pleasure, and I no longer thought of him or desired him. I simply drowned in my own being, in me and me alone, and I was the only thing that mattered to me and the only thing I could see in that uncertain, comforting darkness. And as my imminent orgasm became more than I could bear, I opened my shirt, took it off, removed the last traces of Pulga, and covered Santiago's head with my hands so I wouldn't have to look any longer at the fragment of that man, who in that instant was nothing to me. I looked instead at the outline of my fingers and my abdomen arching upward in search of the highest point of desire and my vagina and my quivering breasts and my airless chest and my shoulders that I kissed a moment before my body dissolved into the cry from that rabid, liberated orgasm which screamed in search of me, only me, and didn't look for help from anybody else.

Santiago wanted to continue kissing me; I pushed him away, gently. I felt rather bad about manipulating him that way, but I didn't admit it.

'My God!' he exclaimed. 'You're terrible. Look what you did to my face!' And he laughed out loud.

I still hadn't quite pulled myself together. His hands, resting on my still-shaking body, made me edgy, annoyed. Anyway, I was bathed in perspiration. The blanket, coarse and scratchy against the length of my back, was another irritant.

'So, what do we make of this?' Santiago asked me.

I sat down. The burning air in the bedroom began to cool down, into a refreshing, icy breeze.

'I don't know,' I answered him as I unglued my sweat-stained hair from the side of my face. 'Well, if they hadn't been so late, you and I wouldn't have done anything.'

'That's life, Sofía dear,' Santiago pronounced, imitating Pulga and the didactic tone of his discourses, which Santiago never ceased to make fun of. 'A person is drawn by destiny, inexorably, to arrive late everywhere.'

'In every relationship,' I said, smiling, 'there comes a moment in which one must confront infidelity.'

Santiago quickly changed his tone, and returned to his normal voice, and said:

'I like you. A lot.'

I didn't have to answer that. Before I had a chance, he covered my mouth with the palm of his hand, to prevent me from saying anything. From downstairs, we heard the sound of a key turning in the lock. We had totally forgotten that Pulga and Francisca could arrive at any minute. We remained there, paralyzed, caught by surprise at the advent of reality. Now we would have to stay up there for who knew how long; it might be another week before Pulga decided to leave the apartment again. Whoever had just entered threw some things onto the table and exclaimed:

'I don't believe it!' It was Pulga.

He wasn't talking about us, of course. There was no way he could see us. He was referring to the clean plates in the kitchen, which filled him with bliss. Jubilant, he hummed a tune and clapped his hands. Then he turned on the television and inserted a video, as he continued babbling absurdities in a loud voice.

'The motherfucker is talking to himself.' Santiago nudged me.

I had to bite my tongue not to laugh. Side by side, we leaned back against the mattress, very carefully so as not to make it creak, facing the glare that shone up the staircase. The video that Pulga had rented, we soon realized, was pornographic. Then a slight trembling sound was audible from downstairs.

'What's that?' I murmured.

The noise from the floor beneath us became louder and more intense, building up to an almost deafening pitch.

'The bastard is jerking off,' said Santiago, still whispering.

There's always something slightly obscene about listening in on someone's private business. To me, that felt like the ultimate disloyalty to Pulga, much more so than my cheating on him with Santiago. After a while, there was silence as Pulga walked into the bathroom, and we could hear the sound of rushing water as he washed his face, and then he returned to the living room. A yawn, just like a roar, emanated from the room. Already wiped out, exhausted from an activity much too strenuous for his constitution, Pulga watched the movie dispassionately. An erection. Then another. The doorbell, then another rustling of keys, and Pulga – with the remote control, no doubt – briskly switched from the porno video to the weather report on the news. I deduced that it was Francisca who had just arrived so unceremoniously, since she also had a key to the place. We heard her greet him, joking as always:

'How are you, you old good-for-nothing, lazy bum . . .?' She continued with a few other colorful synonyms.

Francisca was the only one allowed to talk that way to Pulga. She always liked to say that when the city inaugurated its monument to Pulga, they would hold an unveiling, only to reveal absolutely nothing, nothing at all, because that's what Pulga was: an absolute, utter void.

'Oh, it's you,' said Pulga. 'Come on in.'

Santiago stroked my legs and looked me in the eyes. We kissed. He still held the bitter taste of semen in his mouth.

'Those two haven't arrived yet?' Francisca asked. 'That's impossible.'

'Someone has been here, but they left.'

'How do you know?'

'Because the dishes are clean,' Pulga answered.

'Hmm,' she replied. 'You've never washed a dish in your life, so clearly someone has to have been here.'

'Right. It must have been Sofía.'

'Why not Santiago?'

Pulga didn't appear to have heard that.

'I always said that that girl would one day give up her princess attitude and return to her healthy provincial roots.'

Slowly, very slowly, Santiago removed his clothing.

'And what if those fuckers took off together?' Francisca countered. 'By now they could be halfway to the moon.'

'Well, at least they did the dishes before they left,' Pulga said sarcastically.

'You're such an asshole, Pulga. So unpleasant, sickening, hateful . . .'

'Enough with your nonsense, already. They're probably on their way. Why don't we start the movie.'

'Don't you want to wait for them?'

'Francisca, dear, you have to understand that everyone is responsible for his or her actions. If they arrive late, they have no right to protest.'

Santiago moved closer to my ear and whispered:

'That's what I say.'

Pulga busied himself with the videotapes and the television. Obviously, he'd rented two movies, one for private use and the other for public consumption. He inserted the second tape. It was one of those sick horror movies that he liked so much. He hated movies that made you think too much. The longest

'books' he'd read in the last few years were the libertine calen-
dars his father printed.

'Even death won't come between our love,' said one of the
characters in the movie. 'I'll come back for you from the Other
Side.'

Santiago was still at my side. I sensed the humid echo of his
tongue in my ear and a tickle which made me tremble. The mattress creaked ever so slightly.

'I like you,' he repeated in my ear.

'They can hear us,' I answered, also whispering.

We then shared a long kiss, which held the indiscreet flavor
of our respective betrayals, and which lingered like our
remorse. *He doesn't have a beard*, I said to myself. And I murmured that I liked him, too – but my response wasn't without a
bit of cowardice, because I emphasized the 'too' so he would
understand that I was simply responding to his declaration. He
caressed my back as if to show concern for me, but the gesture
implored something of me, as well. I rested my hand on his
chest to feel the rhythm of his anguished heartbeat. With infinite
grace, he placed his rigid penis between my legs and we stayed
like that for a while – no rush, no urgency.

'According to records, Mary died ten years ago in Tucson,
Arizona.' The movie was still running downstairs. 'However,
since then her body has remained intact. There is no sign of
decay.'

At that moment, as our lips reunited, Pulga said something
we didn't hear, and it was then that the gravity of what we were
doing fell upon us, the ghost of betrayal came between us, transforming the relatively relaxed state of things into a scenario of
savage desire, expiation, and violence, and our kiss rapidly

degenerated into nothing more than an exchange of drool, insults, and incensed bites on one another's skin. Santiago grabbed me by the arm and threw me over his shoulder, turning me upside down as he repeated over and over again what a whore I was, that I was cheating on my boyfriend. Shit, who could ever trust you? he asked. Then he climbed on top of me and penetrated me, with all the cruelty of his rage. The blanket fell to the side, the metal bed frame dug into my flesh, and Santiago's penis shot through me, wounding the deepest part of me.

'A dead person's heart can beat exactly like that of a living person.'

His penis burned against my abdomen, and my immobilized arm was beginning to hurt. I had to go to the bathroom. And so I did. I peed with the inflexibility of vengeance, I peed and peed. The heat of the urine excited him even more. He perforated my body, slamming himself into me in search of every square millimeter of body space that he could invade, lacerating and flattening me. He didn't want the bed to creak, so he kept his body as still as possible. Instead he simply pushed, bearing through me, and crushing me with his unrelenting weight against the bed. He wanted to destroy me, at the same time he destroyed his own conscience, to turn his organ into a knife with which to slice my vagina, in search of my soul. And at the same time I wanted him to do it – I didn't want him to comfort me with sickly sweet sentimentality. I was hungry for his rage, for his punishment, and I wished desperately that my cunt were smaller so he could rip it apart and out of my body. Our fucking was made all the more brutal and insane by the harsh, solemn silence which enveloped us.

'Oh, my love, I will love you in the crypt just as I have loved you on your bed, only as two dead people can love each other.'

Santiago brought his mouth closer to mine and I thought he was proposing a truce in the form of a kiss, I thought he was ready to abandon the game and surrender to the soft sweetness of emotion. I wouldn't have heard of it, though, because I didn't want to see him soften. But he didn't kiss me. Instead, he spit on me and inundated my lips with his rabid saliva. I insulted him again, and I realized he was at the verge of coming. That was his way of being cruel to me: he would leave me dangling at the height of pleasure, in the swamp of unsatisfied desire, and would forge ahead on his own into the dominion of orgasm. I tried to lift up my stomach, and with my free hand caressed myself. I began at the sweet hollow of my ribs and lingered in the furrows leading into the vagina. As I stroked my belly, I also stroked the protuberance of his penis, and my flesh was cradled between our two bodies. I could sense my abdominal muscles tensing from a combination of suffering and effort, and I reached my cunt – my very own cunt, being assaulted by a foreign invader – and gave him the real pleasure he sought. I tightened my muscles around him with an intimate intensity, abstracting myself for the moment from the fury. But my body alone didn't have enough rage for him. I managed to insert a finger into my vagina, parallel to Santiago's penis, and I dug a nail into his fragile skin, just as he was digging into my interior, and then we returned to being two people, as my hand led me to absolute pleasure. There was a second, a brief second in which everything stopped, suspended in the pregnant silence, just like the silence that precedes music.

'We found Frank's body next to the grave of his beloved.

Both have deteriorated into ossified specimens, barely covered by the purulent skin and worm-infested flesh.'

Then both of us came, with the urgency of sobs, and I could no longer contain the moans that were drowning inside my chest, because the orgasm traveled across my entire body, reached my throat, and emerged through my mouth in a cry of pleasure and pain. It was the cry of a wounded animal, a beast whose ability to respond has been impaired by the perverse attack of an arrow. The television was turned off.

Only after several months did Pulga go upstairs again to the attic.

How distant, how uncertain the past seems without you. It's mere history, a biography that no longer applies to me; to recall it is like recalling someone else's past. In this darkened room where I spend my life, so removed from the world that I almost seem dead, I'm as far from everything as you are, Marina. My days seem like a row of lights that turn off, one after the other like lightning, in the vortex of time that devours everything. And I can see the last ray of light beneath the weak and unsteady glow of my memory. I first knew you beneath the glow of the sun, but I remember you at nighttime, between the shadows of dawn or under the benevolent twinkle of the moon. Time is nothing to me anymore. The pain of my childhood and the betrayals of my youth are as far from me as is this instant, this very instant, which I cannot cling to because it has already fallen into the abyss of the past, it has become reunited with the past which was stolen from us. The only true, authentic past: you, Marina, you, my love.

As he leaned against the staircase railing, Pulga rearranged his eyeglasses, patched together on the bridge by a piece of electric tape, dumbfounded. His mouth wide open, he just stood there watching us, unable to utter a reproach or even a response. After a few seconds, Francisca's head appeared. She, on the other hand, did venture to speak, and did she ever. She lit into us with a litany of every last insult, invective, and dirty word you could imagine; vocabulary certainly is her forte. If we had felt like it, Santiago and I could have defended ourselves just for the hell of it, by attacking her rigid, Stalinist morals and by throwing a few other daggers in for good measure. But we didn't, of course. Anything we said would have only made the situation worse. Pulga didn't even have the nerve – or maybe it was the energy – to throw us out. But Santiago and I left, anyway. We dressed quickly, and exited the apartment beneath the torrent of insults that that Andalusian witch continued to unleash upon us.

We walked around in silence for hours, whipped by gusts of hot air and by the cold wind of remorse. At Peña Prieta he took my hand. Our palms were soon glued together by one another's perspiration, but we didn't let go. We felt like accomplices to a crime that neither one of us had been looking to commit. We reached the Parque Retiro, and crossed into the center of the city by way of Alcalá, and stepped up the pace when we reached Puerta del Sol. Then we turned and headed toward Preciados, up San Bernardo to Bravo Murillo, the stadium, and then all the way back down the Castellana to Plaza de Colón. A wonderful tourist promenade for a couple of idiot peasants that don't know what the hell to do with their time or their lives. We finally said our good-bye around midnight, in front of the Prado, and weeks went by before we saw one another again.

On the other hand, it was years before I found out what became of Pulga. He had inherited his father's printing plant, and had revived the business by churning out little stamps of saints. It's a great enterprise, and not even all that much work, since hagiography is such a slow-moving field. Aside from a few beatifications every few decades, there isn't much action. Francisca ended up in rather strange circumstances: she married a Senegalese man named Mbe, or something like that, so he could get his citizenship. But that was much later.

Ever since that night, I had cut off most contact with the friends I'd had before the Betrayal, as I – or my guilty conscience – had begun to call it. I felt alone. I had guessed, perhaps irrationally, that my friends wouldn't want to talk to me when I called, that they wouldn't answer the door if I dropped by, that they would turn the other way just seeing me. I ran into a few of them in my department at the university, and I felt like they greeted me coldly and then used some trivial excuse to hurry off. So, fearing that my friends would reject me, I ended up rejecting them. Santiago did the same with his friends.

With that pathetic sense of pity that is the exclusive domain of twenty-year-olds, I gave up my studies, closed myself off from the world, and cried all the time. I talked to myself, as a way of making myself feel better. Sometimes I'd be serious – Come on, Sofía, you were never in love with Pulga anyway – and sometimes I'd be silly – At least you won't have lice anymore, right? But it was all in vain. I cried and cried for days. I cried until my eyes were red and sore.

I went to the doctor, an old bald guy with little tufts of white hair on either side of his head. He was very good, although he was a bit nosy about his patients' private lives. Like all doctors, he had this obsession about keeping a strict schedule, but in order to satisfy both his curiosity and his punctuality, he would schedule long appointments, and he wouldn't examine you until you'd discussed every single thing you'd done since the last visit – or since birth, if you were a new patient.

'Sofía, dear! How are you?' He came at me with his usual string of interrogatives. 'It has been months since the last time I saw you! How is everything at the university? And your boyfriend? Did you go on vacation?'

I really didn't want to talk to anybody, not even with him, really the ideal listener for anyone who needed to open up. So I went straight to the point:

'My eyes are a mess.'

He stood totally still for a moment and then took out a strange-looking lens to examine me.

'My God!' he exclaimed. 'What on earth has happened to you?'

'I've been crying for days.'

He looked closely at my eyes again.

'You're right,' he pronounced. 'You have no tears left to shed.'

'Doctor!' I sighed. 'Don't say it, or else I'm going to start crying again.' And I wasn't kidding. Little by little, I started to sob. I covered my face with my hands, trying to hold it in. First I pouted, then I whimpered a little, and then I let loose a wail, which turned into a tumultuous spasm of tears.

'Come now, Sofía, tell me what's wrong.' The doctor patted me on the back.

His kindness had a soothing effect, and I took my hands off my face. My resistance to talking crumbled away. I had suffered in solitary silence for so long, and at that moment, during my last and most emotional outburst, I guess I would have confessed myself to just about anyone. I told him what had happened, although of course I cleaned up the story a bit. Mainly I kept the focus on the punctuality aspect of things. I figured the doctor would understand that part of it.

'All right, already!' he exclaimed when I was done. 'I never liked that boyfriend of yours anyway. And if I may be honest with you . . . look, if you really have so much in common with this young man . . .' – everyone under the age of fifty was a 'young man' to my doctor – 'What did you say his name was?'

'Santiago. '

'That's right, Santiago,' he repeated. 'If the two of you are so well-matched then marry him and that will be that.'

About a year and a half before that, the doctor had taken care of my mother during her last few weeks, and he felt somewhat responsible for my future, as if he were my godfather, sort of. I was truly fond of him and, in his fatherly advice did make me feel better. My crying jag slowly ebbed, with short, jerky little hiccups. I dried my tears and sat there, staring at the doctor.

'In the meantime,' he said, grabbing a pad, 'apply this eye bath four times a day, no more. That should be enough.' He wrote the prescription on the pad, tore off the sheet, and handed it to me. 'All right, go on already, I'm in a rush today. It's five and Martinez González's wife has probably been waiting. Now there's a woman who's really in a mess! Much worse than you.'

I got up, trembling a little, and silent. I walked toward the door.

'I hope you remember to invite me to the wedding,' he said

before I closed the door behind me. 'Good-bye, dear, and don't get lost!'

I went down to the pharmacy to fill the prescription. I was still disoriented, confused, but after a while I did come to a few conclusions. It occurred to me that the doctor's suggestion was really the only possible solution to my dilemma. After all, I said to myself, you're not getting any younger – why on earth should you wait any longer? A wedding is a serious endeavour, of course. But so were my feelings for Santiago – I loved him, I wanted him, more than I had ever loved or wanted any other man. I felt that he was the love of my life, the love I'd been searching so hard for.

The cashier at the pharmacist's was an older woman with short hair and delicate hands. They reminded me of my mother, and that inspired me in the same way as my doctor's words had.

Without another thought, I asked to use the telephone. She placed it on the counter. I had to think in order to remember Santiago's number. In those days, he worked at the ad agency only in the mornings. In the afternoon he worked at home, drawing all sorts of things: blueprints, comics, fashion sketches, whatever he could get his hands on. I had to find him. I dialed his number.

'Hello?' I heard someone say on the other end of the line.

'Let's get married!' I shouted, out of the blue.

'Great idea!' the person said. 'Of course, I hope my wife doesn't object to a divorce.'

'This is Sofía,' I muttered. 'Who is this?'

'A pleasure to meet you, Sofía.' Laughter. 'My name is José Mariá San Juan.'

I hung up and then tried another number. This time I got it right.

'Sofía, what a surprise! How are you?' Santiago seemed pleased by the call. 'I was going to call you this week, and—'

'Listen,' I interrupted him. 'I have to talk to you.'

'Well, go ahead, talk. I'm listening.'

'Um, well, this is the story . . . I want to marry you.'

'My God!' he said, a bit perplexed. 'Well, why don't we get together and discuss this.'

'How about now?'

'Right now I can't.'

'Oh, come on, Santiago. You have to.'

'I can't, Sofía, I can't get away right now. I'll tell you in two words: impossible. Tomorrow evening I'm free, if you want.'

'Oh, for God's sake!' I roared. 'I propose marriage to you and you tell me you're busy? Get over here now! Otherwise forget about the whole thing!'

I gave him the address of the pharmacy and hung up without saying anything else. I went over to the woman who reminded me of my mother.

'How much is it?' I asked, pointing to the eye bath.

'They're all the same,' she said. 'Terrible. But what would we do without them?'

'What are you talking about?' I thought she was talking about the different brands of eyewashes, although I couldn't be sure.

'About men, what do you think? If I had any strength at all, I'd be a nun. But I'm so weak . . .'

I limited myself to a nod of the head.

'You did a good thing,' she continued. 'There's no other way to treat them. Tough.'

'Excuse me, but I'm in a slight rush,' I interrupted her. 'How much do I owe you?'

'Nothing, girl! Nothing at all. Consider it a wedding present. Best of luck to you two.'

I said thank you and went out to the street. I paced back and forth in front of the pharmacy, with the firm conviction that I would wait one hour, then I would leave. I resisted staring at my reflection in the store windows, lit up by the late afternoon sun. Farther away, the entrance to the Metro alternately devoured and spit out crowds of people. I squeezed out a few eyedrops, which were nice and refreshing. Thirty-five minutes later a taxi pulled up to the curb. Santiago. Before he could get out, before he could even pay the fare, I jumped into the taxi. The driver looked at me, slightly shocked.

'Listen . . .' he started. The cabbie wore thick glasses, big and round, just like the headlights of his car.

'To Barajas Airport,' I commanded. We were downtown, near Atocha Station.

'Miss, please. Won't you first let the gentleman out? Then if you want—'

'Sofía,' Santiago interrupted, even more put off than the cab-driver. 'I don't understand. What the hell is going on with you?'

'Nothing,' I spat out. 'You and I get married, and that's that.' I said it without realizing that I was repeating exactly what my doctor had said.

'You're out of your mind.'

'Shit!' the driver exploded, breaking all rules of cabbie etiquette. 'Why don't the two of you pick out your kids' names while you're at it? Why not? I've got all day to listen to a couple of lovebirds. Sure, I'm a real romantic.'

'Take us to the airport, please,' Santiago said, confirming my earlier request. Then, once we were on our way, he turned to me and said, 'Tell me, what do you propose we do?'

I didn't answer; even I didn't know where all this was going. I rested my head on his shoulder, not really listening to all the things he was saying: I've never seen you like this before; What bug bit you, anyway, tell me?; Don't think I'm going to get on the next plane just like that, you know . . .

'Hey, what are you doing?' He covered himself as if he were naked and a gust of wind had just blown off his fig leaf.

I pinched the back of his hand, a tiny, painful squeeze – 'nun's pinches,' my mother used to call them. First he let out a yelp, but then he let me continue. The taxi driver didn't even flinch; by now he was already used to our bizarre behavior.

I slipped my hand into Santiago's pants and reached for his penis. It appeared quite contracted, nothing like the wondrous specimen I'd had in my mouth so many nights ago. *Oh, Sofía, you're crazy*, he whispered. I began to caress it, lightly, running my fingers over the swollen veins and massaging the head beneath the thin film of foreskin. I moved my hand up and down, relaxed and calm, and then I noticed how his breathing changed, as did his *Oh, Sofías*, and I felt his penis grow larger in my hand. To move up and down my hand now had to travel a longer stretch, and the distance kept increasing. I pushed back his foreskin and out popped the red tip, rebellious thing, a vital organ if I ever saw one. I brought my fingers up to my mouth; they tasted acidic. I covered them with saliva and then brought them back down, drenching the tip of his penis, and he was murmuring *Sofía, Sofi*, the whole time, and I noticed that it was already wet. I never knew that penises could sweat – or maybe,

I thought, it was my hand, from before. Anyway, what with the movement of the taxi and the warm wetness of his penis, I practically didn't have to do anything at all – the rest of it took care of itself, really: *Oh Sofi, Sofi*, etc. He seemed to be delirious with pleasure. I, on the other hand, still resting my head against his shoulder, was not experiencing all that much pleasure, mainly because of the taxi driver, who drove on impassively. All he had to do was turn his head to the side when looking out for oncoming traffic and I'd have to look at him: not only his pimply neck and his cap, but his face, and the poor guy was pretty unattractive. He had a long, bony face and a prominent nose from which thick black hairs sprouted. They were none too pleasant, so I opted to look instead at another set of hairs. That is to say, I glanced down at Santiago's hair, from which his penis shot out, by now rather vertical, straining itself to the very limit of its possibilities.

My hand, rising and falling in quick rhythm against that hard flesh, felt almost imperceptible granules, like seeds almost, or the atoms that made up his granite penis. His neck was now arched back, his head resting against the backseat. At this point, he had lost all of his previous composure. *Sofía*, he said, *tighter, tighter*, and so I held it tighter. *More, Sofi, more*, and I squeezed it, I strangled it, but it still wasn't enough for him. He wet it himself, he gripped it himself, and I gripped the hand that gripped his penis. He let his pants drop down a little bit more and returned his cock to my hand alone. He then wet a finger and stuck it in his anus: *More, Sofi, more*, he gasped as he grabbed his balls and pushed his finger farther and farther in. Now, the taxi driver was beginning to get a little curious, and every so often would peer at us through the rearview mirror, without saying a word. He didn't have to, really – Santiago was saying more than enough already with all his *More, mores*. Then I got down on my knees and took his penis with both hands; it was really at its breaking point by now, an imposing, a truly formidable erection. I still was able to continue my up-and-down routine with both hands, but it was no easy task. *Come on, Sofía, come on* – he practically was shouting by now, burying even farther the finger he had inserted in his anus, and I got the message that now he was ready. With all my might I tightened the pressure around his penis, dug my nails into it, and then with a gust of energy squeezed one last time, giving it a final, violent jolt.

What followed was an ejaculation that was truly worthy of such an erection, an exuberant, impetuous stream that must have reached the ceiling of the cab, though I didn't think to look, and then spilled onto his pants and my hands. From my crouched position I looked up to see if the cabdriver had witnessed the apotheosis, which surely would have irritated him plenty. But he hadn't; luckily, at that moment the only thing on his mind was a tourist bus hogging up two lanes on the highway.

With little gasps of pain, Santiago slowly extracted his finger from his anus. Then he passed me a handkerchief, and we cleaned ourselves up as best we could, which wasn't much. I resumed my position next to him on the backseat as he attempted unsuccessfully to put his pants back on. His erection hadn't quite subsided; in fact, it looked as straight and hard as it had before. *Oh, Sofi*, he said yet again, *you're such a little tart*. I rolled down the window; it didn't smell good at all inside the cab.

'The worst thing of all,' I said to him in a low voice, 'is that now we don't have anything to do at the airport.'

'True.' He smiled. He understood. He covered his penis with the dirty handkerchief. 'Is this how you ask for someone's hand?'

'It was a pretty cheap trick,' I admitted. I wanted to say that I had actually asked for much more than a hand, but I let the joke go. 'So, what do you think of my proposition?'

'Here we are. Where do you want to go?' said the cabbie. We were approaching the main terminal. I had never flown before, and for an instant I was tempted to just hop on a plane to any-where and leave Madrid behind forever, just like they do in those American movies. It would have been a happy ending for us, but it turned out to be nothing more than a brief stopover. 'Did you hear me, you dirty little lovebirds?'

'Excuse me?' Santiago pretended to take offense. 'What do you take us for?'

'No, sir, don't bother with the act,' the driver said. 'What you take me for? All I care is that you don't ruin the upholstery.' And he threatened to inspect the backseat.

'Listen,' Santiago stopped him. 'I've changed my mind.' And then he ordered the driver to take us back to the pharmacy at Atocha.

'Whatever you say,' said the driver, shrugging his shoulder.

'That's right,' Santiago whispered in my ear after a long silence. 'When do you want to get married?'

There was something rather comical about discussing mar-riage in that particular scenario. His erection still hadn't died down, and his upright penis rocked against the handkerchief as the taxi lurched through the traffic.

'The sooner the better,' I said. 'And you can speak up. After all your shouting, there's no need to keep this conversation a secret.'

He smiled, revealing a long white row of teeth.

'Well, the surprise,' he started to say, 'you know, the shock you gave me' – Santiago first looked over at the cabbie, red, and then fought to stuff his penis back in his pants – 'I couldn't even look you in the face. So, now tell me . . .'

'Yes?' I hugged him, and he hugged me back.

'What is that in your eyes?'

He laughed when I told him the story of the doctor, the pharmacy, and José María.

'Lucky you remembered my phone number,' he noted.

'All right, that's enough!' the taxi driver interrupted as he came to a halt in front of the pharmacy. 'If you two don't get out of here for good, now, I'm going to hit one of you. What do you think of that?'

That useless ride ended up costing us a fortune. When we finally got out, I saw the driver give Santiago a wink through his big round glasses. The handkerchief fell to the curb.

'Santiago,' I murmured, now outside.

'We have to celebrate.'

'Santiago.'

'Let me take you out somewhere. Somewhere elegant and expensive. We'll drink champagne.' He looked truly enthusiastic now; it was that provincial enthusiasm we both had. 'I have to finish up some sketches for tomorrow, but I don't care. I'll stay up all night if I have to. Now I want to celebrate!'

'All right, Santiago,' I said. 'But first pull up your zipper. It's open.'

'You're right!' he said, moving his hand to his boxers; then he interrupted himself. 'But first I want to give that big mouth a lesson.'

He grabbed my hand and we went into the drugstore. He stopped in front of the woman that looked like my mother. She stopped what she was doing to contemplate us, stupefied. She couldn't help her gaze from wandering downward, toward Santiago's dirty, open pants. Santiago then asked me:

'Is this the woman? Is this the woman you and I owe so very much?'

'Yes,' I answered.

He grabbed her hand and began to kiss it, very theatrically.

'Thank you, ma'am! Thank you so much!' he shouted. 'Thanks to your advice, we've decided to get married. And to you we owe nothing less than our eternal gratitude!'

He had now gone from her hand to her whole arm, and he kept on going, slobbering all over the woman with big, wet kisses. I'd never seen him do anything like this before; he was usually so discreet. Now, though, you could tell he was exultant, as was I, and I loved him so much. Certain acts of silliness, when done in the presence of another person, seem much more meaningful than they really are, because they offer the illusion of complicity, of shared happiness, of mutual trust. You think you're having experiences that you'll remember for the rest of your life.

The cashier managed to escape, horrified. As she retreated, Santiago continued shouting:

'We'll never forget you, ma'am! We'll invite you to the reception! You'll be our children's godmother!'

'Mr. Cordoba! Mr. Cordoba!' the woman shrieked, sneaking into the back room. Santiago realized that this was the moment to disappear, so we ran out like a shot.

In November, when we got married, we didn't invite the

woman to the reception because there wasn't any. But we did invite her to the ceremony, and of course her presence was sorely missed. Those not absent included my doctor – who, along with Manolo, was one of the witnesses – and one of the few friends of Santiago's we still kept in touch with. He was not part of Pulga's circle, obviously. It was a sad sort of marriage ceremony, as you can imagine. We couldn't invite anyone other than these people, because little by little, we had isolated our-selves from everything and everybody. Nevertheless, I still entertained the hope of being happy and I thought that sooner or later we would put the past behind us.

When you're as young as I was then, you always think there will be another chance in the future – that is, until you're left with unfulfilled illusions in front of you. I thought it was possi-ble to invent love if you found the appropriate person to do it with, and I thought – I made myself think – that Santiago was that person. If I were to search now for the real reasons we got married, I think I'd find them in something that has little or nothing to do with love: pride. Without a doubt, both Santiago and I felt the need to prove – not just to the world but to our-selves as well – that our encounter hadn't been chance at all. That it hadn't been capricious, futile, guilty. We had been dis-loyal to our friends, and the only thing that could justify our actions, or absolve us, was to blindly obey the idea of love.

Nevertheless, it was inevitable that a veiled resentment soon set in between the two of us. When we looked at one another in the eye, we both feared being considered a betrayer. This weighed especially heavy on Santiago. So many people in his life had disappointed him, and he seemed so unable to endure any more humiliation that he felt excessively indebted to anyone who trusted him. He was like one of those beaten-up old dogs who warm up to anyone who pets them in between beatings. Of course, he was also very jealous. *You've been unfaithful before*, he would say; *what's to say you won't do it again? You came into my life through a window and you'll go out the same way*.

The wedding ceremony seemed somehow to mark our entire marriage. We hardly pulled any more of those juvenile stunts like the one in the taxi, or in the pharmacy, and those were little events that I had interpreted as signs of happiness. The very same afternoon in which we decided to get married, as we sipped champagne in a bar near Retiro – which ended up being expensive but not elegant – Santiago began to sing that bolero whose name I can't remember. And he sang it for a while after that afternoon. '*Amor, nada nos pudo separaaaar . . . Luchamos contra toda incomprensióóóón . . .*' He sang off-key on purpose, and sometimes I wondered if he wasn't disguising the anger he really felt toward me. Then, little by little, he began to forget about the bolero, and after Laura died, he never sang it again.

His anger – latent at the beginning of our relationship, but thoroughly exposed by the end – led us toward a succession of perversions that finally caused us irreparable damage. We acquired a repertoire of repugnant little behaviors, which we repeated when we were alone, night after night, just like a nightmare.

We both knew that things couldn't go on like that for much longer, but we both lacked the conviction required to end it for good. I can't blame Santiago entirely for that, nor would it be true, exactly, to declare myself a martyr. My conscience won't let me: my thirst for the erotic could be satisfied only at the tumultuous fountain which we tapped from our very first sexual encounter, violent and charged with rivalry as it was. We shared a shameful bond which was rooted in the intersection of only partial aspects of each of our personalities – mere potentialities that had previously been untouched and unrealized. That's why I insist that Santiago not be held entirely accountable for my misfortunes. We were both executioners and victims of our own sick relationship. And now I can do nothing more than lament my pain and remorse, because I no longer can rely on the alibi of innocence. I pushed Santiago, far beyond where we'd been. With him, it seemed like I could try anything, everything, and that hadn't occurred to me before him. I judged myself to be outside of the sick games and the cruel passions; I hadn't foreseen the possibility that pain was just another of the many faces of pleasure. On the contrary: the unpleasantness of my childhood catapulted me into a constant search for the serenity and comfort to be found in love.

But from my first brush with Santiago, I began to feel a confusing attraction to danger, and I felt the same fascination that people who walk along the ledges of tall buildings must feel, or people who bet their entire fortunes on a number on a roulette wheel. In the most trivial of moments, we would risk our lives with the idea that the danger would somehow make our lives meaningful. Nevertheless, the inherent triviality of risk perpetually prevented us from ever truly feeling satisfied. So, each time, we would try to outdo ourselves with yet another compromising position, one after the other, truly unbelievable feats, really. And they should have been able to satisfy us, but nothing did. And we'd try to stop, but the cycle would inevitably begin again. Each time, it would start from some imprudent whim, and then there would be no turning back. And at this jaded point in the road, there was another added element: guilt. Our actions were wearing us down, but instead of giving them up, we punished ourselves with further excesses. It's so difficult to save yourself once the wheels of degradation have begun to turn. Only a catastrophe can stop you from doing it. Santiago and I stopped when it was already too late, much too late, and we paid the price in blood.

By that point, curses, scratches, and depravity had long ceased to be enough. I remember we would stand there, looking at each other, unsatisfied and slightly alarmed as the question hung in the air: What would we do next? Once we'd crossed the line that we had previously held to represent the upper limit of our recklessness, the adventure suddenly was no longer an adventure but had instead become routine. It wasn't enough; we needed more.

The first time he tied me up, it was just mischief, an experiment. We were lying face-up in bed, naked and gasping, after failing at an attempt to fuck in the conventional way. He suggested it hesitantly, the way you suggest something you assume is going to be rejected, as if going through the motions of a request.

'You wouldn't want me to tie you up, right?'

The question was framed in a very unexciting, casual manner, but it turned me on anyway. Immediately I felt that damning sense of guilt that infiltrates temptation. I was ashamed to feel desire for such an outrageous suggestion, and to teach myself a lesson, I submitted to it.

'Why not?' I said. 'Do it. Now.'

He hesitated a moment, and then rose. He rummaged around the closet until he came up with two leather belts.

Before I knew it he had tied my ankles to the bed frame, leaving the knot loose enough for me to free myself with the most minimal movement.

'No, not like that,' I insisted. 'Tighter! Don't be a coward.'

He adjusted the belts. My open legs were now entirely immobilized. We watched each other, I suppose with the secret hope that the other would put an end to this deviance. But neither one of us said a word. And with that, we lost the opportunity to ever turn back. Santiago left the bedroom and returned with an electric cable. He tied one end to the headboard and the other to my neck, with a slipknot. Only my arms were free now; I could barely move without choking myself. The cable was short, so there was no way to pull on the knot to make it looser.

'What are you waiting for?' I spat. 'Fuck me.'

He shouted at me, saying that I was a whore for wanting to be fucked that way, and then he slapped me. My teeth bit into my lower lip from the force of the blow, and I felt the heavy, obscene taste of blood in my mouth. I told him I was much more than a whore, which got him to insult me even further, and he struck me again. His penis grew harder with each blow. I put a hand on my cunt and began to masturbate.

'You like to touch yourself, don't you?' he asked.

'Yes, yes, yes,' I answered. 'You do it, too.'

With his five fingers, he encircled his now erect penis. Then he began to masturbate, about ten centimeters away from my face. His right hand came and went over his flushed penis, in brusque, short strokes, while his left hand grabbed me by the hair, forcing me to face him, to move my eyes away from my own body. *Touch yourself more*, I said to him, caressing my breasts, *do it like I'm doing*, and he imitated me. He let go of my hair and brushed his fingertips across his nipples, hidden underneath the thick hair on his chest, and he shuddered, the victim of his lonely spasms. We were two lonely dogs that didn't know how to give each other pleasure, and so had to stimulate ourselves individually. Santiago now caressed the muscles on his chest, his abdomen, his thighs, before placing both hands on his rigid cock.

It made me heady just to watch him work like that, as my own expert fingers worked their way into my vagina, and the ties on my ankles and neck tortured me, reminding me that I was a whore, much more than a whore . . . *How could I be enjoying this so much?* I asked myself again and again, under my breath; *I like this, I like this*, and my climax was then stained with reproach, I reveled in the distaste of it all. I know because my vagina became swollen, and inside it, the most sensitive nugget of joy was already hard, as hard as Santiago's cock, bitter, and I suddenly felt obliged to press hard against it, with all my fury, and come, finally come, so Santiago could see the rhythm of my contractions and accelerate the rhythm of his masturbation, and spill the flaming stream of semen on my face. Yes, like that.

We barely had a moment of pause. But we were hot, like two wild beasts, and we both wanted more. I grabbed his arm and pulled him toward me. He got up on the bed, kneeled over my chest, and placed his penis in my mouth. As I sucked it, my lips covered in semen and blood, I felt him still trembling from the previous orgasm. It was like sucking on the last leftovers, the bottom of the barrel, the backward echo of everything. It took a while to revive his erection, and my own arousal pushed me further into it: I clawed my fingernails into his buttocks, and then, yes, then he began to get hard again, less than before but enough to penetrate me. He got it in, and I was at his disposal, his prisoner, with an open cunt in between his open legs. I anxiously accepted that burning bit of flesh, slightly soft, and although it didn't fill me entirely, it managed to inflame me all the same. I began to berate Santiago, as a way of urging him on. And it did. He and his member responded, and as both of us approached another orgasm, I dug my fingernails farther in, into his shoulders and his back this time, till they bled. I kissed his blood with my own bloody mouth and he kissed my face, and licked me up in order to swallow every last trace of his semen. When I felt his ejaculation inside of me, I tensed my neck so the electric cable would suffocate me, and I pressed my clitoris against his pelvis, and came.

There was no third time. Like a magician who has run out of tricks and, in the midst of the audience's boos, collects his top hat, rabbit, and magic wand, Santiago untied me in silence, with that same sense of failure. We then washed off, treated our wounds, remade the bed, and slept in each other's arms, as if afraid of falling off some imaginary precipice.

The next day we did it all over again, and slowly it became something we couldn't live without. We couldn't fuck any other way now.

Santiago's back was red and raw as a result of my scratches. But he made me keep my fingernails long, because that little trick made him enjoy it even more. For my part, I was reduced to wearing dark glasses to hide my blood clots and the contusions that had begun to appear on my face, although there was no way to really hide them. And then I would invent the most outlandish excuses to justify during the daytime those signs of my nocturnal life. After a while, Santiago limited himself to hitting me on the body – clothing hid the bruises easily enough. To think we'd gotten married in an attempt to find some kind of simple, quiet refuge in one another and that, ironically enough, we now found ourselves in a vortex of blind lust, whose intensity drew us in with a morbid seductiveness. In an effort to create an escape hatch, in a moment of lucidity (which were few, since we rarely spoke about it, as if it weren't our problem) we decided to have a child. But when I got pregnant, nothing changed at all. We went on in that same hell – that is, what we considered to be hell, in the belief that if we'd given ourselves up to our desires less obsessively, less violently, perhaps it all would have been different.

And, after a while, doing the same things over and over again, that idea which had originally seemed such a novelty turned into a habit. Santiago did everything he could to prevent it from losing the element of risk, until it bordered on the absurd. He bought an enormous vibrator, which was filled with prickly things at one end, and tried to stimulate me with it. Our acts became more violent, and he began to replace the belts with heavy electrical cord, and sometimes he would tie me to the floor, or on the bed like the first time, in an effort to remove the comfort of the mattress beneath me. He suggested we invite someone else to join us, so we wouldn't always be so alone, and he bought awful pornographic videos for us to watch as we fucked. In total, we tried all the classic activities that go along with disenchanted eroticism – which, of course, were of no use to us. We always seemed to feel that there was something missing, and the scenarios invariably acquired an air of exhausting theatricality, a play whose outcome could be nothing less than tragic.

There was only one territory we didn't dare enter, by mutual accord: anal sex. Once, in an allusion to our little scene in the taxicab, I tried to insert my finger into Santiago's anus, but he rejected it, flat out. He was the only one that could do that, he said, and then only rarely. Men give but they can't receive, he explained; they can fire the penalty shot but the goalie never can. Maybe it was a tormenting reminder of his days as a prostitute, I don't know, but I did understand that it was an area I should steer very clear of. As far as I was concerned, on the other hand, the only thing I objected to was sodomy, and that was because from experience (a couple of early boyfriends had attempted it, to no avail), I was certain that pain would significantly outweigh any satisfaction I might get out of it. And he resigned himself to my position on the matter, in exchange for my willingness to accommodate his preferences.

When Santiago untied me, I would go to the bathroom, turn the key in the lock, and, my body in pain and my soul unfulfilled, masturbate. That might sound strange, but my solitary pleasure felt like a kind of purification after those frenzied sex scenes. It helped restore the equilibrium and well-being I had thought marriage would bring. The bathroom became my den of pleasure, and I (and I alone) was the only person who knew how best to give it to myself. I masturbated in the shower, on the bidet, or in a corner, my eyes filled with tears or with a vengeful smile, and completely at ease. Sometimes I would cover my body with cream or soap until I was all slippery and soft. Then I would look at myself in the mirror, my skin shining, and arouse myself with my sensual shape. I'd spread my hands across my smooth flesh, across my hot flesh, I'd suck my soapy breasts, I'd gently bite at my shoulders, and searching for my cunt with my slippery fingers became the most irresistible thing of all to me. That was when I could finally satisfy myself, without ties or slaps, without intrusive cocks . . . myself alone, with one hand going up and down my leg while the other stroked my genitals, me alone, my double, the real me in the mirror and the image of myself there in the bathroom, standing up, with my face renewed by satisfaction and my knees weakened by the orgasm I reached.

But it happened. One tormented morning Santiago tied me to the bed, as usual. He was drunk. He had spent the previous night with his nose in the computer, firing missiles at spaceships and martians, with a bottle of whiskey for company, while I had lain in bed reading a book. I think it was a Saturday, because that was how we spent our evenings when we didn't have to work the following day. He went through the whiskey and ordered me to get him the bottle of rum.

'Don't drink any more,' I dared to say.

'Shut up and do what I say!' he yelled.

I knew something was about to happen: he never shouted at me. That is, unless we were turning on the machine of our mutual sexual dissatisfaction, he didn't treat me like that. Usually he was even kind of loving. I brought him the rum. He finished that, too. He asked for the vodka. I obeyed and then went to the bedroom. I got undressed and into bed, and soon I was asleep. I woke up to the sound of rain falling, a savage, unbridled storm. Santiago was tying my feet to the bed.

It wasn't the first time he'd awakened me with the tying-up ceremony, so I didn't object. The lights were on, and in their electric clarity everything seemed less ominous. He insulted me, smacked me, and ripped my panties off in one quick motion. He told me to start masturbating in front of him. His penis, however, resisted. Being drunk had rendered him practically impotent. To spur him on, I whispered:

'Hit me harder. Your slaps don't hurt me.'

It was true. That's what I said. I was three months pregnant then, and I knew better than to provoke Santiago, but I said it anyway. I couldn't help falling into the trap of my own will. Failure, alcohol, and my words sent him over the edge. He hit me all over – on my face, and on my stomach – as he blamed me for his impotence. *Now I'll never be able to fuck again. You've ruined me forever, you slut.* He hit me until he had exhausted himself.

'Give me the vibrator,' I said to him.

He squatted down on top of my chest, his back to me as he leaned over my cunt and prepared to penetrate me with the substitute for his virility. I clung to him with my hips and guided him toward me. I passed my tongue along his buttocks, rubbing them against my teeth. He didn't complain. In fact, he adjusted his ass right at the level of my mouth so I could suck on it. No question, this was a special day for us.

It tasted sweet; a pleasant flavor spiced my saliva, which, oddly enough, reminded me of the milky treats my mother used to prepare for me when I was a little girl. But this wasn't exactly the moment to take a walk down memory lane, because Santiago's penis had been slowly awakening and now decided to become hard. He had abandoned the vibrator between my legs and dedicated himself to enjoying the sensation that was so forbidden. My tongue darted inside him and he let out a gasp of pleasure. He relaxed in order to open himself up to the blossoming of my kisses, and I extended my tongue as far as it could reach. I couldn't raise my head any farther, though, because the tie held my neck back and cut into it. Santiago let himself fall onto me even more, and I caressed his ass as I continued sucking. With the tips of my fingers I flirted with the entrance to his anus, to gauge his reaction. No, he said, no, but I was familiar with that kind of negative and I could tell that he said it more out of habit and fear than anything else. I continued. I wet my index finger and as my tongue licked the tense edges, I slowly introduced it inside, to the first ridge, then the second, and then all the way in.

His erection was ready. I took his penis with my left hand, encircling it fully and shaking it lightly to the rhythm of my now sticky index finger as it moved in and out of his anus. He shouted yes, now he wanted more. So then I added my middle finger, and then my ring finger to the index finger, but he still wasn't satisfied. He wanted me to penetrate him even more profoundly; he wanted to feel that hole completely filled.

'Give me the vibrator,' I ordered.

He hesitated. His agitated breathing was in step with my fingers now, which continued repeating the crazy metronome of the rain beating against the windows. Finally, Santiago decided to pass me the dildo. He howled when I impaled him on it. In each hand I held a cock: one real and one fake. I could have distinguished between the two blindfolded from the way the real one grew in size. Between my thighs I felt the warmth of my own organ. It made me crazy to see him like that, surrendered to my whims, enslaved and at the mercy of my tyranny. I could strip him, degrade him, or give him pleasure. I buried the fake cock still farther and he twisted his body in satisfied response. I didn't even have to wiggle the dildo inside his asshole, because he came with a vengeance and ferocity, even harder than he'd come in the taxi. His body shuddered several times and finally was spent, sprawled out across my stomach. Then he complained it hurt. I thought I shouldn't prolong the suffering for much longer, so I pulled the dildo out in one swoop. He howled again, and tears poured out of his eyes.

'I feel sick,' he babbled. 'I feel sick.'

His body arched suddenly, shocking him. Without managing to extricate himself, he vomited all over my groin. He fell again, facedown on his own excretions.

'What have you done to me?' he cried. 'What have you done?'

'Calm down,' I said. 'Don't take it so hard – you loved it.' He got up slowly; he could barely walk. 'Now me; you left me hanging.'

With the perplexed countenance of a drunk who feels he's been violated, he weakly placed the dildo inside me, but he didn't have the strength to jiggle it around at all. He must have noticed how crestfallen I was by the look on my face, because he then asked me:

'You want more, right?'

I nodded yes. Unsteady, he hobbled into the living room. I stayed there in the bedroom alone listening to the rain, still tied up, with my fingers dirty and covered in semen and vomit. I had to see the insanity of the situation; nevertheless I was more excited than ever. I smoothed the hairs on my vagina, separated my lips, and located the rigid lump of my clitoris. I caressed it, put pressure on it; my only thought, my only obsession was to achieve a new, better kind of orgasm, one that would take away the tedium I found myself in.

Santiago knew what I was thinking: he came back to the

room with one of those large, stiff plastic tubes that he used for carrying his sketches to the ad agency. It was about five centimeters in diameter, and at least forty long. My heart was pounding in my chest, wildly. Santiago seemed to have recovered some of his energy; on his lips was a sardonic smile. It wasn't about satisfaction anymore; now it was time for revenge.

'That's too much,' I dared to whisper, my eyes fixed on the dimensions of the plastic tube. 'Give it to me up the ass, if that's what you want, but don't stick that thing inside me.'

I was terrified of the consequences of our recent frenzy, and I was prepared to make whatever concession was necessary to avoid them. Yet at the same time, I secretly prayed that no scruple would hold Santiago back from doing what he was going to do. He punched me in the throat. Momentarily forgetting I was tied down, I tried to get up, and the noose choked me with a sharp yank that sent me straight back down on the bed. As I fell, Santiago hit me again, in the nose this time, and my face was soon covered in blood.

'Shut up!' he bellowed.

He had never punched me before; just slaps up until then. I begged him for mercy and that infuriated him even more. My only hope was that a furious orgasm would justify the pain, and pacify him.

He placed a hand on my belly and with the other began to insert the tube into my vagina. The pain was devastating. I wanted to scream but my voice drowned in a suffocated sob that didn't manage to escape my throat.

Santiago kept on going. Half the tube was now inside me. I felt as though a bonfire was raging through the remains of my charred flesh and my dislocated bones. At that stage it became clear to me that no way would I be able to come in such circumstances. I stroked my clitoris in an attempt to isolate it, to provide solace from the world around it, from the pain. I could taste the blood that continued flowing from my nose. *I don't like anything you stick inside of me. Just me, me alone, can make me feel pleasure*, I said, or I thought; I'm not sure. The excessive amount of penetration had sent me teetering into a kind of delirium where there was no line between nightmare and real life, between language and hallucination, between memory and the present time. The tube was bisecting me, worse than the blade of a knife would have felt, and it seemed as though it had reached all the way up to my throat, against my spine, through my kidneys, and into my brain. It couldn't go any farther now, I was certain; there was no way.

And then Santiago gave the back end of the tube a hard slap with the palm of his hand and somehow buried it deeper inside of me, beyond my vagina, beyond me myself, beyond my body, far beyond our mutual disillusion and bitterness. I don't know what he did after that. I fainted. When I came to, my vagina and legs were numb. I was sitting in a lake of blood that had stained the sheets a bright red and swamped the mattress. Santiago was crying inconsolably over his vomit. I couldn't move, but even so, I cried buckets. And then I realized why I was hemorrhaging so much.

'I'm losing it!' I screamed to Santiago, but he didn't respond. 'Quick!'

I couldn't get up, because I was still tied up, and I knew that every second lost was critical. I grabbed him by the hair and shook him, desperate. He opened his eyes.

'Hurry up! I need to go to the doctor!'

He untied me. He covered my bloody body with a jacket and rushed me out the door. Rain fell on us like some kind of scolding. We stumbled into the car. I didn't lose consciousness again, but I still can't remember how Santiago was able to drive in that state, and I don't remember how we got there, or even which hospital we went to. Everything after that happened too fast: all those attentive nurses; Santiago's excuses; the doctor with the accent from Extremadura (memory is an odd thing: I can't recall his face, but his accent stayed with me); that doctor who threatened to call the police on Santiago until I managed to babble that it was my fault, it wasn't him, it was another man; the doctor's insults; the harsh light shining down on the surgical table; the anesthesia. After a few days, I was able to go home. Santiago had changed the sheets, but he'd forgotten to untie the belts from the bed frame.

I'm sorry about that. It's not without disgust that I narrate these events. It seems that these days, desperation has become sort of old hat. A couple of tears roll down your face, and you get labeled pathetic. I would have preferred to omit this disgrace, and the one that followed, Marina. I would love to write a frivolous, carefree book, and talk about love and death as if they were refreshments in the park. What I mean, really, is that I wish these things hadn't happened. But they did happen, and that's what I regret most of all. That wasn't the first time I'd aborted. But in the past, I'd done it of my own free will. Now it was different; I had placed so many of my hopes in that birth that never arrived. I had thought it would take me back to that placid realm of a life without chaos, and, through the fruit of my womb, allow me to make up for all the injustices I'd suffered as a child, as a way of reconciling my history. Of course, it all ended before it could even begin. I imagined that the dead fetus had been a girl. I called her Laura. I never smoothed her hair, never dressed her after a bath, never walked her to school. She finished her life which never began in a garbage can of a hospital whose name I can't recall.

Santiago cried and cried, asking for my forgiveness. But it was a fatality that we had both participated in, propelled by our intemperate passions. After the incident, we tried to take care of each other, so as not to fall back into that abyss we had created for ourselves. He tied me up just once more after that, and it was only after a long, long time. Too long, perhaps.

We renounced all emotions, all ideas of being happy, and we gave up the thought of having another child. We abandoned violence and adopted a cordial indifference toward one another, trading old regrets for new sorrows. Physical contact between us became sporadic and lifeless: reaching orgasm required so much more effort than we were usually willing to expend.

From those useless attempts, I remember endless bouts covered with sticky sweat, and our irritated and alienated genitals, and Santiago's agitation, his gasps, the remote glimpse of pleasure which always ended up getting lost in the labyrinths of an incomprehensible chill. And then, when my body finally overflowed with an unquenched ardor, I would escape to the bathroom to conjure up the shining secret of Narcissus, and my apathy would disappear as if by magic, from the lightest contact between a fraction of my hand and a fraction of my cunt. Years went by like that.

During that time, we didn't fight, not even once. Santiago was a perfect gentleman with me – objectively speaking, he was exemplary, and he tolerated all of my silence and disdain with a patience I'd hardly imagined him capable of. If I hurt his feelings, even indirectly, he would clam up for a few seconds as if silently reminding himself not to resort to violence, as if he had to force himself to repress brutal instincts that were always on the verge of exploding. Then he would respond with some loving comment, and touch my face and ask me if something was bothering me. Now I know that each one of my rebuffs, one by one, nourished his rage, strengthening it, multiplying it, waiting for just the right occasion to release it. But he never talked about it, and in our conversations he made a conscious effort to avoid all talk of the past.

That was why after the miscarriage he never sang that bolero, which now seemed to be on the radio all the time – as I drove to the pool beneath the suffocating May sun.

Perhaps this brief escape from my daily life in Madrid was nothing more than the most minimal of transgressions against my familiar routine, the childish, secret mischief of a married woman. But to me it felt like an extraordinary event, whose origins could be traced back to the exalting dream of that morning. In general, I didn't see the light of day at this unusual hour, unless it was through the window of some disgusting restaurant or the gallery. Today it shone directly down, and it comforted me, it seemed to promise me it would clean the shadows out of my eyes, which were tired of squinting around me in a fruitless search for happiness. Through the open car window, I felt the fresh breeze of velocity, which I enjoyed with that physical appreciation only experienced through the most elemental forces of nature.

I was certain that there had always been something missing in

my life. Inside me there was this feeling of indefinite expectation, and none of the men I'd known before Santiago had been
able to fulfill it. Santiago hadn't been able to either, nor had our
violent love, or my work, or anything that I could have imagined
back then. Nothing could placate my anxiety, intangible flare
that it was, not the nights of solitary sex in which I would masturbate in front of the bathroom mirror nor even the pregnancy.
It was an intimate, inexplicable sensation, which I felt right
there in the car as I drove down the luminous highway, in search
of something I wanted but couldn't identify.

The pool was farther than I'd calculated. At first I was afraid
I'd lost my way, because I don't usually drive outside the city and
I have a terrible sense of direction. I got misled because I kept
looking out for those gypsy settlements that had been in
Santiago's photos, but they were no longer there at the side of
the road. Finally, just when I had almost given up hope, I drove
past a billboard that said something like 'CAMPING ATERPE ALAI,
8KM.' Behind it, I spied a sign, smaller and a bit beat-up, that
said, 'Piscina El Tórrido Trópico, 200m,' and a little arrow
pointing toward the right. My heart seemed to flip over. I
turned onto the side road, drove past a row of houses, and
arrived at a kind of Caribbean-motif hut, from whose roof a
half-lettered sign seemed about ready to fall off:

EL TO RID T O IC .

Another, newer sign, stuck to the window by four little suc-
tion cups, announced that the pool was open from May 1 to
September 30, from 9 A.M. to 7 P.M. It was none too tempting.
I parked alongside a gravel driveway, under the shade of a linden

tree. I turned off the engine and sat there a few seconds, my hands on the steering wheel, asking myself if once more my hopes were destined to be dashed. But this time I was not the victim of disillusion, or illness (as Manolo had feared), because I met you. Your love was waiting for me there.

How can I honestly say that we met for the first time that day, when we had always known one another? We had seen each other every morning in the mirror, and every night in both happy dreams and hallucinatory nightmares, and always in the defective photos and prophetic portraits, in the hopes and in the horror, in the imminent passion, and in the unbroken solitude of our separate lives. I had already heard every one of your heartbeats, Marina, before feeling them pound against my finger entering your sex. It is the same heart of flesh that still tries to measure the presence of your absence. One beat, and you leave me. Another beat, and you escape. Another beat, and you go farther, and farther still, another beat and you disappear in the savage swamp of time. Another beat, another beat, another beat of my dying heart.

The attendant with the chubby arms gave me a key and a brass plate with the number 5. Then, without even looking at me, she subjected me to an exhaustive medical inquiry, the purpose of which was to assuage any doubts I had as to the pool's standards of hygiene. Of course, it produced the exact opposite effect.

'Do you suffer from mycosis, pediculosis, venereal diseases, tetanus——?' She interrupted herself, suddenly appearing like an electric appliance whose current has just been cut off. She didn't seem thrilled about running down that long list which she clearly had to repeat to each and every swimmer. 'Tetanus . . .

tetanus, herpes' – she stopped to think for a moment – 'or any other illness?' she finished.

'No.'

'That's all!' She gave me the nod. 'All right, go ahead.'

I entered a locker room, which was indeed as torrid as the tropics. I undressed and hung my clothes in a beat-up metal locker, the fifth in the row. Then I put on my bathing suit, which still carried the scent of gasoline. A bathing suit is the definitive test to see if you're fat; the evidence is almost as conclusive as an X ray. It doesn't matter if you've seen yourself hundreds of times in the mirror, naked and dressed – until you try on your bathing suit for the first time, in season, you won't know for sure exactly to what extent obesity has conquered your body over the winter. I had no big complaint; it could have been worse. I grabbed my bag and went outside to the pool area.

The intense sunlight blinded my eyes, which had adjusted to the darkness of the dressing room. I walked slowly, feeling the grass brush against my bare feet. The pool was shaped somewhat like a deformed kidney. On one side, between mutant palm trees and gray rocks, there was a fake fountain which spouted water from a fake waterfall. The noise of the rushing water gave a bit of equilibrium to the atmosphere, which was pierced by an overexcited South American melody. I walked down a stone path, avoiding the outdoor shower where we were to wash our feet: in its turbulent waters I saw several items floating, including dried-up blades of grass, a half-smoked joint, dead bugs, and a used Band-Aid that had lost its master but still retained its cylindrical form. At the far end was a counter, about thirty meters from the locker room. It wasn't much more than a stand, covered poorly with a cone-shaped straw top.

This wasn't exactly the kind of spot one would go to for making important life decisions. In fact, every element of the place had a vulgar, artificial quality, and the whole purpose of it, to foment a forced feeling of happiness, was just depressing. I lost my appetite, so when I sat down at the bar after crossing the little park, I only ordered a beer.

The waiter moved with the effervescence of a civil servant and sweated like a slave. The poor guy was pretty old and very bald for the blinding floral shirt he wore, which appeared to be another of the institutional obligations of the place, much like the litany of infectious diseases presented to me earlier by the locker room attendant. He alone, however, was responsible for pulling his pants so horribly far up from his waist, no doubt to draw attention to the large lump before which all women were expected to prostrate themselves. I did not. I took a sip of the beer; it was lukewarm, and the smell of the waiter's perspiration seemed to be mixed in.

There couldn't have been more than seven people at the pool. We were seven embarrassed, antisocial people who were trying anonymously to overcome, as well as possible, our unfortunate decision to spend an afternoon at El Tórrido Trópico. In the farthest corner of the property, two people sat playing cards in the shade; Manolo would have surely identified them as dentists. A guy and a girl, lying on the grass near the fake fountain, were locked in an endless kiss, uninterested in pausing for breath or whispering sweet nothings in one another's ears. A man slept face-up to the sun, floating in the curve of the kidney atop an inflatable raft. A girl with a huge sty near her eye wrestled with a crossword puzzle as she leaned against the bar, three seats over. Everyone (myself included) had that winter pallor, superficially burnt by the intense rays of that premature May sunlight.

The waiter walked toward the locker rooms, furthering the development of his pestilence by exposing the skin of his arms and face to the oppressive sunlight, and after a while returned with a bag of ice, which dribbled onto the grass.

Then he announced to me that my sister had arrived.

I thought he was trying to pick me up with some tired old conversation starter, so I just nodded, and didn't tell him that he was mistaken, or that I hadn't made a date with anyone. Nor did I mention that I was an only child.

But a few minutes later I saw two women in the distance, exiting the locker room and walking toward the pool. The first one was around middle age, short and robust, slightly bow-legged – her legs looked as if she were about to ride a horse. She wore a robe, like the kind boxers wear, and it hung on her, half-open. The other one seemed a bit younger, although I couldn't tell exactly how old she was because she wore a pale rose dress that went down to her ankles and a huge yellow hat which totally covered her face.

A strange curiosity came over me. I could not take my eyes off the second woman. What was she doing with the other one? I asked myself. Her appearance revealed that they were clearly from two very different backgrounds; they didn't look like friends. I also dismissed the idea that they were related. At a loss for any other explanation, I told myself that they must know each other through work.

I was darkly attracted to the younger woman. I longed to know her – not in that particular moment, though. I wanted to know her already, to have known her all my life. Clearly, her yellow hat didn't match the pink dress, and she kept touching it, as if it were uncomfortable. I figured the other woman must have lent it to her.

In general, though, she had an air about her that reminded me of me, even though the distance between us and the clothing she wore prevented me from knowing exactly how similar we were.

As she spread a towel over the grass next to the pool, the other one removed her boxer's robe, showing off tanned skin that was unusual for this time of year.

The younger woman did look like me, although her gestures were different; she walked and gesticulated calmly, serenely. Like the sudden wallop of a wave against the beach, the image of my own naked body in the mirror came rushing into my mind. My own body, burning with happiness beneath the stimulus of my loving hand. I felt ashamed of myself.

'Did you hear what I said?' A voice behind me was saying something.

'What?' I stammered. I turned around, like someone coming out of a fainting spell. It was the waiter talking to me.

'I made this for you.'

In his hand was a gigantic glass filled with fruit and ice cream, with a brilliant green liquid.

'I don't want it,' I said. 'I didn't order anything.'

'Come on, lady, it's on the house. The golden rule at El Tórrido Trópico is to please the clients.'

'Thank you very much, but I really don't want it.'

'Oh, give me a break! I went out of my way to get the ice and everything for you.'

'I couldn't care less,' I said. 'I'm not thirsty.'

He insisted. I guessed the best way to get rid of him was to accept the repugnant beverage. I took it from his hands and placed it on the counter. But he was persistent, all right. He threw me another overused pickup line and pointed out the woman he thought was my sister, thinking I hadn't seen her yet.

'The name is *Diez de Richter*.' He hiked his pants up even higher.

'Who?' I thought he might mean the woman; I didn't know yet, of course, that Marina was her name. Marina.

He nodded toward the glass.

'What do you think, woman? The drink, of course,' he said, exasperated. This was the kind of man who liked to be called the 'barman' and not the 'waiter.' He went on, 'It's a killer. I invented it myself.'

He moved closer to me, forcing me to inhale his offensive breath; then he lowered his voice, and leaned into me, to whisper:

'It's an aphrodisiac, you know.'

'Oh, shut up already,' I snarled.

He left me alone after that. When I looked over at them again, the two women were sitting on their towels, chatting animatedly. The short, stocky one was facing me, and the younger one had her back to me. She had removed the pink dress and was wearing a mustard-colored bikini. I still couldn't see her face, but the delicate shape of her legs caused me to tremble in such a way that felt improper, even shameful. Unconsciously, I ran my hand over my own legs, almost caressing them. I was becoming aroused, without even trying, without knowing why.

Forgetting for a moment the crossword puzzle girl and the overbearing waiter, I surreptitiously stretched my finger across the smooth, synthetic fabric of my bathing suit, and made out the concave form I desired: my sex, which was now beating as hard as my inflamed heart.

She took off the incongruous hat and threw it rakishly to the side. She had brown hair, like me, and she sat with her back hunched over, more likely out of modesty than because of some spinal aberration. She wore her hair short, and as I contemplated the nape of her neck, I felt a chill run through my nerves like a spark ignited. What did she possess that catapulted me into these new sensations? Was it the mere coincidence that we resembled one another physically, or was this the transcendental moment that I had been waiting for all my life? If it was, it had certainly crept up on me unexpectedly – I had never desired a woman before, and I didn't hate or fear men, I'd always been satisfied with them. Yet there I was, perturbed by the distant image of a woman, even though all I had to go on were her legs and back – and her haircut, which was enough to arouse me beyond belief.

If you only saw her hair, that inverted triangle with a truncated point, that perfect trapezoid sitting above her neck, you might think you were looking at a man, or a soldier, even. But it didn't take much for me to look elsewhere, and to notice the indisputable hallmarks of a beautiful woman. The tips of her soft cheeks, her light jawline, her delicate shoulders, the peeping chest, the waistline that led to the curve of her hips, her thighs and then once again the nape of her neck, the virile cut of her hair, her cheeks.

I pressed my finger against my vagina even harder now; this

was really pushing the limits of decorum, I thought as I felt myself fire up in the heat of the day. In the mirrors, in my solitary joy, I always saw myself head-on. Now, as I watched her from behind, I could close my eyes and cut her out of the shape of the world and see myself from behind. I could now slyly discover the other side of myself, the diaphanous side, the side that could free me from the shadows and direct me into the light, into a clarity I had never known. My body shook and I wanted to cry, out of impotence and fear. My excitement was infectious; it invigorated every one of my senses and faculties. I felt I was doing something wrong by watching her, but at the same time I felt I would be doing something worse if I stopped watching her. I was desperate to conceive of a love that was just beyond my reach; and I furiously, secretly reveled in my intimate glimpse of her – her profile, her contours. And, for the first time, my hand wasn't enough; it cried out, it demanded another body. The body of a woman. Your body, Marina, your body, just like mine.

'See how my magic potion turns you on?' The waiter, again.

He wasn't looking in my eyes; he was staring at my hand, which was tucked between my legs. Had he not been, however, he would have seen my tears. On the counter, in my drink, the ice cream had melted, mixing in with the bright green liquid and the bits of candied fruit suspended in it. And I hadn't even taken a sip. I felt a terrible shame wash over me. I was going crazy, that was it. Luckily, the waiter's stupid remark had served a purpose, and brought me back to reality. I was afraid something was going to happen, something I wouldn't be able to undo. I should leave, I said to myself. Forget about that woman, get on with my life and my void; I should go back to normality.

When I got up, I inadvertently knocked over the glass with my elbow, and the contents of the mystery drink spilled all over the waiter's flowered shirt. I babbled a few words of apology and jumped up from the bar. I strode toward the locker rooms, intent on getting out of there. I would circle the pool from the other side, to avoid bumping into the two women.

But then it happened – the event that the premonitions, dreams, and coincidences had all indicated ever since the early morning of that one crucial day in my life. Until then, my existence had gone by uneventfully; I woke up every morning in the same state as I had gone to bed the night before – until dawn broke on this one unpredictable day, a day that turned everything into chaos. I've only had two days like this in my life, two days that essentially changed the course of my destiny. The first, Marina, led me to meet you, and I wasn't prepared for it, even though I had received so many incontrovertible signs. I had tried to read into them rationally, but of course there was no way to interpret them that way, because the coded language of augury is only accessible through the innocence of love, the inspiration of poets, and the madness of visionaries. The second day came suddenly, and that was the day they ripped you out of my hands and expelled me from Paradise. I had feared it for a while, and was on my guard, but that wasn't any consolation. A tragedy foretold can sometimes be more painful than an unexpected tragedy. Fate gave me something and took it away, and even so I knew that it wouldn't change anything, that I would love Marina no matter what, in spite of everything.

On the other hand, the day at the pool I knew in an instant – before we even looked at each other – that nothing would ever be the same after that, even if I had left that instant, and had refused to confront the woman I had spied on. Even if I had gone and never seen her again. Her mere presence in the world was enough to change my life from what it had been before. My certainty was not just a result of our surprising physical resemblance, either: it was the rapture that robbed me of breath, and filled my chest with ecstasy. Remember, Marina, how I used to hate Borges? He was one of your favorite writers, and I only began to read him because you had asked me to, but I wound up loving him one afternoon in the Campidoglio, when I came across a passage that expressed the certainty I felt those days. 'Any destiny, no matter how long or complicated it may be, consists of the reality of one single moment: the moment in which a man realizes who he truly is.' I knew it like nothing I had ever known before. And I began to be a better person than I'd ever been. The same thing happened to you, Marina. You became part of me, my life became your life. We understood you as I had never before understood anything.

So that was when it happened.

The woman that looked exactly like me, the sister that the pool waiter had announced, also got up. She said something to the other woman while shaking out her legs. She turned around halfway and walked toward the bar. Toward me.

Part Two

We moved toward the encounter, one toward the other, around the edge of the pool, and each step we took brought us closer to confusion.

It wasn't that Marina simply resembled me. She was identical; not even sisters could look so much alike.

My stride slowed down to the rhythm of my stupor, and I felt as if I were before some kind of abnormal mirror, or a photograph from some forgotten moment in my past, or a sorcerer's enchantment. It was like that feeling you have when you wear new clothing, or cut your hair, when you're shocked by the first image the mirror reflects back to you, or when you look at photos taken by surprise, before you've been able to imprint your will upon your facial features. There is always an imbalance between the reality and the myth of a person, between the old and the new image, and nothing but a new habit can correct it.

I had that feeling of being slightly off-balance as I mentally catalogued the superficial details that distinguished me from Marina. They were almost imperceptible, characteristics that only someone with a sharp eye would even notice. Beyond that, of course, the main thing was that I had discovered the existence of my perfect double.

We advanced in slow, hesitating paces, and finally stood face-to-face.

No words found their way to my trembling mouth. It wasn't really necessary anyway. My bag slipped from my shoulder and fell to the ground. I barely lifted my left shoulder and stretched my palm out to Marina, as if to prove the physical reality of my dream, and at the very same moment she stretched her right hand out to me. We didn't touch. I looked her in the eye and there I saw my own eyes staring back at me. I turned; we turned. We contemplated one another in the broken, repeated reflections of the water and we were four Narcissuses in one, and two. You looked at us, we looked at me in the undulations of the pool, in search of our true face and our name written in the water, and an impulse incited me to escape that dream by diving into the water, and Marina did the very same thing.

The mirror broke at that moment, and I found my shadow, my reflection; I found you, I found myself in the water's limpid vigil. There, my tears evaporated forever in the pool, along with the gasoline smell of winters past, and love was like the water that wrapped itself around us without fissures or wrinkles, and the world, our undulating, multiple reflections. I opened my eyes and saw more clearly than ever, because I saw you, my love.

We touched, fearfully at first, barely brushing against each other, and even that light contact made me dizzy. I forgot who I was, my modesty, my virtue. It was so incredible that I couldn't even begin to describe what was happening within ordinary parameters of description, nor could I stop to observe the usual urban rituals — *I like you, I have to think about it, Call me next week, Don't go so soon, We need time to get to know each other*, and all that nonsense. No, this was something beyond normal experience, beyond the rules of flirting and seduction.

I surrendered myself to her. There are things you do sometimes, actions that you take by obeying sudden impulses, without stopping for even a fraction of a second to think, and then you spend the rest of your life either lamenting it or thanking yourself for it. They are rare, unique, and perfect moments.

We embraced, and that first embrace in those infinite, remote depths separated us from the past and united us: Narcissus held Narcissus, we squeezed each other tightly, amid the bubbles of our breath and the foam of light; we caressed one another beneath the water, until our lungs had reached the point of explosion, and then we rose up, returning to the world once again. But we were no longer the same people: we had crossed our river of forgotten memories, through the threshold of mirrors. We had shed our old skin, and initiated ourselves into the mysteries of an identity that divides itself in two, to find itself baptized by an uncommon sensual ritual. And now that our wet hair clung to our heads, those insignificant details that separated us disappeared, and we were the same, we were hidden beneath the surface of the pool but entirely visible in the center of the center of our being.

At first, I didn't want to kiss her, because I still couldn't comprehend this miracle that had been bestowed upon me, but it was enough to contemplate the lips which I had kissed so many times before against the cold surface of the mirrors, leaving the disappointed imprint of my lonely mouth, which I had hoped would erase my doubts, and I kissed it, I kissed it with the same desperation that my lungs lived on to breathe. I searched in her mouth for the air to fill my own, I held on to her face, grateful for the lips and sweet tongue now upon my own, and I didn't even stop to remind myself that I was a woman and this was the kiss of another woman, because I was crossing the boundaries that separate love from scruples, shaking myself out of the splintered remains of the mirror. And I was afraid, if only for an instant, or maybe less, or maybe I just thought I would be afraid but wasn't really, and in the cold water my hard nipples made contact for the first time with another pair of nipples, and I touched a cunt that was not my own but that felt as if it had always been part of me. At the same time, a light feminine hand was searching for my sex underneath my bathing suit, and it was exhilarating, like an electric charge running through the water in the pool, setting us on fire. Everything toppled over right then: I could no longer resist the irrational frenzy I found myself in, I couldn't think, I wasn't ashamed, and I felt no qualms at all. I surrendered myself to that urgent desire of twenty-eight years of abstinence, and I witnessed once again the love of two identical bodies reaching one single orgasm, locked in an embrace and submerged in the water of two mouths joined together in the one kiss that truly held love.

I don't think anyone saw us kissing in that shadowy corner of the pool – well, with the exception of the waiter, who stormed off toward the locker rooms, cursing under his breath, with his Hawaiian shirt slung over his arm. Dumbfounded, he stopped, and went behind the trampoline to spy on us, but we barely noticed him. We only separated our lips for a moment, gazed at each other, and then the kiss resumed, sweet and liquid, filling our mouths with water. Our hungry tongues tasted the same, they sought each other slowly, recognizing each other like two angels lost in the rooftops of a hostile city, and when they met, reveling in the love they had discovered.

An unexpected guest interrupted the scenario: the man who was dozing on the inflatable raft. He had drifted toward us, carried by the undulations of the water, but he didn't wake up and continued snoring. He was better off that way, anyway.

Under no circumstances would he be able to sleep that night – the sun had burnt his skin to a crisp. In any event, Marina and I finished our kiss and left the pool, although both of us would have remained in there forever if we could have.

Sprinkling the ground with thick droplets, which also contained a bit of the saliva left over from our first kiss, we walked together around the perimeter of the pool. We didn't bother with the waiter, who continued watching us, paralyzed. What he had just witnessed – homosexuality and incest – must have seemed like the epitome of depravity and must have exceeded the limits of his understanding. His stupor shook me, and all of a sudden I was overwhelmed by a wave of fear.

We didn't say a word, but we still couldn't separate. Our damp, chilly arms brushed against each other in that May heat, and it seemed that every one of our erect hairs were joined in mutual contact. We approached the short, robust woman who Marina had come with to the pool. We kneeled down on the towel.

'I don't believe my eyes,' she stammered when she saw us. 'You are one and the same person!'

Marina looked me in the eyes.

'My God! It's incredible!' the woman exclaimed. 'It sounds so obvious, but you're like sisters. You're identical!'

We were. Weeks later we would search for differences; there were so few that they only served to remind us how alike we were. Her sternum was a bit more prominent, her nose slightly longer, her voice grittier, her arms and legs more delicate than mine, she didn't gesture as much when she talked, and little dimples appeared when she laughed. I, on the other hand, had wider hipbones, smaller ears, narrower shoulders, a higher voice, my eyes were set farther apart, and I blinked more often. Long, intimate evenings of discovery revealed these things to our reawakened senses. I will never forget how, during a naked afternoon in Siena, surrounded by the sounds of people returning from modern life through the medieval streets as the cathedral bells rang for the Angelus, I will never forget how there, in the darkness, in front of the silent mirrors, we compared our navels, brushing them lightly with our index fingers with a touch more sensual than penetrating, feeling their distinct shapes in the blind darkness. Mine protruded outward, and hers was like a concave star. From there we took the first step on that long road leading to pleasure, as I ran my tongue slowly across her navel and she, on all fours above me, did the same to me, and our navels burned between the beats of our kisses, which alternated in perfect synchronization, in momentum with our bodies. I was now nearing the breaking point of ecstasy, my body wrapped around your legs and your excited breath against my skin as the sound of the cathedral bells outside greeted our rapture. Every encounter left us weakened from the sheer voluptuousness of it all, from the renewed awe and ever-increasing devotion we felt. In no time, we wore our hair and dressed the same. It's true, we did lack those gestures that family members share. The shock of the world would separate us before that kind of mimicry would become second nature to us.

As I looked at Marina, next to the pool where we had just kissed in silence, I realized that she – not I – had been the person I'd seen in my dream the previous night.

'I'm leaving,' announced the other woman. 'I think I should leave the two of you alone. You have a car?' she asked me.

I nodded yes. The woman gathered her things and before she left said to Marina:

'Keep the hat as a gift! Even if you don't like it so much.' She smiled. 'It will be your souvenir of this afternoon.'

Marina and I were now alone, for the first time. Both of us were anxious, terrified. Where was this going to take us? We still hadn't said a thing to each other. I didn't even know her name. I thought, We should at least introduce ourselves, like two teenagers who fall in love at a dance. But she spoke first:

'Shall we go?' she whispered. She had a serious voice, rough but sweet.

Logic told me it was impossible – absurd – to fall in love with a person with whom I literally had not exchanged a single word. But it was true. I also knew that I would never be able to love anyone else as I loved that woman, that stranger, right then.

The shadow of the waiter darkened our faces. He was standing next to us with his arms crossed, and his face was filled with curiosity. He had changed into a newer, cleaner shirt; this one featured palm trees and parrots. My handbag dangled from his fingers; that was his excuse for approaching us. I said a curt thank you and silently wished him away.

'Let's go,' I said, and ran my hand quickly over Marina's short hair – secretly, of course, to touch the nape of her neck. I could no longer resist it, and I felt strangely content when I did it.

I don't know how we got to the locker room to change. In a strange moment of modesty, I dressed with my back to Marina; she hadn't put anything in the lockers, so all she did was throw the pink dress over her bikini. She didn't put the hat on. The attendant with the chubby arms sat there staring at the counter in front of her. We went to my car. I started the motor and turned onto the road. Very long moments passed before either of us dared to say anything. The damp outline of her bikini appeared on Marina's dress.

'My name is Sofía,' I murmured, finally.

When she told me her name was Marina, I realized she wasn't Spanish, but South American. Marina, I repeated to myself, and – can you believe it? – the name still didn't mean anything to me.

'Where are you from?' I asked her.

'Want to guess?' she joked, and I realized she was trying to relieve the tension created by the fear we felt.

Colombia, I said. No, she answered. Chile. No. Mexico. No. One after the other, I rattled off all the countries I could think of, without luck. Marina then pressed her fingertips against my exposed legs, on the insides of my thighs. The midday sun had burnt my skin, and the contact with her hand was refreshing. Venezuela. No. Nicaragua. No. Marina's caress was not allowing me to think particularly clearly.

'And it's in South America?'

'Yes.' She laughed. 'I'd say so. You can leave out North America and Central America.'

'But there are no more countries left,' I said.

'Obviously, the old colonies are not your forte,' she observed, as she pushed my skirt up to the waist.

I slowed the car down. Her hand was already working through the hair on either side of my panties, and I felt an infinite sense of well-being, protecting me from fear, and forgiving me for all the things I perceived as impure thoughts and behaviors. In that moment, however, I did not experience the need to be punished for my shocking thoughts, as I had when I was with

Santiago. In fact, I felt the opposite: I found myself in such a state of serenity that I saw in this passion a perfect wholeness rather than an expiation of remorse.

'What do you mean there are no countries left?' she whispered. 'You forgot about Ecuador, Argentina, Uruguay, Paraguay . . .'

I stopped at the side of the road, because I knew I couldn't keep driving like that. I said she was Uruguayan, but we got off the subject of geography because our lips had found each other once again. I felt as if we were sharing a single kiss – in fact, the same one we'd started in the swimming pool – and that it would last forever. I touched her breasts, with trepidation at first, and then with increasing excitement, like someone trespassing on private property. The sound of a truck horn startled us. I rested my head on her shoulder and kissed the pulse in her neck. I remained there for a while, my heart pounding nervously in response to the booming horn, and that shoulder was my refuge, my peace. For the first time in my life nobody asked anything of my silence. Marina simply allowed me to prolong that harmonious tranquillity, embracing me as she gently sketched the lines of my ear with her fingernails. The sun was moving toward nightfall, but I didn't move. Sitting there, I let the day melt into shadows.

It was then that I left the protection offered by Marina's shoulder, as I began to feel the incipient desire to bring her a bit of pleasure. I leaned over her sex. I licked it, I licked it until she came, again and again, and I perceived a new appreciation of the female form, savoring the thing that until now I had only touched with my hand, grasping a groin which wasn't my own, burying my fingers into unknown depths, arousing myself with my initiation into a cursed, forbidden, sweet passion, rising up on either side of that seductive triangle of her sex, until reaching its vertex. This triangle was the inverse reflection of the nape I desired so deeply, and I willed Marina to ecstasy with my desire for her, I wanted her to feel my gratitude, my refuge in her shoulder, my scorn for the passing time.

Cars passed us on the road, illuminating us in long sheets with their headlights. No truck horn would startle me now. A little farther up the road, the luminous letters of a neon sign indicated the presence of a furniture factory, in regular intervals of green, red, and darkness. Marina asked me to tilt my seat back and she undressed me there, in that sordid spot which felt like paradise to me – there, on the edge of a river of indifferent, fast cars; there, in the hollow shape of a distant city, where a routine that no longer belonged to me could continue on without me. I looked at her in the darkness, in the brilliance of the headlights, in the red and the green neon. She was the reflection that had come alive out of the dead mirror, to exist, to breathe on my body, to cover my breasts with her lips, to take my hands inside hers, to travel over my skin, burnt and stiff from the sun, to guide four identical hands toward my sex, over my sex, into my sex, and out of my sex, enveloping it, penetrating it, kissing it with my own mouth, with another identical mouth that allowed my lips to reach what had always been beyond my reach. I thought I was ready to melt, but no, it wasn't over yet, the orgasm was endless, lasting longer than any other ever had, elevating me to the highest levels of rapture, to a place I had never been before, beyond which there was nothing at all; but there was something, there was always something else, a new limit that would soon be achieved and surpassed, the green

light, then red, the night. That was when Marina smoothed out
the waves generated by so many hands, and slipped her index
finger into my vagina, placing pressure on the upper wall, on
that wrinkled, sensitive island, as her thumb rested on my clitoris. It was nothing more than a pea, and the island stiffened up
like never before, and I felt a totally new kind of pleasure which
enveloped my entire body. I thought I was going to pee, and I
said so.

'Give me everything,' she said. 'It isn't pee.' And it wasn't, I
realized for the first time. I had had to wait twenty-eight years
to find out: women ejaculate as well. And I relieved myself. It
wasn't pee, nor was it the habitual moisture of excitement, but
rather a clear, light liquid that spilled out onto the seat. I had to
look at it, touch it, even though I was in the middle of a hasty,
precipitous orgasm, and I laughed and I cried out loud with
laughter inundating my cries, Marina, and the wonder of watching myself, my double in that living mirror, beautiful, agitated
by the passion and the pleasure, the rapid succession of headlights, the distant city, the water, my water, my reflection.

It was almost eleven when we reached Madrid. We didn't say a
word during the ride back. Marina asked me to stop the car near
the traffic circle at Bilbao. She said:

'I live nearby. I can walk from here.' Perhaps she sensed my
imminent protest, because she added:

'I don't want you to take me there.'

Now that I was back in the familiar territory of Madrid, the
sense of security I had achieved so recently seemed to dissi-
pate, as if Marina were a witch whose powers lost their magical
effect once removed from their environment. All the shame I

had accumulated swept over me at that instant. How could I have been so crazy, so foolish?

Some time later, Marina would tell me that she too had felt all the certainties of her life being swept away. We both had the feeling that it was not going to be easy to surrender to the kind of blazing love we felt. Nothing worth doing is ever easy; I know that now, and I knew it then, too. Still, it paralyzed us. And it wasn't that we were trying to make things more difficult or create a fuss out of it, either; our bond had been established, far beyond the usual rules of seduction. No, we felt as if we had desecrated a sacred temple, usurped the throne of the gods or invaded the domain of dreams. We were frightened by the significance of our actions, the uncertainty of finding ourselves before a definitive future, a future that from beginning to end would put our entire lives in question.

'I'm afraid,' I confessed. 'I'm afraid of seeing you again, and of losing you.' I turned off, then turned on, then turned off the headlights. 'I've never been with a woman before.'

A car passed in front of us, and it reminded me of the furious love we had made on the side of the road.

'I have, many times,' she said. 'I've always liked women, and I've never even been with a man, but that isn't the problem. I'm afraid now, too.'

The car stopped behind a garbage truck, as did what few other cars were out on the street at that hour.

Fear was paralyzing her as well, I thought; if that was so, nobody would be able to rescue us from this abyss, from this almost wordless, painful dialogue. This was insanity, I said to myself. The illusion of leaping to the other side of the mirror, things that don't happen in real life, that shouldn't happen at all.

I tried to convince myself that by tomorrow, I would forget all about this. But I knew that I wouldn't and I knew that the anxiety wouldn't go away, either.

A group of animated teenagers ran by, playfully punching and swatting at each other; they didn't even look inside the car, where Marina and I were each contemplating the other with the bitterness of an executioner who has to kill the person he loves.

I put both hands on the steering wheel as if to drive, my eyes gazing out into the distance beyond the windshield.

The lives we had led up until then lost all meaning. It was a birth, in a way, but also a death. How can you erase an entire existence in one fell swoop? It was too much, too many changes all at once for me, and I knew that Marina was pondering the very same thought.

It was a clear night, with that fresh serenity that follows periods of intense heat. A light breeze blew through the plants on a balcony above.

I'm afraid, I repeated to myself, I'm afraid of being alone again, of starting my life over with the wrong person.

I saw my reflection in the windshield, but I had a difficult time recognizing myself in that distorted, depressed image.

Alone, alone again. Maybe we would end up drowning each other, wounding one another like two beasts locked in a cage, like Santiago and I had. Maybe our love would turn to rot.

I felt an overpowering fatigue, like someone who has lost faith in the one thing he had always believed in.

I tried to console myself by thinking that perhaps we would see each other again. And that if this encounter wasn't chance, then why wouldn't fate intervene by reuniting us?

Marina touched my chin and lifted my head so I could look at her.

'I don't want to hurt you,' she whispered.

She walked off in silence, and I let her go.

'I love you,' I said, once I was alone.

A cat walked down the street toward me, indifferently sniffing the remains of the garbage that had fallen from the truck. All of a sudden, another car approached.

'I love you.'

The car's headlights blinded the cat, which was caught, paralyzed, in the middle of the street. The driver slammed on the brakes, but not in time. The car thumped over the cat's body and continued on, not bothering to stop. The cat lay on the asphalt, dead, and a slow stream of blood trickled down from its mouth onto the curb.

That night I didn't go straight back home; I stayed in the car for a long while, devastated. After everything that had happened to me, it was going to be difficult to face Santiago, to lie to him or to offend him with that painful silence. My mind was filled with a jumble of images: Marina, my dream, the cat's terrible death, the neon sign, the waiter, the water in the swimming pool. How could I go back to my life? Just like cities destroyed by hurricanes, I felt I had before me two possibilities: either abandon the remains of the catastrophe and construct a new city, far from the old one, or rummage through the rubble to save what was left and begin the arduous process of reconstruction. For a moment, I leaned toward the first option, and cursed myself for letting Marina go. The next moment I decided that the second option was the better one, and I repeated to myself over and over that I had made the right decision. Then I changed my mind again, and bounced in this way from one decision to the other.

I got out of the car and walked over to the dead cat. I wanted to take it and bury it somewhere, but I didn't have the strength. I went back to the car. I started the engine, and drove aimlessly through the streets of Madrid, feeling more foreign than ever. I saw things without nostalgia, without passion. The only thing that keeps me here in this city, I thought, is Manolo.

I remembered the painting he had given me in the gallery that morning. It seemed as if months had gone by since then. Maybe he could tell me what to do, or offer some patient understanding in the face of my confusion. At the very least he could keep me company so I wouldn't feel so lonely. Perhaps this was the right moment to initiate the true friendship we had held off on for so long. I accelerated, having decided to head for his studio.

As I drove, I weighed the various possibilities for introductions to this thorny topic of conversation: melodramatic ('I'm losing my mind'), discreet ('I'm confused'), intriguing ('I have had the most incredible day'), direct ('I'm in love with a woman'), slutty ('I just had the ride of my life'). I even practiced them out loud, to make sure they sounded convincing enough, and this provided a great deal of entertainment for the couple sitting in the car next to me, waiting at the stoplight. Just like when I was a teenager and had to go to church and confess, I wished there were some kind of formula for revealing scandalous intimacies like this one.

As I repeated my speech, practicing the different variations of it, I began to realize that nobody — aside from me or Marina — could give me the right advice, the final word, the explanation

that would reveal every one of the innumerable nuances of my
state of mind. This realization, in addition to the absurdity of the
preambles I was preparing for my confession, didn't divert me,
exactly, but offered me a brief parenthesis of serene resignation,
like those afforded armies that establish a truce to count losses
and reassess their strength for the next battle.

I reached Manolo's house, which was in the front part of a
house in Salamanca. He had knocked out all the interior walls so
he could have one giant room, where he could leave easels,
stretched canvases, and paintbrushes all over the place. Tucked
away in a corner, practically hidden, was the bed (usually a
mess) where Manolo slept when he was too tired to do anything
else. I pushed the gate and walked into the yard. The window
was open. I cautiously spied on him from outside. From somewhere inside, I could hear Manolo's favorite music, Haydn's
Saint Cecilia Mass. He could listen to that over and over again
nonstop. Like all of us, Manolo was an avowed atheist, but he
frequently worked to the austere rhythms of religious music –
which embarrassed him; he never wanted anyone to know about
it. On the several occasions I had visited him in the past, all I had
to do was ring the doorbell and he would replace the mass or
oratorio of the moment with something lighter. His purpose, I
think, was to hide a habit which he feared would be interpreted
as affected or pompous. I had never let on that I knew, and I
didn't this time, either. I stood there, watching him through the
window, observing him as he painted. Maybe I was caught in the
spell that the music cast in the silent darkness, but Manolo
seemed to have been transported into an extraordinary other
dimension, parallel to this world, or perhaps in its inscrutable
center, that dimension so rarely attained, ever-changing like

the smell of jasmine, the fog of early dawn on empty streets in a strange city, the trace of a wave breaking on the beach, the whistle of wind in trees, the taste of a first kiss from the person you have waited for all your life.

I realized that I shouldn't interfere in Manolo's life, nor should he in mine. Both of us had to continue on in that perfect, marginal reality, which both united and separated us. I got into the car and drove around, wandering, until about two. Then I decided to go home.

I inserted the key in the lock with an uncommon shame. Santiago was wide awake, waiting for me.

'Are you crazy, or what?' he said, before I'd barely crossed the threshold that instilled in me that feeling of blind everyday monotony. 'I've been looking for you everywhere.'

I didn't answer him. I threw my bag over a chair and remained standing.

'I see you've gone out with your car!'

I turned around so Santiago wouldn't see me blushing. I felt trapped, transparent, naked, unmasked, like a person who's just had plastic surgery and realizes that everyone's gossiping about her new face. I figured he had to notice the lassitude of my tired legs, the satisfaction in my body, and most of all, the transformation of my soul.

'The lady from the gallery has called four times – she's furious at you,' he said. 'And you were supposed to call me back about going to the movies. Where the hell have you been?'

'Around,' I said.

'Where "around," if I may ask?'

I named all the places I had been since morning. I had the upper hand here, though: my bizarre conduct had begun so early in the day that there was no way Santiago could figure out that my current state of mind had its origin at the pool, which to him appeared just another stop on my springtime pilgrimage. In any case, obviously, I omitted all mention of Marina. Nevertheless, I felt that perverse temptation that assassins are prone to feel when they offer veiled clues to the police as a kind of personal dare or a subconscious desire to be caught. I rummaged through my bag until I found the photos. I handed them over to Santiago. As he looked at the repetitive images, I asked him:

'Hey, what would you do if there was another me? Someone identical to me, I mean.'

'Listen, I don't even want to imagine it. I have my hands full with you!' he replied, smiling to let me know that he was ready to give up his anger. 'One Sofía is enough to worry about; two would send me over the edge.'

I left him as he gleefully looked through the horrible photographs he'd taken of the gypsies and the ocean. I kissed him on the forehead and went in to bed. As I undressed, I had a different impression of my naked body. I had acquired a sort of multiplicity, in which each gesture was followed by a corresponding echo – distant but alive, not like in the dead reflection of mirrors, those slaves to human will. Knowing that I wasn't unique made me feel unique two times over, Marina's accomplice in the conspiracy against the tedium of solitude. I lay down on the bed, my mind unable to focus on any one thing in particular. It was a long time before I fell asleep that night.

Nevertheless, when Santiago entered, I closed my eyes and breathed with slow regularity to suggest that I was sleeping. He lay down next to me. I assumed he was staring at me, but I didn't move an inch. Moments later I sensed his hand between my legs and felt him smell my vagina.

He was sniffing me, to see if I had been with another man.

I want to dream about you tonight. I want to find you in that world that seems so much like death, but isn't death. Funny that it's something life blesses us with, and yet it isn't life at all. It's that inconsistent reality with its own logic, where one thing can be two things at the same time, where a face can have two faces and time doesn't exist. I want to dream that you're by my side, that you are Sofía and Marina, Clara or Laura, and that you hug me, that I can see the dimples in your smile and hear the tickle of your voice in my ear. I want to dream about complete happiness, with the rapturous balance of your breasts pressed against mine, locked in a love that lasts and hasn't died.

The journalist chasing Manolo was called María del Carmen Chazarreta. She was a rather whiny girl who wore her bangs dyed blond and her clothes as masculine as possible. I saw her at the next gallery opening, although if I could have avoided her, I would have. One of my duties at the gallery, unfortunately, was to pay attention to the reporters, so they wouldn't ignore us when it was review time. And I really had to be on my guard these days – the gallery owner still hadn't forgiven me for my long afternoon at the pool with Marina, and I was sure she was just looking for an excuse to get rid of me.

I moved closer to the blond-banged journalist, said hello, and gave her the catalogue, which announced the painter on exhibit as the greatest artistic discovery of all time. All around us, a multitude of guests and crashers seemed to swim amid an

ocean of overheated bodies. The smell was intolerable. María
del Carmen did most of the talking: art, painters, galleries,
'cultural politics' of the government, and the like.

I heard her, but was distracted, really only listening for key
words, just in case she asked me a question which obligated me
to respond. No matter where I looked, however, María del
Carmen's voice had a way of pulling me out of my ruminations,
with a surprising tone of reproach:

'You're late . . .'

I realized she was talking not to me but to another person
who had just arrived, with whom she evidently had made a
date.

'I'll leave you two alone now,' I stammered, taking advantage
of the escape opportunity.

I looked at the other person. It was a woman – the short,
robust woman who had accompanied Marina to the pool. I recognized her immediately because of her bowlegs and deep tan.
Clearly, she was María del Carmen's girlfriend, I realized suddenly. In two seconds I was on top of her.

'You're – you're – ' I stammered.

'Yes, I am,' she said.

She was also taken aback at seeing me. Maybe it took her a
moment to realize that I wasn't Marina, because I had cut my
hair short by then.

'Oh, you two know each other!' said María del Carmen, visibly put off.

'We met once, in passing,' the lady informed her.

'Well, this is Emilia,' María del Carmen said to me, indicat-
ing that she had authority over her friend. Then she insisted on
showing me that she knew everything about her friend. 'Emilia

Faustina Gesualdo Cortés, that is.' And then, without much
enthusiasm, she nodded her head toward me. 'And this is . . .
Oh, what's your name again?'

I doubt she forgot my name; she was just trying to be con-
descending, to stab me with her last little bit of disdain. But I
wouldn't give her the satisfaction and so I didn't say my name
(Emilia probably already knew it anyway). I thought about how
destiny had brought me closer to Marina through the last people
I would have expected would be intermediaries: first Carranza,
now María del Carmen. Unconcerned with the curiosity or
annoyance of the reporter, I grabbed Emilia by the arm and
pushed her past a desk beyond which the other people didn't
venture.

'You have to tell me how to find her,' I said.

'Who?' she asked.

'Oh, come on, don't play coy!'

She paused.

'Well . . . I don't know what to say, exactly.'

On the other side of the desk, the crowds continued mingling, oblivious to our conversation.

'What is it?' I blurted out, making a bit of a scene. 'Are you
jealous of me?'

To calm me down, she gently pressed her left hand onto my
shoulder, even though I had just grabbed her arm. In a kind
voice, she said:

'You should know, there once was something between
Marina and me, but that was a long time ago.' She hid a smile.
'We're friends now, and I just want her to be happy.'

'The fact that you and I have run into each other,' I said, not
without a certain solemnity, 'is a sign from destiny.'

'The incredible thing, really, is that we haven't run into each other before,' she said. 'I generally come with María del Carmen to all these gallery openings. And I assure you, I would have noticed you.'

'So what does that have to do with anything now?'

'Don't you see? ' she continued, as if she hadn't heard me. 'By pure chance Marina didn't come with us tonight. I try to get her to go out; she seems very depressed these days.'

If anything, I guessed that I was the likely cause, and it was the first time that the news of someone else's pain had ever caused me such joy.

'Did she say she wanted to see me again?' I asked, desperate.

She didn't say the one word that would hurt me, but then again, she also didn't say the word that would make me happy. I pressed her, and she was forced to shake her head no.

'"No," what?' I clung to the vaguest hope. 'She hasn't said anything or she doesn't want to see me?'

'Look, don't think I don't understand your anxiety,' Emilia said after a brief pause, breaking the silence that had descended on us in the middle of the continuing din of the crowds.

'Well then why won't you tell me where she is?'

A waiter with a tray of drinks reached the desk. I signaled for him to get lost.

'Well . . . you know, Marina is a little confused,' Emilia said. 'It's not as simple as you think. She has the same concerns as you.'

'Well, tell her that I don't have any more doubts,' I said, firmly. 'I'll do anything to be with her. Do you understand?'

'Oh, Emilia!' It was Blond Bangs again. 'I'm drowning!' She had already gone through the exhibition, painfully, examining just enough to be able to leave and write her review.

Emilia looked at me as if to apologize, and said:

'All right, I'll tell her. I see her every day.' She winked at me and threw me a bone: 'She's living in my house, you know.'

With that, Emilia and the reporter with the blond bangs sank into the crowd of guests and made their way to the door. I stood there, alone among all those people. The opening continued on its inexorable, frivolous path. I talked, I greeted, and I smiled, showing off my teeth. I said things I promptly forgot, and I maintained my genteel, carefree demeanor, even though inside I was far away, miles and decades away, pondering my fate, lamenting, imagining Marina's reaction and our next encounter, which now didn't seem so improbable as it had before.

Since our separation in the car three weeks ago, I had been living through some truly terrible moments. Nothing excited me, or even piqued my interest in the slightest. I berated myself for having let Marina go, for having been such a coward. All it took was an ephemeral flash of memory, and the insufferable weight of how stupid I was came crashing down on me.

In the middle of all that unhappiness, interfering in my solitude and calm, Carranza appeared – the man who had invited me to the pool. He had taken to appearing at the gallery, every day around noon and even sometimes in the afternoon, always with some excursion planned for the two of us, always in that tight gray suit (either he never washed the thing or else his closet was filled with dozens of identical ones). I had a tough time getting rid of him; he was always ready with some comeback to the excuses I tried to give. His courtesy was infallible, it made you feel bad for trying to avoid him. He followed me when I would go out into the street, pretending that he was accompanying me. He said he did it to protect me. Once he followed me all the way to my doorstep. Luckily, Santiago had come home early that day and we ran into each other in the intersection in front of the building. Carranza didn't escape — the opposite, in fact. Just as he had done with me, he introduced himself to Santiago, using that same, vaguely menacing formula ('My name is Carranza') he had used on me. He told Santiago to take care of me, because strangers could take advantage of me; he was only looking out for my well-being, he said. Then he tried to invite himself up to our apartment, but somehow we managed to refuse, and he walked away, waving good-bye as if we were old friends. When I told Santiago who the man was and how he'd been following me, he didn't pay much attention. Oddly, he didn't even seem jealous.

The truth is, at the time Santiago was up to his ears with lots of other things, as I would realize a little later on that afternoon. This realization would be a decisive one in the long days that I waited without Marina, and without love. A fact, a fact that appeared to have nothing to do with me, led me to the decision that I had to find my double no matter what. One night, only a few days after he had sniffed me to check if I had cheated on him, Santiago came home unusually late. Without my asking him, he assured me that he'd been working at a client's factory, and followed with a torrent of details. It wasn't the first time he'd ever been home late and he never gave me explanations like that, so I was automatically suspicious. I was lying in bed, watching TV without really watching it. I also found reading impossible. My mind was on other things and I felt a profound sense of dejection. I told myself that I had to do something, snap out of it, but I couldn't, and that most sensible command made me even more apathetic. So despite my suspicions, I didn't bother with proving to myself whether or not Santiago was telling the truth.

He stretched out next to me, still dressed, and rested his head on my chest. I felt an urge to caress him, but I held it in. I asked him if he wanted something to eat. He didn't answer; he'd fallen asleep. I felt a wave of tenderness come over me – he was like a little boy, who, like all other little boys, could be violent sometimes, but in the end was always just a little boy. Whenever I watched him sleeping, I always felt that way – that desire to take care of him. It seemed as though he was at my mercy, help-less, showing me with love his weakest, most intimate side. I stroked him. He turned over in his sleep and mumbled that he had to get undressed.

'I'll do it for you,' I whispered.

I untied his shoes. I took them off and then did the same thing with his socks. I loosened his tie, unbuttoned his shirt, unzipped his pants, and removed his belt. I stripped his pants off, and with them went his underwear. Gently, I ran my long nails up and down his legs, so he would feel a pleasant, light tickle, and I rubbed his thighs and took his penis in my hand. That piece of flesh made me shudder a bit; at that moment it really was nothing more than a piece of flesh to me. I covered it completely so only his pubic hairs were visible, and my eyes clouded up as I tried to imagine that I was actually with a woman. But it didn't work. The contact from my hand caused Santiago's cock to grow, and I turned toward him again, with a sharp look on my face. I liked his masculine body. He smiled in his pleasant dream-state, and said:

'I'm so tired . . .'

His passivity felt like a dare, and it excited me. I wanted to feel him inside of me, the way it had been that very first time when we were twenty years old, before disenchantment had set in. I wanted him, as if he were an instrument that could remove my anxieties. I didn't regret having cheated on him with Marina: the two sides of my sexuality — my marriage and my love for Marina — were mutually exclusive. You couldn't compare the two, really, they were two irreconcilable aspects of my being, two riverbanks that no bridge could unite. And I had to choose; in my hands I held Santiago's penis, which had been inside me so many times, and which had come to symbolize security, tradition, the light of day, the naked face. And the decision became impossible. At that moment, the pleasure I had achieved with Marina disappeared into a foggy, confusing memory — it stuck in my mind as just another one of the times I had masturbated alone. And that's why betraying Santiago didn't bother me. Strangely enough, it actually made me want to be a good wife, a textbook wife, detached and devoted, the kind of wife that does nothing other than minister to her husband. After all is said and done, I said to myself, this is what my life is and will always be.

I decided to wake Santiago up by sucking on his penis. When I leaned over him, though, I saw traces of lipstick. It wasn't a clear mark, like the kind you sometimes inadvertently leave on someone's cheek when kissing them hello, but rather a little halo, a sort of pinkish cloud that ringed the base of his penis. But it was unmistakable.

'Son of a bitch,' I said. I felt betrayed by him, not for cheating on me, but for robbing us of that one moment of tenderness, of useless devotion. 'Son of a bitch.'

I realized then that both of us would always be living a farce, hurting one another with dissatisfaction and lies. I realized that one of the two sides of my being was nothing more than the illusion of tradition and custom. And I also realized that one moment of thirst for those illusions is better than a lifetime of monotony. Santiago's secret life, so far from my true self, had the indirect effect of making me see more clearly the opaque aspects – the shadows – of my own character. And even in her absence, Marina helped me to think, as well. Not because she poured ideas into my head like liquid in a jar – something she never would have done – but because the mere fact of her existence awakened certain dormant faculties, latent possibilities that lay inside of me.

It was as if someone, without saying anything, was telling me what I had to do, telling me the best road to follow. I knew I had decided what to do. Only with Marina would my life have any meaning. If I couldn't have her, I realized, I'd rather be alone. I had to risk the quiet security of the life I was accustomed to and go in search of something unknown and uncertain. I didn't know how I could find Marina, but I knew that if I did, something more than love would enter my life. Loving a woman would turn me into a different person, and it would also turn me into a victim of disapproval, even in these supposedly tolerant times. Loving a woman who was my double, who looked more like me than a sister or a twin ever could, would make our relationship appear dirty, an aberration of nature. But I knew that I could withstand it. I could even resign myself to never having children, despite all the pain it would cause me, after Laura, the child I had and then didn't have. I had made up my mind. And you and I, Marina, we both understand those moments in life when a person discovers who she really is.

Santiago woke up as I was putting things in a bag, preparing to leave, not knowing where I would go or where I would find myself the next morning.

'What are you doing?' he mumbled.

'Son of a bitch,' I repeated. I couldn't seem to say anything else.

'I don't know what's wrong with you, but we'll talk about it in the morning. Right now I'm too tired.'

'You're tired because someone's been sucking you off.'

He sat up in bed, resting on his elbows. He looked ridiculous like that, half-naked and his dick still half-cocked in the air.

'I haven't been with any woman.'

'Right,' I answered. I was so certain about my decision that I was able to remain cold and focused, at my most cynical. 'So I guess the person wearing the lipstick must have been your client, the guy from the factory.'

He sat up in bed, and saw on his penis the irrefutable evidence of his betrayal, and he knew. He was silent. When I finished packing, he jumped up and grabbed the bag out of my hands.

'You aren't going anywhere!' he shouted.

Then, without letting go of the bag, he slapped me with the back of his hand, slamming me against the closet. The buckles on the bag cut my cheek, confirming that I had made the right decision to leave. He hadn't hit me in a while; I wasn't used to it anymore. And I didn't miss it.

'You're the one who cheated on me!' he howled.

'You would know better than I would – you smelled my cunt to find out, didn't you?'

He hit me again. He had gone from lethargy to fury in nothing more than a brief moment of silence.

'You didn't find anyone else's smell, did you? But you accuse me anyway, to justify what you did.'

'No! My only justification is your indifference. You despise me!' He threatened to strike me again.

'Don't you dare hit me,' I warned him. 'Don't you ever hit me again.'

This time, he didn't.

'It's been weeks since we last had sex!' He was shouting now, and the tone of his voice changed as he went on. 'Weeks! Weeks . . . You don't let me touch you . . . you've distanced yourself from me . . .'

His mood changed again, almost imperceptibly from rage into an uncontrollable sobbing. It was only the second time I had ever seen him cry. I repeated to myself that nothing should steer me away from what I was about to do, not even the sympathy I felt for Santiago's suffering, his helplessness.

'I . . . I've been with another person,' he sobbed. 'But it doesn't have anything to do with you.'

'I don't want to know who it is. That's not what hurt me,' I said.

He fell down on the bed, covering his face with the sheet, ashamed. I heard him whisper:

'I was with a transvestite.'

I have to admit that my first impulse, in the middle of that scene, was to say, *You're a faggot, you always have been, you were lying when you said you were forced into prostitution — you loved it*. But I quickly realized that, if my love for Marina was to be consummated, I would have to endure those kinds of insults. So I shut up. Now that he had confessed, Santiago dared to look for my reaction, peeking through the sheets that covered him. And I can't say that I didn't listen to his story with a strange and slightly morbid curiosity.

'I used to see him when I was in the car, almost every afternoon. He would be all decked out, ready for the night to begin, and I, as you know, would be on my way home. The first time I went down that street was pure coincidence. But after that, I would go out of my way to drive past, to spy on him. And about ten days ago, just seeing him gave me this totally irrational turn-on. I told him to get in, and . . . and . . .'

'You don't have to tell me if you don't want to,' I said. Although I did want to hear the rest of the story, even though it sort of pissed me off that he had gone through a fear similar to the one I had gone through after my encounter with Marina.

'He sucked me off,' Santiago whispered. 'And when I came in his mouth, I felt this horrible shame, just like I felt during my first months in Madrid. I practically kicked him out of the car and drove off. But the next night I went back. He was waiting for me. He knew I would come back. And I've gone back every night since then.'

He wiped his tears with the back of his hand. He had nobody to talk to, and it was clearly weighing heavily on him. That was why, after his initial hesitation, he was now spilling his guts.

'Tonight, for the first time, I undressed him. It's weird, you know? To see the body of a woman, perfectly shaped, attractive, and instead of a vagina, to see a dick. Because he hasn't had an operation . . . I had touched him with his clothes on, but to see it is different. And . . . I sucked it. I sucked him off, you know? And then I . . . I gave it to him up the ass. But I was so turned on that before I left him I asked him to suck me again.'

'Don't be ashamed. I'm not judging you; you can do whatever you want,' I said. And I decided that my curiosity had made him suffer enough already. I had to interrupt him, with:

'But I think the best thing is for me to go now, quietly.'

'Why?' He sat up in the bed again. 'I'll never see him again, I promise. We can keep trying, Sofía, can't we?'

'Of course we can't!' I answered. 'You'll find me distant again, you'll see your transvestite again, and you'll hit me again, to satisfy our conscience.'

For a second I was afraid that his mood would change again, all of a sudden like it had before, and that he would slap me right then and there, but he held it in, and only whispered:

'I knew this would happen sooner or later.' Then, like Carranza, he acted like he was worried about my safety. 'And where are you going to go at this hour?'

'I don't know.'

'Don't worry,' he said. 'I'll go.'

I figured he was suggesting this so he could keep his eye on me, but I accepted his offer. He got up from the bed. He emptied my bag, throwing my things on the floor. He filled it haphazardly, with two shirts, three pairs of pants, four pairs of socks, two ties. He threw in his electric razor, toothbrush, cologne, and deodorant. He got dressed and from the bedroom door looked me in the eye. His sad face really seemed sincere. He didn't say a word. Beaten, he lowered his head. He left the bedroom and then the apartment. I don't know where he spent the night.

Rather than pain, I felt only anxiety. I had turned a page in my life, and I was waiting for the next one, one that hadn't yet been written. I used the solitude to look for Marina. Several times I went, uselessly, to the Tórrido Trópico, and once I glimpsed Carranza there, although I hid so he wouldn't see me. I never went in; I stayed inside the car, in front of the entrance. I would go on my free lunch hours, and then I would return to the city, slowing down as I drove past the place on the road where Marina and I had made love. When you've only seen a person one time, you always think you'll find her again in the same place you first saw her, as if the world is supposed to stop on the wavelength of your expectations.

When I came home at night, it would frighten me to see those lonely rooms; sleep in that cold bed, eat dinner alone as I watched television, and wash my clothes every five days. I had dreamed of being separated from Santiago, but I surprised myself at the many things I still did that were reflexively meant for him. Habits have a way of constructing a false life on top of real life, and it takes a while before you can distinguish between the two. Often you never can.

The second night alone, when I came back from work, I cut my hair in front of the closet mirror. I did it to see Marina. Then I sat down on the bed, without taking my eyes off my reflection, and removed my skirt and blouse as I tried to evoke the body of a woman sunning herself at the pool. I finally took off my underwear, and was left with nothing on but my high heels. They elongated my legs, lengthening their line to the tip of my sex. I wet my index finger, circling it with my tongue, and placed it inside. Using my fingertip, I placed pressure against the precise spot I desired the most. Looking at Marina, I came. Then I was overcome by a feeling of spiritual misery and void. That night, masturbating gave me a bitter pleasure, but I did it again and again, desperately, until my strung-out body couldn't stand any more and I fell asleep with my heels on. I woke up in the middle of the night, hugging myself, my cold hands caressing my shoulder blades in a false embrace. I was talking in my sleep. I washed my face, and said to myself that this solitude was good and awful at the same time, because it was really made up of two separate solitudes. The first one was something I wanted – to live without Santiago, to free myself from a present filled with unhappiness and desperation. The second one, on the other hand, was the solitude I suffered from – Marina's absence, the dream of a future happiness.

My hair was a mess, so the next day I closed the gallery a few minutes early and escaped to the hairdresser's. Carranza was by, as usual. I didn't tell him that Santiago and I had separated, although I'm sure he realized, because he decided to accompany me to the salon. He sat down in a chair in the front, and while he read about the love lives and the splendid yachts of our modern nobility in old dog-eared issues of *Hola*, I got the hairdresser to give me a cut as similar to Marina's as my lovelorn memory could re-create.

I didn't know what places to check, because I really didn't know anything about Marina, so I was on a sort of blindman's search. Nobody mistook me for her, to my relief. I was an unknown ghost. I started worrying that she had been just a tourist passing through Spain and had returned home.

I began to get desperate, and then I found myself at the gallery opening, where I bumped into Emilia.

All the rules of good breeding flew out of my head when I jumped on Emilia, ignoring the annoyed grimaces on the face of the blond journalist. The information I got calmed me down a little. Marina was still in Madrid, and now I had a pretty good lead to track her down with.

That night, when I went back to the party for 'the greatest artistic discovery of all time,' I called Manolo. He answered, but didn't say anything. I knew he was there because I could faintly hear the sound of his music, the mass by Haydn.

'Manolo, I know you're there,' I said. 'I'm not a reporter. You can talk.'

He hesitated for a few seconds, and then finally said, in a low voice:

'And who are you?'

'Sofía.'

'Oh, Sofía!' he exclaimed. 'I didn't recognize your voice. Is something wrong?'

'So many things . . .' I answered. 'If you only knew . . .'

'I know some,' he said. 'I saw Santiago yesterday.'

I was the silent one now.

'Let me know if there's anything I can do,' he continued. 'But don't tell me anything I can't tell Santiago.'

'Oh, come on, Manolo!'

'I'm serious.' His voice had a touch of consternation in it. 'I said the same to him. It's very hard to be between two friends who are breaking up, you know.'

'Whatever you say,' I said, and then I cut to the purpose of my call. 'I need the address of María del Carmen Chazarreta, that reporter who's after you.'

'Shit! What for?'

'Well, let's just say that María del Carmen is a friend of Emilia's, who is a friend of Marina,' I said, not stopping for breath 'And I'm looking for Marina.'

'I don't know what you're talking about, honey.'

'Of course you don't. You've asked me not to tell you anything compromising. Don't change your mind now. Just give me her information. You said she'd invited you to her house a bunch of times.'

'Wait a second.' I heard him rustle some papers, open boxes, walk to the other side of his studio. He returned after a bit. 'Here it is!' he informed me. 'I knew I had her card, I just didn't remember where the hell it was.'

He read me the address, and I copied it down into my date book. Then I said good-bye to Manolo.

'Good luck' was the last thing he said to me.

I didn't have much luck that first afternoon, but the second afternoon I did. The gallery owner was in Paris, so I took advantage of the opportunity and escaped early once again. I stopped the car near the curb and began my vigil at the front door of the blond-banged reporter's building. It was beautiful at that hour, as the horizon sparkled at the end of the street with that intense blue of late afternoon.

A little after eight, I saw her approach the building. She was walking up the sidewalk. I shot out of the car and within half a second, quick as a mousetrap, landed right in front of her. Seeing me jump out of the shadows like that startled her. She was clutching a folder to her chest, filled with papers, and when she saw me everything went flying – from the surprise, I guess. The papers fluttered through the air like little birds that disperse at the sound of a rifle shot. They fell down to the pavement all around us. I bent down to help her pick them up.

'Oh, look what you made me do!' she moaned.

'I'm sorry.'

Then she stared at me, quizzically. Outside of the gallery I was nobody to her. I told her my name and where we knew each other from.

'Oh, Sofía,' she finally said. 'What a coincidence.' Her voice didn't betray a scintilla of enthusiasm.

'It's not a coincidence, actually,' I said. 'I've been waiting for you.'

Her pitying look lasted for about a second, and was soon replaced by her customary suspicious one.

'Give me Emilia's telephone number,' I spat out.

'What do you want with it? ' With her free hand, she brushed off the dust that had settled onto the papers. Maybe she wanted me to beg for it.

'That's my business,' I answered.

'Well, I'm not giving it to you,' she replied, defiant.

I grabbed her by the wrist and the papers flew out of her hands again. She cried out, theatrically. I didn't really hurt her – she just wanted to show that I *could* have hurt her.

'Listen to me.' I moved my eyes closer to her bangs and let go of her wrist. 'I don't care about Emilia. I'm looking for Marina.'

Much later, I would learn that María del Carmen was a jealous person – that's why she treated me this way – and hated Marina with all her heart, because she was always afraid Marina would steal her girlfriend away, even though she had never seen her try. Of course, to see me with short hair in the gallery, she must have thought that she'd been plunged into some kind of horrible multiplicity out of her worst nightmares. She had launched into a thunderous tantrum of jealousy when Marina moved in with Emilia, who subsequently decided to keep her girlfriend at a distance.

Now that she was free, the journalist exclaimed:

'The blessed Marina! Because of her, Emilia and I are in a fight.' She bent down to pick her papers up again. 'This is all I need.'

She apologized and then reluctantly gave me the number.

I called her that night from a phone booth. Emilia answered. I hung up without thinking twice. I called again when I got home and then had the courage to speak.

'Emilia,' I whispered. 'It's me, Sofía. Do you remember me?'

'Of course, dear! It's so nice to hear from you.'

'Your friend María del Carmen gave me your number.'

'That's odd,' she exclaimed. 'Well, anyway, I suppose you're happy now.'

'Why?' I asked.

'What?' she said. 'Haven't you seen Marina?'

'No!'

'Well, she went looking for you at the gallery.'

'I don't believe it!' I could have kicked myself. 'She had to do it today.'

'Listen, I don't know if you know that . . .' Emilia trailed off. I sensed her waver, and her breath quickened.

'Please, tell me everything,' I exhorted. 'I want to know.'

'Fine,' she conceded. 'Look, this is the situation: Marina has to leave Spain . . . very soon.' A long silence fell between us. 'But don't worry. As soon as she comes home I'll tell her you called. Tell me where she can find you.'

I told her. Before hanging up I added:

'Thank you, Emilia.'

'Don't leave your house.'

A few minutes later, the doorbell rang.

It wasn't Marina. It was Santiago. Through the door, he said that he only came by for a few of his things. I let him in. He looked totally wiped out: he had huge circles under his eyes and his skin was wan. His restless eyes moved about, looking every which way. I saw how he glanced sidelong into the bed-room, no doubt in an effort to see if he could detect signs of the presence of a third person. I was in the middle of changing when he arrived, so I was dressed sloppily, in a big, open shirt. My anxiety was uncontrollable, and it grew with the disappointment of seeing Santiago there instead of Marina.

'I'm waiting for someone,' I warned him.

'Just a few minutes, Sofía. A cup of coffee and then I'll leave,' he said in a heavy voice. 'You cut your hair . . .'

I went to the kitchen. I prepared the coffeepot and put the water in. As we waited, he asked me straight out:

'Have you been with anyone?'

His voice didn't indicate the least bit of resentment, although it did reveal some kind of deep fatalism. At that moment, I decided the most honest thing to do would be to destroy all hope for a reconciliation, so he wouldn't suffer from entertain-ing any pointless illusions. So I said yes, I had been with someone. His silence was painful. I saw that he was fighting to hold back his tears, which he managed to do.

'You see!' he whispered, dejected. 'I'm still in love with you, and I'll do anything to keep you. Anything.'

The coffee wasn't ready yet, and, though I didn't detect any veiled threat in his words, the scenario was making me uncomfortable.

'And you?' I asked, to break the silence, and also to satiate that strange curiosity that had overtaken me when Santiago had told me for the first time about his transvestite encounter.

'Me what?'

'Well, have you been with anybody?'

'What are you referring to, exactly?'

'Well, you yourself said you'd been seeing a—'

'Shut up!' he said. His cheeks reddened with anger, and then his voice lowered. 'Don't make fun of me.' I had given him the perfect excuse to emerge from his depression by the quickest exit possible: rage. He repeated:

'Don't make fun of me, Sofía.'

'But I'm not. I'm simply asking a question.'

'Why the fuck did I ever trust you?' he shouted. 'Goddamn you on your mother's fucking grave!'

It wasn't a random curse; I'm sure he said it on purpose. He knew all too well that my parents were always on my mind and that an insult like that was particularly hurtful.

'You're a pig!' I shrieked. 'Get out of here, you fucking faggot. Go sit on it somewhere.' That was no innocent slur, either: there's nothing worse than calling a man a faggot, most of all if he really is one but wishes he weren't.

'We'll see about that.'

He grabbed me by the wrists. In a way, I thought that – without knowing it – he was making me pay for my behavior with María del Carmen.

'Let me go,' I said. I tried to sound intimidating, but it ended up more like a plea.

'Why should I?' he answered, smiling. 'Don't you like my kisses the way you used to?'

The coffee filled the pot and bubbled noiselessly. Santiago tried to press his mouth against mine. I kneed him in the groin. He doubled over against the door, cursing me. There was no way to get out of there, though, so I decided to hole myself up in a corner of the house. I paused, then decided to try for the bedroom, but I didn't do it fast enough to be able to lock the door behind me. Santiago came in after me and tossed me onto the bed, facedown.

'You're still my wife,' he said.

I turned over. I tried to dissuade him.

'Don't be an idiot, Santiago. I know you . . . you'll regret it later.' In response, he grabbed me by the lapel and threw me down as he caught me across the face. The buttons flew off my blouse without a noise.

'I had my IUD taken out.' It was true, but he didn't believe me. 'I don't want to be pregnant by you again.'

'Don't lie! You just told me you were with another man!'

'There's no other man, Santiago.'

He slapped me again with the palm of his hand.

'Have you been with anyone?' he shouted. 'Yes or no?'

'Yes.'

Another slap, this time with the back of his hand.

'Then there's another man!'

'No!'

Another slap still, with the palm.

'Well, let's see now, who have you been with, then? A woman?'

'Yes.'

He was silent. Then a hysterical peal of laughter erupted from his mouth, and it turned my blood cold.

'I don't believe it.' He continued laughing. 'I don't believe it. You've always loved this.' He unzipped his pants.

'No, Santiago. Please, no.'

'Calm down, I won't get you pregnant,' he assured me. 'Now let's see who gets it up the ass.' He turned me over with a shove, facedown again. 'This is the only ass I've ever wanted.'

I tried resisting, but he immobilized me, tying my arms behind my back and kneeling on the backs of my thighs. He had the decency – albeit a questionable one – to take his free hand and run a finger over the hole to lubricate the opening. I felt his cock fighting to enter my anus. For years, ever since the day of Laura's death, he had been hanging on to one half of our incomplete agreement regarding anal sex – the part that referred to me, that is. And he wanted me to pay. I kicked a little, but didn't get very far, since he had my legs trapped from the bottom up. The pressure became more intense and an excruciating pain shot up through my insides. I jerked upward, I dug my teeth into the pillow, I shook myself from side to side, but that only added fuel to the fire which was already burning through my rectum.

'Don't fight me. You'll only make it worse.'

The worst part of all was that he had a point, but I didn't want to give him the satisfaction. In the end, I surrendered. His penis went in a little farther, then a little farther still, and now it felt as though it had reached my stomach. A hot stream filled my entrails with a savage spurt and Santiago trembled over me, and then it stopped.

'I love you,' he whispered in my ear. 'I did this because I love you.' In the collapse that follows the satisfaction of desire, he was suddenly overcome with scruples.

'Get out,' I said.

I didn't think he'd do it, or I would have prepared myself. When he withdrew his penis, I felt as if a hurricane were ripping my body apart from the raw inside walls of that torture chamber. I cried out with the pain. It had all happened so fast. When my crying subsided, I heard Santiago leave the apartment, slamming the door behind him.

I woke up to the sound of someone banging on the door, and it was only then that I became aware of the smell of gas that filled the apartment. Somebody was knocking, anxiously. Limping, I opened the windows and went into the kitchen. The coffee had long since spilled onto the burner, extinguishing it. I turned off the gas and walked to the door. On the other side, as if standing inside the welcoming frame of a mirror, was Marina.

'Sofía!' she said in a worried tone. 'What's wrong?'

It dawned on me that I was half-naked, my blouse ripped to shreds. I felt dirty, damaged. Without another word, I grabbed Marina and held her. Having waited and hoped for that embrace for so long, I was finally receiving it, but only after I had been broken in pieces, the victim of an irrational, degrading intrusion. We closed the door and walked into the bedroom. Stains of blood and excrement were visible on the sheets. I was going to attempt an explanation, but I didn't, because I didn't want to take advantage of the pathetic nature of the situation. Marina, nevertheless, understood. She put me to bed and stroked me so gently that it seemed as if her fingers barely touched me.

'I didn't want to hurt you, and I hesitated too long in

coming,' she whispered. 'This is my fault. But I won't leave you now. Nothing's going to happen to you, my love, my love.'

If there is a God, only he can know how grateful I was for Marina's presence that moment. Even if she hadn't said anything, even if she hadn't offered me her weightless caresses, I still would have felt the relief of being with the person who inspired in me the most complete trust and the most profound serenity. I babbled something unintelligible, but thankfully, Marina's lips, placed squarely on mine, interrupted my broken words. Her lips were warm and pretty, just like mine; I hadn't noticed them before, not even that day at the pool, and I drank now from the fountain of her mouth to calm myself down. Like some kind of sign from the hostile external world, a shooting pain through my rectum doubled me over in pain. Marina placed me facedown. She massaged my back with the palms of her hands, and then she kissed me in the very same spot where Santiago had humiliated and desecrated me, in the epicenter of my pain and shame, and her loving tongue brought me peace, gave me back the dignity I had lost, took care of me, quieted my cries of pain with the murmur of her tender lips. That was when I understood that I could never not love her. That love is nothing but the tranquillity of a kiss upon the horror of an open wound.

I told her that I felt dirty, and that I wanted to take a bath with her. 'All right,' she replied.

'I'll take off your clothes.'

'We'll put bath salts in.'

'And lots of soap.'

'And I'll kiss you again.'

'And I'll do the same to you.'

We went on talking like that, in those sweet and silly phrases of intimacy whose meaning exists only for the lovers who utter them, like hugs or silences. I got up. Another sharp pain reminded me of Santiago's visit, but I controlled my nausea. My kiss had stained Marina's mouth. I cleaned it with a corner of the bedsheet and then ran my tongue over her lips.

I stroked her silk blouse, sliding my hands down languidly from her shoulders to her breasts, enjoying the sensation on my fingers and the surprise of not finding a flat chest in front of me. I opened her blouse and instead of hairs I discovered a soft, luminous skin. I unhooked her bra and then two breasts just like mine asked me to kiss them, and I drank pleasure from them, slowing the tip of my tongue so I could travel within that tiny, infinite moment through the space that separates the soft skin of the breast from the irregular surface of the nipple, until I reached the crowning tip, upon which a minuscule crevice signaled the center of the center. I went in and out and in again, like the moth that searches for light in hopeful flight, and whose impulse sends her out and back, making her spin around and around the object of her desire. I finished undressing her and we went into the bathroom.

In the whiteness of the bathroom, our naked bodies stood out against everything else, stripped of all scenery and masks, separated from the world and from the past, one duplicated in the other, and unique in their peerless doubleness, submerged in the calm, warm water as we were before in the chill of the outdoor pool. Here we were glued together by the soapy foam, our caresses, our desire, slightly cramped in the tub, but happy. Happy.

Marina got out before I did, and I found her in the bedroom.

She dried her hair with a towel, sitting in front of the mirror on the corner of the bed. It was the same place where days before I had searched for her image through the simulation offered by my own reflection. I sat behind her, still in pain. I wrapped my arms around her waist. I pressed my cheek against her cheek. The towel fell to our feet, creating a strange figure, and Marina smiled at me through the mirror. Our faces, one next to the other, were uncanny in their resemblance; we would never get used to that.

I opened her legs and slipped my fingers into her vagina, which was warmer than the bathwater, and I realized that this was the refuge for them as I watched that strange creature with four legs, four arms, two heads, and one torso that we created, sitting in front of the mirror. And I stroked her, and us, as my breasts became more agitated against Marina's back, which seemed to breathe in sync with my lungs. She arched her neck back, resting it against my shoulder, twisting fingers through the tangle of my wet hair and you said you loved me, that you would never leave me . . . just like I love you, Marina . . . and in my hands I felt her come with a pleasure that was mine as well, even before she knelt down at my feet and stroked me, stroked us, locking her eyes in mine, allowing me to reach ecstasy for the first time without looking at myself but rather at the person who was fucking me, and then she made me lie down, on my back, so she could lie on top of me, pressing her pelvis against mine, rocking lightly, unhurriedly, until we reached the point at which our bodies moved in perfect tandem, and not for the last time. It was incredible — that light contact was all we needed, and the entire surface of my skin had become a limitless cunt, pene-trated in every single pore at the same time, and penetrating

Marina to the tiniest corner of her body. Our lips met, and continued kissing that first kiss in the pool and on the side of the road, and then our skin ceased to exist altogether, our flesh touched, our souls were glued one to the other, and our nerve endings jumped out of their tunnels and all other passageways, to join together, to rediscover each other, and the orgasm reached us at the same time, one single orgasm that came over us simultaneously in two twin creatures. It was slow and perfect, like two tributaries spilling into the same river, the two frayed ends tied together in a single knot, the two inseparable faces of one single coin, like a broken bone that has just healed.

I know the word 'destiny' can sound empty, just a simple noise, a question mark placed at the end of our ignorance to close it up in some appropriate way. But I don't know any other way to explain how two people, born in such different places, and without any trace of common ancestry, could be as identical, indistinguishable, as Marina and I were. And how else could our chance encounter be explained, if not through the intervention of destiny? She was a foreigner passing through Madrid; she stayed just over a month. And in that handful of days we were struck by that coincidence (or providence) that is desired by everybody with more than a quarter-century behind them: the encounter that only seems possible in dreams, the date that we had unknowingly made at the beginning of time. No. For me, for us, 'destiny' will never be a hollow concept, because it affirms the central role love plays in the universe. If destiny weren't responsible, we would have to resign ourselves to chance and leave our future in the hands of shadows. One time, after kissing her, I read to her in a whisper that held the sweetness of our kiss: 'Think of all the thousands of years it took for the rain, the wind, the rivers, and the ocean to transform the rock into the granules of sand you play with. Think of the millions of people it took to allow your lips to burn beneath mine.' I remember it, Marina, and I remember how you kissed me again after I read it to you, and now my lips burn with unquenched desire, with devastated love, with loneliness and nostalgia for the lost orchard of your mouth.

'I'm leaving Madrid next week,' Marina said. 'Let's go together, let's forget who we were before today, before that night.'

Up until the spring when we met, Marina had worked as a translator for UNESCO in Paris. Through a contest held for employees of international organizations, she'd won the chance to work for the Food and Agriculture Organization, headquartered in Rome. Marina had thought that Italy would be the best way to escape from the web of apathy and status quo that seemed to cover France. She'd entered the contest and won, and she was supposed to start her new job in September. After leaving UNESCO and before starting at the FAO, she had decided to go on vacation in Spain, to visit a woman with whom she'd been involved some time ago, but who ended up becoming a good friend: Emilia. She'd sold some of her things, given other things away, and kept only a few books she still wanted. She'd then left her apartment in Paris for good, leaving that cloudy phase of her life behind her forever. She'd arrived in Madrid around the middle of May. It wasn't odd for her to stay with Emilia; Emilia visited her often because she was a travel agent, and always got good discount flights through the airlines. (Manolo wasn't mistaken with respect to the professional pursuits of those people

who frequented the swimming pool at El Tórrido Trópico.)
And now Marina had to go to Rome to give herself time to
settle into the apartment left for her by her predecessor at the
FAO. According to Marina, it was right in the center of the
city, and it was said to be quite nice.

'Nobody knows us in Italy,' she added. 'We could pass for sisters.'

I accepted the first part. And if I had a bit of apprehension
about the uncertainty of our future, and such an abrupt change,
I said to myself that I had to conquer my fear, that extraordinary
circumstances require courage. It was all the same to me,
really – I'd have gone to Italy or any other corner of the world,
as long as I could be with Marina. I wanted to be with her, only
with her. Just like the idea of destiny, the idea of a trip – an
escape, really – with a lover might seem ridiculous or corny to
some, but not to the people who find themselves in the situation
that I found myself in then. Before, when I was living with
Santiago and was totally unhappy, even I would have made fun of
something like this. But now, before the concrete possibility of
doing it, my decision was firm, certain. I wasn't about to let this
opportunity slip by, I wasn't going to let Marina go again without me.

Despite the physical pain that tormented me, I sat down on
the bed next to Marina, and we held hands, exultant as two
teenagers. With our naked hearts pounding, we began to devise
a plan for our imminent life together. When dawn broke, we
were startled.

Although we didn't have sex again, the night was filled with
love, long and intense, as can only be experienced by two
people who know that they will never be apart again, and in that

peaceful fervor of real, true passion. If I had known what was to happen later, I would have reached out to you, Marina, in an endless embrace. Look at my hands now, Marina, look at them. They are alone, cold, and helpless without yours. It's a lie that people die only once. Only lovers, lunatics, criminals, and poets know that. One of them, a man who was once all these things, raised his voice from prison to sing that he who lives more than one life must die. And I die every morning. The dreams that we will be together have all evaporated, as I remain awake in my loneliness and remember that first dawn in which we found ourselves together, and I die, I bury myself in my condemned flesh, soulless.

I offered to take her to Emilia's house, even though I had difficulty moving.

Before going down to the street, we got dressed together. I put on Marina's miniskirt and silk blouse (it smelled of you, my love), which, naturally, fit like my own. She poked through the closet and picked out an old pink dress of mine, short, with a square neckline. As she looked, she threw some other dresses onto the bed, with their hangers still in place.

'This you have to bring to Rome,' she said. 'This one too.'

'No, not this one,' I said.

We almost finished packing my suitcases for our departure the next week. In the apartment, we stopped what we were doing several times to kiss, long and slow. But in the elevator we did it with that illicit, impassioned urgency of adulterous, prohibited love. Elevators were invented for nothing else, I'm sure of it.

We climbed into the car. As I sat down, I felt the pain run down my backside, with the burning sensation that still hadn't dissipated from my insides. I put the key in the ignition, but didn't start the car. In our long night of planning, Marina and I had decided to take the old Marbella to drive to Rome, and at that moment, even an object as common and meaningless as a car seemed dear to me, like an accomplice, the only thing that knew our secret.

Unfortunately, someone else discovered our intimate secret. We were filled with anxiety and we wanted to continue sketching out the details of the trip. But at a certain moment in which we had simultaneously come up with the same idea, we erupted in laughter and hugged. Over Marina's shoulder I caught a glimpse of someone watching us, a few centimeters from the open window. Carranza. My blood ran cold, and Marina picked up on it.

'What's the matter?'

I moved away from her and signaled toward the snoop, who hadn't moved and stood there smiling, silent. I started the car and got ready to escape. En route, I explained to Marina who Carranza was, how I had met him, and how he had been following me around lately.

We continued our conversation as if nobody had interrupted us, although we couldn't completely regain our previous euphoria. I took her to have breakfast at the same bar where I had first met Carranza, the morning that everything began. I told her about my dreams, my premonitions, Manolo's portrait – all the signals that had heralded her arrival. For Marina, on the other hand, it had all begun several weeks earlier. She had been feeling expectant and anxious, as if she weren't alone, even when she was in a room by herself.

I left Marina on the same corner where we had separated that first afternoon. How different it looked now, how luminous. No dead cats, no night, no good-byes.

I took the car to the mechanic, an endearing Portuguese man who knew Santiago before we were married. He was always saying he was up to here with the weather and European women and that in a couple of months he'd sell everything and move to Brazil. Then, for one reason or another, he wouldn't do it, although he always kept the flame of that dream alive in his heart. Today was no different: he told me that this would be the last time he serviced our car, because the day before he had finally bought his ticket to Rio de Janeiro. I congratulated him and asked him to prepare the car for a long trip.

'You're going to use the Marbella?' he asked.

He was surprised that we weren't using Santiago's Renault. I managed to change the subject so he wouldn't get suspicious.

At the gallery I answered the phone call from the owner, the same one she made every two days. I told her that she had better return soon from Paris because otherwise I might not be there. She practically had a heart attack when I said that but I hung up and let the phone ring and ring, without picking it up. The dice were tossed. I just hoped that she didn't take it out on Manolo, who had found me the job in the first place.

I went to the bank to find out about opening up a new bank account, with a credit card in my name, that I could use out of the country. A married couple that has just separated has to sort through an endless string of practical issues, none of which Santiago and I had taken the time to resolve. One of those issues was financial. We had a joint bank account, and I figured that I had deposited about a third of the money in it. Nevertheless, I was told, I still needed my husband's approval to close it.

Naturally, I could have withdrawn the money and just taken it with me on the trip. That would have been too risky, though, and opening a new account with only my name on it would have been such a mountain of paperwork and bureaucratic procedures that – unfortunately for me – I decided to leave things more or less as they were. I figured I would simply note down all the expenses I made on the credit card, and that I would just have to make sure that I didn't go over the one third of the money which belonged to me. Given everything, the fact that I had no idea how I would make a living seemed like the least of my problems. I've never been very good with financial matters, anyway. My mother – and later, Santiago – never stopped nagging me about it.

The most nerve-wracking thing was my anxiety and desire to leave, to get out of there once and for all. The planning seemed to take so long, it was all so tedious. Marina and I barely saw each other during those feverish days of preparation. Just like two people engaged in the traditional way, we had decided to remain apart until our departure, as if this were our honeymoon.

The gallery owner, back from Paris, didn't throw a tantrum as I had expected. She was, in fact, very happy for me and wished me a bon voyage. Basically, she was relieved not to have to deal with me anymore. Moreover, she would save a lot of money now that she didn't have to fire me. She was so pleased that she even took it upon herself to write me two or three letters of introduction to gallery owners she knew in Rome.

I also went to the cemetery, to put flowers on my parents' graves.

One afternoon, when the pain in my insides had finally begun to subside, Santiago called the gallery, as if it were the most normal thing in the world. I didn't curse him, as he deserved, because my goddamned scruples were making me feel guilty about escaping to Italy and leaving him alone, with no friends, with no me, in the midst of all the hostility that still hadn't gone away and which we were both to blame for creating. Over the phone, he didn't indicate the slightest bit of remorse. He had been almost proud of what he did and now that his desire had overtaken him again, he assumed that he could reconquer me with the old, violent habits of our marriage. I didn't discourage him; what was the point? I also didn't mention that I was leaving Spain. That would have been the right thing to do, since he was living in a *pensión* and the apartment would be empty, but I feared that Santiago would be capable of anything, even the most depraved behavior, to prevent me from leaving. I knew it wouldn't be long before he found out, anyway. But until then, he still wouldn't know that I had fallen in love with a woman. And he kept on insisting that I tell him the name of the person I was involved with.

'It's not Manolo, is it?' he asked.

I started to panic, the way innocent people who have been accused of a robbery start to act all guilty in their efforts to prove their innocence. To leave Manolo out of it, to protect Santiago, I said:

'Carranza. He's the one.' That way I killed two birds with one stone: I disentangled myself from Manolo and I avenged — though in an indirect fashion — my pursuer and his harassing ways. Now Santiago would put him through exactly what I went through that morning when Carranza was spying on me from outside the car.

'That son of a bitch! If I ever see him . . .'

'It's nothing serious,' I assured him. 'I don't think it'll last.'

'You still love me, darling. There's no question, I'm still the man for you.'

I would have liked him repentant and tormented, but it was better this way. Still, I knew I shouldn't forget what he had done to me, that I could not let him make me feel sorry for him.

'I have some photos I'd really like to show you,' he said, which I figured was a pretext. 'So, when should we get together?' He had this cocksure attitude of someone who knows his demands won't be rebuffed.

'Thursday,' I answered. The departure was planned for Tuesday. 'I can't do it before. Come on Thursday. To the apartment.'

I know he showed up. I know he was infuriated that I wasn't there. I know that at that moment he began to suspect, and that was the moment I began to lose you, Marina.

It was a desperate idea, that of leaving in search of your past as if it were a pilgrimage. I went through with it even though it was senseless. I flew to Montevideo, and from there to Buenos Aires, and then from there I went to Rome.

On the plane (KLM), a man whose face I didn't see (and didn't want to see) waited for me to use the bathroom and pressed up against me before the door closed behind me.

It was night-time up there in the firmament, and I couldn't sleep. The other passengers scattered around snored away, sprawling into the aisles. The movie had finished and I was afraid that sleep would only bring me nightmares. 'Don't shout,' said the man as he locked the bathroom door behind us. He didn't have to threaten me; I would have done anything, really, because it was all the same to me. At that moment, anybody could have used me for whatever he fancied.

I had just lost you, you see, Marina? It hadn't been much more than a year, and I wanted you, and I would have given my life to make love to you once again. What could be better than giving myself to someone I'd never see again? Who better than that individual who looked nothing like you and couldn't fool me with the illusion of your return?

I decided that the refuge of your memory would be the last kiss I gave you on New Year's Eve. I wouldn't let him kiss you, rest his mouth on the lips that you had kissed.

I clung to the sink, my back to the man who panted behind me. I resolved not to turn around, not even one step toward his anonymous mouth, when I realized that he did not have the slightest intention of kissing me, because now he was lifting my skirt, moving my panties to the side with his fingers, and he stuck it in. He had an enormous cock – it had been a long time since I'd been fucked like that.

I became aware that he was much more aroused than I had initially thought. I pressed myself against this stranger, so he would penetrate me to the full extent possible of his oversized prick, and I didn't look at him once, not even the hands that gripped my waist and pulled me close, then shoved me away, and I didn't look at your face in the mirror, or Clara's face, or my own. Instead I focused. On the metallic washbasin, the drain, my struggle not to revel in the pleasure for too long, to simply come in accordance with my physical desire, the instructions printed in English, the outlet, and that orgasm took with it all possibility of tenderness, and then my excited body obeyed, and it began to come, the soap, the paper towels, and then he came, the lights, the faucet, and we hadn't even uttered the name of the beloved person who wasn't there, nor did we come down sensitively or lovingly, nor did we ask for each other's respect. We had fucked like two pigs and neither one of us wanted anything else. We were caught in the middle of that empty hum of airplanes, which invades your ears like the voice of memory, and we maintained the tacit agreement of silence, of love without love or kisses. He left.

I heard him unlatch the door, open it, leave, close the door, and once again the void of air ten thousand meters above the ocean. Then I looked at you in the mirror, and I saw your tears, and down my legs trickled the now cold semen of a strange man whom I would never even be able to recognize amid the other passengers, and the door opened once again.

It was a stewardess; maybe she thought the man had tried to rape me. She came in to check that I was all right, hoping to avert a scene. Because the first rule of conduct in an airplane is discretion, at all costs, that reserve that borders on indifference. She rested a light hand on my shoulder, and whispered, *Do you feel all right?* This stranger was black, much taller than I was, and spoke in English, but she looked like you, Marina, because she was trying to console me, be friendly, make me feel at ease. 'Marina,' I said to her, 'is that you, Marina?' breaking the silence of the sky, crying for your lost love, wishing that this intruder – now doubling her efforts – was you and not the intruder, and that was the danger I had to avoid, Marina, that someone might replace you. I had to do everything I could to remain indifferent and cold, so nobody would be able to take your place in my memory and to ensure that nothing could be even remotely similar to our love. You gave me that, and dignity, too. Degradation was the furthest thing from that.

To keep the memory of our purity intact, I had to revile myself, debase my body, and dirty my hands with bodies I didn't want.

But it scared me to see that black stewardess naked, to stroke her skin, so different from yours, the negative of your skin, it scared me to kiss her exposed neck and sink my fingers into her hidden hair.

I turned around and embraced her. She hesitated for a moment, and then went on consoling me like one would a little girl, patting me on the back and pulling her warm body away from mine, running from me, as I pressed against her, until I couldn't resist any longer and just like a ferocious vampire lunged at her neck to bite into it, to feel the flavor of skin that wasn't yours, Marina. And then the stewardess pushed me away, stammering, What . . . what are you doing? She tried to untangle herself from me, but I wouldn't let her. I begged her to let me desecrate myself in her arms, even though she clearly didn't understand a word of my gasping Spanish, and did nothing to hide the disgust she felt for me. I bent over, tried to push my mouth through her tidy uniform, to conquer her foreign sex, and like a tiger before the scent of flesh, I smelled the unmistakable smell of her cunt, that perfume you taught me to love, but the stewardess was not another victim of our heartbreaking love, she didn't hesitate, and with a sharp knee under my chin she cut me off and ran from the bathroom, leaving me on the floor, alone, running my hands across my legs the way you did to satisfy me. Although I did this to stain my fingers with the strange man's sperm, and then suck them, inundate my mouth with the dry taste of your absence, alone, alone on the floor and in the sky at the same time. I wanted to cover myself in repugnance so my infidelity to you would be sinister and painful, but I only managed to make myself feel ridiculous, like someone who, all alone, tries to carry out rituals she doesn't believe in, like the monkey who imitates human gestures that she doesn't really understand, like the priestess of a religion whose god has died. I was alone, Marina, without you, like I am now, and my throat tightens up as I uselessly call out your name. I was alone, aroused, happy to have been humiliated and happy that my betrayal hadn't touched your memory. I was lost, corrupted, thrown to the floor of absence and ten thousand meters above the ocean, my face smeared with tears and bitter semen, abandoned, dead, and once, we loved each other.

Monday, the eve of our trip, Emilia organized a good-bye party for Marina. I didn't know what kind of gathering it was, until, rather innocently, after half an hour there, I exclaimed:

'Hey, Emilia, only women showed up.'

She let out a laugh, as if to say, 'You're still a novice, but you'll catch on.' Then, before she went off to put more plastic cups on the table, she whispered playfully:

'Relax – nobody's going to do anything to you.'

I began to observe the other guests a little closer, and I noticed little gestures, caresses, looks, that proved the naïveté of my exclamation. It was the first time I'd ever been to that kind of party. And while it's true that nobody did anything to me, I can't hide the fact that I felt a sort of aversion to it all. I have tried to be honest with myself, in an effort to understand – without reproaching myself – the reasons behind that feeling,

and the only answer I've been able to come up with is that I
suffer from a bit of stubbornness, blindness, a certain shame, or
whatever you call it, with respect to my homosexuality. I always
thought of myself as normal, as normal as a person could be,
and the presence of those women revealed to me my true
nature, placing me in a category I'd never suspected I belonged
in, classifying me with a label that I had rejected up until that
day. With time, I would understand that what is called 'normal'
is nothing more than a question of statistics, but right there at
that party, although I seemed to find in Marina the perfect
mirror of my own desire and my own true self, in the other
women I saw the deformed mirror of my scandalous abnormal-
ity. But it wasn't their fault. Many times what you consider
'deformed' isn't a mirror at all but rather the figure placed in
front of you – you know, it's easier to criticize the photographer
than the model. And it only makes things worse when the figure
itself isn't deformed at all but your eyes see it as such because
you don't like something, or you reproach yourself, or you're
afraid of things simply out of habit, or upbringing, or prejudice.
In all honesty, I think that's why María del Carmen, the
reporter, made me so nervous.

So there I went, thrown down that road of self-analysis, and
gradual self-acceptance, that night at Emilia's party. And I still
haven't reached the end. At first, as I looked at the people
around me, they all seemed ridiculous, monstrous, aberrant,
like those marionettes that speak in falsetto. Some of them were
calm, others seemed scared, and still others hid their insecurity
with attitude. Some dressed like men, others like prostitutes.
Some truly loved each other, while others found only a passing
fancy in women as disillusioned as they were. Some were ugly,

others beautiful; some weren't the least bit interested in men while others hated them with an irrational kind of rage and still others feared them either out of ignorance or one bad experience. Others felt picked over by men, uncomfortable around them, and were only relieved once in the company of women.

Afterward, nevertheless, following my instincts, I began to understand that none of these women were alike in any way, except for the fact that they were consumed by the same honest, painful, and unavoidable passion – one that the world debases with ugly names. They all were or had been victims of some kind of anguished, interior struggle, exactly as I had been. From this perspective – and only this perspective – heterosexual love really is easier. It comes on in such a natural way and doesn't require a conscious, exhaustive examination of one's inner will, doesn't fight against one's inclinations. It receives the beloved fatalistically, without fear, and its demands are nowhere near as intimidating.

Marina and I were, of course, the general topic of conversation, due less to the visible intensity of our love than to our striking similarity. People confused us with each other the whole night long.

A heated discussion erupted, as if the two of us weren't there. Of course, neither of us took offense. Our situation was so unusual that it inspired some fiery debates, and some women openly declared that they thought our relationship was wrong, while others defended us.

To my surprise, Blond Bangs found herself on the side of the latter group, despite the fact that the ire she directed at Marina and me still hadn't quite abated. She was calmer, because our trip to Italy would take two problems off her mind for a while.

But our staunchest defender was Francisca, the Andalusian girl from whom I had stolen Santiago. This was where I saw her again, after years of absence. She greeted me as I was walking in the door.

'Are you Sofía or Marina?' she asked.

I told her. We looked at one another, like two Masons who, after seeing each other every single day for decades, suddenly realize they belong to the same lodge. She was emaciated and lethargic, skinnier than I'd ever seen her. She didn't reproach me, though, for what had happened in the past. In fact, she didn't even mention it, I guess because she didn't care anymore. I asked her if something was wrong.

'No, Sofía, no.' She didn't even have the energy to laugh. 'I just have so many appointments, things to do, all day long. And at night . . . well, ever since I fell in love with her, I'm a mess.' She indicated a girl who couldn't have been much older than twenty, with brown hair and an athletic body. She had a look on her face like that of a little girl who wants to do everything. 'She's just a baby, but she was the one who corrupted me. Followed me and followed me until I finally gave in. You know, have new experiences and all that sort of thing. But I went crazy, really crazy. I was insane, I was tormented, imbalanced, I lost all common sense.' Well, she'd lost her mind but certainly not her passion for synonyms. 'Tell me, Sofía, how could I have been so fucking stupid to wait until now to do anything?'

'I don't know. The same thing happened to me.'

'And we can't get enough sex. Every time we say "Not tonight," we go to bed, touch each other – the lightest little brush – and our good intentions go right out the window. Just telling you about it now is making me horny.'

'You've got to start getting some more sleep, Francisca.'

'What for? All I have is erotic dreams.'

She told me all about her marriage to the Senegalese guy named Mbe, and everything she knew about Pulga. Then she asked me about Santiago, smiling finally, anticipating my answer by tilting her head toward Marina.

'When I saw the two of you,' she said, 'I thought I'd finally gone over the edge. You're exactly alike, identical, the same, mirror images, carbon copies, like what they say about two drops of water. In your shoes I think I would have done the same thing – but I can't even fathom how that can be. Tell me the truth – doesn't it shock you, just a little?'

When the party reached its peak, I decided to leave. I still felt uncomfortable. I didn't want to dance with all those women, and I resisted being the center of attention of that collective hilarity. I was exhausted. I wanted to think only about the trip and nothing else.

There was no reason to change our decision to not live together before the day of our departure, so Marina stayed as I said good-bye to the rest of the guests, who abandoned their earlier squabbles to wish me – all of them – good luck, bon voyage, congratulations, and all those idealistic human expressions that can almost never predict the unforeseeable assaults fortune has in store.

When I arrived home, I put on a big shirt and tried to relax a little, although I knew I wouldn't. I had a hard time falling asleep. To calm my nerves, I rummaged through some papers, photos, dresses – all the bits and pieces you hang on to with the illusion that you're eternal and that one day you'll look at them again, even though that day never comes. I suspected that I would never see that apartment or those objects again, and that was pretty much what happened. In a way I felt like someone condemned to death, that it was my final hour, and I couldn't shake the feeling. With Marina, my life would start from zero, and so it was logical: I would have to leave the old me behind in that apartment I had shared with Santiago, along with the useless leftovers of my past life. They were nothing more than the sediments of habit: shells and remnants of things that other people had tacked on to my character, disguises that I had willingly assumed over the years. I opened the suitcases, removed a few things, added others, and closed them up again. When the sky began to clear, the doorbell rang. It was Marina.

'I couldn't sleep either,' she said, sensing my anxiety.

We clung to each other as we walked into the kitchen. I made some coffee. We stood there drinking it, talking about everything and nothing.

'We should probably get some sleep,' I said. 'Tomorrow . . . today . . . we have to drive all day long.'

'It doesn't make any sense now, though, *che*,' she said, using that peculiarly Argentinian expression. 'If you want to, sleep. At eight, I have to talk to the man from my apartment to arrange things.'

I didn't sleep. And at eight Marina called the guy who would be our landlord in Rome. She spoke Italian pretty well, or at least she yelled and gesticulated convincingly enough. When she hung up, I said:

'Now I see what your real language is. I always knew it wasn't Spanish.'

But she didn't even crack a smile at my joke.

'Bad news,' she said.

'What happened?'

'The apartment isn't going to be ready for another fifteen days.' After a pause, she added, 'And if an Italian tells you fifteen days, it really means thirty.'

'That's impossible.' I couldn't believe it. All of a sudden, I started to feel like everything was starting to go wrong, and I thought about the gallery, and Carranza. About Thursday, and Santiago. 'No!' I shouted. 'No! We're leaving today!'

Marina looked me in the eye, took my hand, and said:

'Yes. We'll leave today.'

A surge of happiness shot through me. In a flash I went to get dressed. I threw off my shirt and put on a long, wide skirt, a blue shirt, and low-heeled shoes.

'You look pretty,' Marina said as she walked into the bedroom. Never before had a compliment felt so gratifying. She looked pretty, too. She wasn't wearing what she wore to the party. Instead she was dressed in black, in a linen miniskirt and a batiste blouse with white buttons. I've never seen anyone wear miniskirts as much as she did. She had great legs – and I'm not just saying that because they looked like mine; hers were much nicer – and a very elegant stride. She never looked cheap – the opposite, in fact. To complete the look she wore high heels, which she always selected with the utmost care: they had to be serious-looking, in muted colors, never too high, never too low, with a pointed but slightly curved toe. In those heels, it was as if she slid around the world without quite touching it, moving her hips with a subtle yet sensual discretion. On the other hand, when she wore low-heeled shoes – and don't think that love is making me exaggerate – she was more like a goddess who had descended to mingle with the mere mortals and copy their

gestures and movements, while maintaining the divine carriage
of her regal lineage. Once, I had lightheartedly assured her that
if I had been a man, I would have fallen for her.

I didn't give the house a once-over before leaving. I closed the
door, relieved, feeling like a person who has just had a tumor
removed. It occurred to me that I should get rid of my keys but
I didn't do it, because I thought that such a typical gesture of
bravado would bring bad luck. Who knows what would have
happened if I had obeyed my instinct to throw away those keys,
which still had Santiago's mark imprinted on them? Would it
have changed anything?

We pushed the suitcases as best we could toward the car.
They weighed a ton and the effort just about wiped us out.
Inside one of them was the portrait Manolo had made for me,
along with the yellow hat Emilia had given us as a gift that day at
El Tórrido Trópico. The luggage didn't all fit in the trunk, so we
had to lower the backseat to make more room.

We went by Emilia's house, where Marina had a couple of
suitcases and a box of books; she had already thrown out everything that wasn't essential back when she'd left Paris. Those
books are the same ones I have by my side now. I've saved them
so I can read and repeat to myself the passages Marina liked. I
look for her little notations in the margins, the angles of the
pages she folded down, her signature on the first page. But it's
too late even for that, and I'll be giving them away soon.

Emilia was a wreck. She had just woken up and had to get to
work. She had an awful hangover and a terrible headache, but
she was very sweet to us. She promised to come and visit, and
before she said good-bye to me she said something I'll never
forget:

'If happiness means deserving to be happy, then you and Marina are happy.'

Once again we dragged suitcases to the Marbella, and the poor thing was more loaded down than ever. I turned the key in the ignition and we left. I hadn't said good-bye to Manolo, I realized, although I knew he wouldn't be angry with me for that.

With which foot did I enter the car?

That day I felt more superstitious than usual, but all my intuitions and inklings were off. When I turned on the radio I thought it was a good omen to hear that song by the Rolling Stones that goes, I think, '*She's like a rainbow.*' I thought that these signs were as clear as the ones I'd received the day I met Marina.

'I love you,' she said.

'And I love you,' I said.

We left Madrid shortly after ten. It was June 25. I felt like I deserved to be happy.

Part Three

'*H*ey, do you have any idea how the fuck we get out of Spain?'

'Not the slightest.'

'We're really something! All that planning, and now we'll just stay here and drive around Madrid all day.'

'We could live in the car. At least we wouldn't have to pay rent.'

'Let's ask someone,' I suggested. It was the first time I was the driver on such a long trip, so I didn't know which direction to go, which road to take.

'That doesn't make sense. We should really buy a map.'

'I'd rather ask someone. If there's one thing I never understand, it's maps.'

'Well, I understand maps better than some random person's directions,' she replied. 'They always just tell you to "keep going straight" when you hit intersections. "And then turn right about two hundred meters before you hit the Housing Department." How am I supposed to know which is the Housing Department? And how am I going to know before I get to it? If I'm asking, it's because I don't know.'

I spotted a woman who was waiting to cross the street, carrying a shopping bag. I pulled up next to the curb and said to Marina, 'There's someone we can ask.'

She reluctantly stuck her head out the window.

'Excuse me, ma'am,' she said. 'Would you be kind enough to tell me which road to take to Italy?'

'Well, I'm . . . I'm from Galicia,' the lady said. 'I'm sorry. I still don't know the streets here.'

We went on, laughing as I went round and round trying to find the way out, going faster and faster. After the visit to the Portuguese mechanic, the car was running great. I stopped at a gas station, where we bought a book with all the European road maps. I didn't even flip through it: I am incapable of going from two to three dimensions.

'Well, now that you've got your map, tell me where to go.'

'All right. All you have to do is follow the signs,' she said. 'We have to go through Zaragoza.'

Zaragoza. The place of my birth. I didn't have very good memories of the place; it reminded me most of all of my father's long absences. He lived going from city to city in search of some job, an illusion that inevitably never became reality. He always wanted a secure, stable job, and to get one he spent his days in perpetual motion. Most times he would go alone, but he took us with him on several occasions. So we went from Zaragoza to Barcelona, then Murcia, Alicante, Barcelona again, León, and finally, when I was almost nineteen, Madrid. And if we didn't go anywhere after that it was only because my father died of a heart attack just when he was planning for us to emigrate to Tangiers. My mother didn't survive him by much. But to recall these things with Marina by my side gave everything a human dimension that was totally new to me. She allowed me to be happy without having to forget my painful history. It meant that I didn't have to block out the sad memories, and in fact turned them into something that strengthened our union. From the dazzling to the mundane, we could find a meaning all our own, in anything, even in the most depressing things. The same

things had happened to Marina, too; she had had a very similar
life. She never knew her father. When she was eight years old,
she left Montevideo with her mother and siblings and moved to
Buenos Aires. She stayed there until she was twenty-two, when
she got a scholarship and moved to Paris. Neither of us had a
country to return to happily.

When we passed Calatayud, she said:

'I want to see the house you were born in.' She rested a hand
on my leg, to transmit some of her warmth. I caressed it and
then placed my hand back on the steering wheel.

Zaragoza was so different from what I remembered that I
didn't feel the usual emotions one feels upon a return. We went
down every last street from beginning to end, but I couldn't find
the house, so I wasn't able to satisfy Marina's desire. I filled the
tank with gas and we left the city. All of a sudden I realized that
my rectum had stopped hurting. We stopped soon after at a
restaurant with a terrace overlooking the Ebro River, beneath
the cooling shade of an oak tree. They were closing, but the
owner took pity on us and gave us a plate of cold cuts, cheese,
bread, and red wine. The sky was clear and the breeze helped
offset the afternoon heat. The wine and the imminent twilight
made me sleepy. Silly giggles escaped from my mouth, which
made me giddier. Then I entered an especially sensitive state of
mind and stopped laughing altogether. I found myself in a
dimension somewhere between sleepiness and lucidity, just like
the day Carranza had interrupted my contemplation of the
woman sweeping the streets. I looked at the bark of the oak
tree, studying its infinite veins, and I saw in them a strange kind
of reality I'd never seen before. I touched the tree and it seemed
to carry the beating of the earth, the generosity of rain, the

precious desire of its roots and their incessant growth, the whis-per of the breeze through the leaves. It was a knowledge that came to me in a nonverbal way, and ran through my body as if it were my very own blood, sap and blood at the same time, and I absorbed it instantly, spontaneously, without thinking. I tried to explain to Marina what I was going through, but I could only manage to sputter out a few disconnected phrases of nonsense in which the only distinguishable word was 'tree.' And then as I tried to express it, my vision ended and I returned to the lucid world around me. Even so, she understood what I had been trying to say.

'When I was a teenager,' she said, 'I would go on walks to smell the perfume of those white flowers that grow in the begin-ning of November – that is, our spring – on the tall trees that they call Paradise . . . I don't know what they call them in Europe. I never saw them in France.'

'Trees of Paradise.'

'Maybe that's it.'

'Maybe.'

'I would go out at night, just to smell that perfume. But it was all very brief, because after the first rain, the flowers, which are very fragile, fall off the branches and start to smell awful, like rotten fruit. They don't last very long. Maybe a few days out of the year, sometimes less than a day even. It all depends on the rain.'

We went back to the car in silence, and left. One, two, three, four roads and finally the road we wanted. We were on our way to Italy. Zaragoza lay behind us.

Where is that memory now, of those flowers lost forever in your youth? And where are your hands, which like the oak tree revealed to me the truths about my life, through the shortcut of your body? And where are your eyes, which answered my own? Where is the love you gave me? Where are the roads to Italy? Where is the tranquillity of your hoarse voice? That's what you taught me, Marina, among so many other things: the scent of Paradise is always fleeting.

We took turns driving and sleeping.

'I have a proposal,' Marina said as we crossed the French border, after the customs officer gave us back our papers through the car window. 'Let's not walk on French soil.'

It was night already.

'All right,' I answered. Marina and I would concur on certain whims like that one.

As she drove, I fell asleep looking out at the highway, something I've always found poignant, I don't know why. I find a beautiful melancholy in all sorts of things – bars, gas stations, bored mechanics, the shape of a spare tyre sleeping under its blanket, the toll taker who spends the night in his microscopic cubicle, maybe with a television hidden some-where, traveling salesmen who sleep in motels and truck drivers who rest at those leafy little pit stops on the side of the road, the waiter who wipes the counter before serving you coffee. If it were up to me, I'd stop at every service station along the road.

I woke up in a gas station near Nîmes. Marina had given the attendant the key to the gas tank so she wouldn't have to get out of the car, even there. I moved over to the driver's seat, a rather complicated maneuver given our determination not to set foot on French land, but we didn't really suffer much more than a brief encounter with the gearshift in certain undignified parts of the body.

'Hey, Marina,' I said, laughing, when we were back on the road. 'I have to go to the bathroom.'

'Well, you'll have to hold it in,' she answered.

'Of course I will! A promise is a promise.'

We passed through Provence, Cannes, Nice, Menton, and finally we entered Italy. The first thing I did in Italian terrain was quite prosaic, but clearly there was no other alternative. I stopped to pee at a gas station. As we had our first Italian coffees, Marina pulled out the map and asked:

'Where are we going?'

'Give me some choices.'

'The most tempting choices are Florence, Siena, Venice, Padua, Ferrara . . .' and she continued reading me all the names that came to mind.

'Florence!' I interrupted her; I had lost her from the start of the list. 'Let's start with Florence. We've got at least fifteen days.'

Without even stopping to say 'You're it!' Marina began to run toward the car, which was parked right outside the café. I accepted the dare, not to be outdone. Like a little kid desperate to run outside and play, I went galloping after her. I won the race and got into the driver's seat.

We arrived in Florence at nine in the morning. With the immunity that our foreign plates gave us, we went straight to the old city, the area that's normally closed to traffic. Marina procured a map and a guidebook to satisfy her cartographic fixation.

A traffic cop stopped us, but right away he let us go. We

weren't so lucky with the next ones. We pretended to be lost, and half the time the policemen would pretend to be making an effort to let us go without penalty. But they gave us a bunch of tickets, too. I didn't worry about them, though; if they get to Madrid, I thought, Santiago won't pay for them.

We found a hotel where we could park the car out front. I think it had a name like Boccaccio, Machiavelli, Petrarch, Dante, or some other Florentine writer. The receptionist, upon looking over our documents, exclaimed:

'I thought you were sisters.'

'We are,' Marina answered. 'We have the same mother.'

After we'd signed in, they took our suitcases up to the room. We laughed when we saw that they had given us a room with two single beds. We took showers and went out to walk around the pedestrian streets in the center, despite our exhaustion, because neither of us had been to Florence and we were dying to get lost in those irregular, erratic streets. We wanted to see it from high above, so we went up to Giotto's bell tower, and through the little windows we could see the city as it shrank, the Gothic contours of the cathedral, the baptistry, until, right in the middle of one of the narrow stairways, a flock of Japanese tourists descended upon us, trapping us in their multitudinous circle and preventing us from moving any farther.

Marina and I were trapped on the same step. I felt the heat of her body against mine. It was an unforeseen contact, and I felt a sudden rush of excitement. I pressed my breasts against her back and ran them from one side to the other, rising up to caress her shoulder blades, one at a time. I searched for one of her buttocks, and cradled it in the nest of my upper thighs, the refuge of my cunt, which grew warm, soaking the inside of my thighs. I put my hands on her waist and pulled her closer to me. The comments and exclamations swirling around me in Japanese – who knew if they were about the bell tower or about Marina and me? – seemed to give me a sort of impunity, in that peculiar solitude that one finds only in the biggest crowds. Acting as if I was going to whisper a secret, I covered her ear with my hand, and kissed the ear. I ran my tongue over those irregular curves and tortuous passageways, so that she could hear the sound of my saliva. I felt five fingers (they were hers, God willing) that rested against the outside of my right thigh and pressed down on it. All of a sudden, the swarm of Japanese people dissolved as quickly as it had formed, revealing the two of us alone, and in an embarrassing, exposed posture.

'Let's go back to the hotel,' she said, yanking me down the stairs.

Upon entering the room, we pushed the two beds together. I asked Marina to move closer. I undressed her, almost not touching her, holding off in my anticipation like someone saving the best for last, feeling my sex get moist instantly. Once again, the miraculous union of figure and reflection was imminent. She remained immobile and docile, submitting herself to my acts.

I was kneeling down with a knee on each bed when I finished undressing her.

Her body fascinated me; I've spent so many hours just look- ing at her. I left her there, only for an instant, to close the window. There were so many buildings close by; I didn't want any strange people interfering with their indiscreet glimpses.

If I had let them, those strangers would have seen two iden- tical women, one dressed and the other naked, feverishly consummating a passion that had been put off for so long.

They would have seen how the clothed woman turned to the naked one, stretched her out in her arms, and laid her down upon the joined beds to kiss every corner of her body and pet all ten fingers with her thumb and index finger, from palm to fingertip, as if she were taking off a ring. They would have seen her kiss the naked woman's knuckles, shoulders, mouth, chest, calves, between her legs.

They would have seen the naked woman's body tremble with pleasure as the clothed woman's face buried itself in her sex, and they would have seen the naked woman's legs cross over the other one's back, a cross of smooth skin on top of the dark background of the fabric, the toes tightened with pleasure, and the face of the other woman shining with the waters carried up from the well of that cunt hidden beneath her lips, the cunt which itself hid a tongue that savored the delicacies of the most intense love, until suddenly the naked woman jumped up and undressed the clothed woman.

And then it would have been impossible to distinguish between the two, because they were two flowers from the same tree, two twins, two images of the same person, because their organs joined, mixed, swirled, fused together. They wouldn't have seen the differences – the dimples of one atop the wider hips of the other, the more prominent sternum of one against the narrower shoulders of the other, the more delicate arms on top of the smaller ears – because by now it was impossible to tell whether it was two women or one, or five, who twisted around those pushed-together beds, the two beds that now, little by little, had started to move apart, the women supporting each other so as not to fall into that tiny abyss and then they moving to the bed on the left, against the wall, and after a while, it was clear that yes, there were two of them, the woman on top of the woman, and they were like figures in a mirror, only in reverse. That is, the legs of one woman were reflected in the face of the other and the lips of one woman in the sex of the other, one body was seeking another body like one who searches for gold amid gold, the girl in the middle of the eye, a search that was a discovery before it even began, and then later, a parade of precise images in the vortex of indefinite, vague images – the wrist bone on the stage of two juxtaposed stomachs, the light sweat of an underarm and the napes of clipped hair, a forehead, a clitoris, the nails that brush but don't scratch, another clitoris, a curved spine and hard buttocks – it was gibberish, a carnival, a substance of skins and kisses and flesh and longing, the sex at the height of sex, a tonic, the doubleknots of desire, a kaleidoscope with bits of moving mirrors, imprinted forever on those who love themselves and their lover.

The strangers would have seen the two images culminate in one single vibration and one single kiss and one single sex and one single body, and then separate. And then reunite in a whole that was so much more than the parts.

They would have seen the mattress fall to the floor, useless, between the two beds, and the woman and the woman on top of the mattress, like a cascade of mirror images, like the incessant current that takes Narcissus's face both from him and to him, and they would have seen the women continue kissing and loving one another, unconcerned by the surface upon which they supported their mutual desire because it was as if they were held up by nothing at all, and the strangers would have seen them float away, clinging to one another, the breasts of the woman against the breasts of the woman, their liquids like water flowing down the same river, and the leg of one intertwined in the legs of the other, although it was hard to tell which legs were whose, but it was all the same rapture as the hours ticked by slowly and the night gave way to day and the day to night in a succession that was as perfect as the mirrored bodies of two reflected women.

But the nearby buildings were too far for their inhabitants to have seen how the eyes of the woman and the eyes of the woman became moist with tears of happiness, before they began again, again . . .

The truth is, I don't know how many days we stayed at that hotel in Florence. Behind the closed shutters, oblivious to the indiscretion of both our neighbors and the sunlight, we consumed our passion outside of time, we lived the most idyllic of solitudes, the solitude of two people in love. Our love was always serene, autonomous, immune to the circumstances of the world. Maybe that's why I also thought it to be eternal, because it needed nothing but itself, like the God of the mystics. But I had forgotten that the logic of rage can be very, very different from that of love. We wouldn't go unnoticed; it's not enough to leave people alone in order for them to leave you in peace.

The person who was really nice to us was the waiter in the hotel. Although he never asked us if we were sisters or lovers, he took care of us in our confinement. He looked just like the actor Vittorio Gassman; no Sooner would he walk in the door than we would exclaim: 'Ciao, Vittorio, come stai?' He always answered the same thing: 'Quiá! I wish I were Gassman! Then you'd see me serving in the bedrooms!'

The hotel didn't have room service; it only made breakfast.

But Vittorio brought us sandwiches, Coca-Colas, beer, coffee —
I suppose from some bar nearby. At first we had to ask him for
it, but later he would note how many hours had gone by since
the last supply had been delivered and would then bring us
something to drink and eat. The last days, when he would rap
on the door to our room, he gave in to announcing himself as
Vittorio.

One afternoon — or was it morning, or night? — I wanted to
see the clothing Marina had packed in her suitcases. Little by
little we emptied them, and then we did the same with mine,
exchanging clothes, trying everything on. Pass me those panty
hose, I would say, and then I would put them on, naked, with no
underwear, and she would caress my legs. Her hands would
slide down that shiny, brilliant surface that covered the delta of
my moist sex. Then she would ask me for a blouse, through
whose fabric I would kiss her breasts, or she would try on a
short shirt that fell like an awning over her pointy breasts, and
we went on, burying ourselves in mountains of clothing, using
one another as a mirror, pausing to make love half-dressed,
concocting the most absurd outfits. Then Marina begged me to
walk around in her shoes and I told her to put on my black
dress, the tight one, and I reached my hands around her waist
and sank my feminine tongue in the décolletage I longed for, in
the furrow of her two breasts, my breasts, before I put on her
hips the bikini she wore the day I met her, before I licked the bits
of down that escaped from either side, before I donned the
gloves to masturbate with as I watched her, and as I did all those
things she brought to me the inebriating perfume of paradise
emanating from her lace panties, corset, bra, miniskirts, robes.
We interchanged everything and everything had a purpose in

our pleasure, because the pleasure was between us and not our possessions.

So, naturally, it didn't take long before the room was a mess – not unlike Pulga's attic, in fact: the mattresses thrown to the floor, the open suitcases, empty bottles, dirty napkins, hard little heels of bread.

Instead of cleaning up, we went to Venice. I had never been there, and Marina convinced me that we should take the train. We left very early one morning and returned at midnight. We spent the entire day walking around that illusory, melancholy, beautiful city, which always looks as if it's falling to pieces, that is if it hasn't already. At the Peggy Guggenheim museum, we saw a painting that left us dumbstruck, called *Two Women Before a Mirror*. It showed a blonde and a brunette duplicated in a mirror, in an everyday kind of moment that was somehow pierced by a profound sadness. We tried to buy a copy, but it wasn't available.

We returned to Florence. We took one final walk through her streets, said good-bye to Vittorio, paid the hotel, got into the car, and once again asked ourselves what our next destination would be.

Before leaving for Italy, many times I asked myself if I wouldn't become a victim of that bitter disappointment that comes over you when you finally get the thing you've wanted for so long. It's funny – it's as if finding something is the same as losing it. I was petrified of becoming disillusioned by the physical reality of Marina, by the discovery of who she was. But on that long trip we took before settling down in Rome, I found that my anxieties were unfounded: the reality I had so longed for was not at all vulgar in comparison with the unconsummated dream; it was rather a culmination, a triumph, something the imagination could never even have dared to envision. It couldn't have. We never disappointed each other, not even in those first few moments that follow physical love. Our experience had taught us that those moments necessarily led to chasms of incurable sadness; instead, we found ourselves astonished that the satisfaction of desire didn't extinguish the love, but inflamed it. We didn't finish our orgasms like people closing doors behind them that they will never reopen. No, we were like two people exploring labyrinths whose chambers have no end, or like two people running through space, sea, air, where there are no boundaries, no beginning and no end, and the journey and the destination are the very same thing.

That's why it's hard for me to remember the different stages of our Italian trip in proper order. I can only hold on to haphazard, isolated fragments; with this rubble, these stones, these ashes, I am trying to fill the refuge of memory. Time blends together and spoils the tyranny of time: if past, present, and future lose their meaning, then my love and my memory can attain a certain immortality, eternal youth. The only true death is the death of memory. The other, the one that awaits me, doesn't frighten me.

These pages branch off, they turn themselves, jumping ahead in leaps, gushing out, receding, stopping to look at what lies hidden in the folds of time, not because of some whim but because they are simply obeying the most basic form of my memory and my hope.

As I threw myself into the happiest days of my life, without losing the tiniest bit of my equilibrium I observed everything

carefully, so I would be able to remember it after – to the point
that I would remember experiences I was still in the middle of
having, and would admire myself for acquiring those new memories even as I did so. To multiply that game of mirrors through
a love stolen from mirrors, to close even more trunks within
bigger trunks, like those Russian dolls, reminded us to record
the steps, the efforts, the hesitations that had led up to our first
encounter, because one of the sweetest acts of love occurs when
two lovers evoke together the infinite proposals, the daring
plans, and the impatient vicissitudes of love's evenings.

I have a hard time establishing any chronology; I should rely
more on the external elements, like the Gulf of Naples, the
colors of Siena, the walls at Monteriggioni, the steps of Gubbio.

Or maybe I should linger in the slow, pleasurable details of
joy, images that I can never forget, like the tepid warmth of
Marina's face against my shoulder as we would drive down a
tree-flanked road. Or the soapy foam on her sex as I washed it
in one of the few bedrooms we had with a private bath. Or the
shadow of a medieval tower in San Gimignano that fell only on
us and seemed to follow our slow journey through the sun-
filled streets. Or the dark sketch against the oblique clarity of a
hotel window, of our two bodies loving each other, one single
fabric that produced the whisper of our ancient, unknown acts.
Or the gully that presided over the cemetery at Volterra (or was
it Cortona?), purple in the afternoon sun amid the green
cypress trees. Or the silent stone monsters of Bomarzo (I
thought of a Wertmüller movie) among whom Marina kissed
me on the mouth. Or when she told me that she loved the way
I look as much as she loved me (by that time we were in Rome,
I'm sure of it, beneath the false cupola of the Church of St.

Ignatius). Or certain gestures Marina had, insignificant, casual, perhaps, but so necessary for me – like the lower lip that slowly dried as she read a passage from our travel guide as we entered and left Spoleto, until her tongue darted over it with a brief flash of moisture, a movement that was both delicate and quick. Or her eyes that were always ready to lock with mine when I allowed mine to stray from the road for an instant. Or the murmur her legs made beneath her miniskirt and in the fishnet stockings if she crossed her legs under the table at that restaurant in Perusa, the one below those ancient archways, where with the tip of my toe I explored every one of those minuscule diamonds woven into the fabric of those hose. Or how she trembled when I would kiss the hairs on the back of her neck. Or the way her fingers grasped the glass before taking a sip.

I remember – and for anyone who has never loved a woman these details will surely seem extraordinary – her bright red lips on my aroused red nipples, the droplets of water scattered across her breasts in the shower, the rhythmic sway of her hips as she walked, the pearl earrings that shone in her earlobes, the same ones I licked when we fucked.

I remember how I helped her get dressed, how I colored my lips by kissing her, how I drank her menstrual blood, how I called her by my name, how we dressed up in party clothes and danced in silence, how I told her I loved her as if she were a friend and not my wife, how I cried for not being able to impregnate her.

I remember when she told me again that she had never slept with a man. I asked her if she wanted to – *I mean, don't worry about me*. Only if you're with me, she said.

I remember every single time we made love and I could

count them all, just like a vain adolescent who writes about his conquests in a secret little book.

At the hotel in Florence, as Vittorio would knock on our door to no avail, I would be lying facedown on the mattress. On top of me, Marina would wrap her arms around my waist, open my legs with her hands, and with scarcely two fingers procure the simultaneous pleasure of my clitoris and vagina.

And right there, or in Urbino, or in Assisi, I would lie her down on top of me, but this time we would both be face-up, her back against my breasts, her buttocks against my pubis, her thighs against mine, and I would stroke her sex as if it were my own, as if we weren't two people. I stroked and I stroked the whole way through and she rose to reach her orgasm and didn't come down and gasped with my lungs and was it her hand or mine that entered my sex to take me to the elevated point where Marina lingered?

Once, we kissed each other all over, allowing nothing to escape the range of our lips: toes, the sweat behind our knees, our back muscles, the valleys of our necks, the cavities of our collarbones, our nostrils, each one of the hairs on our sexes – sucking them one by one like unique, delicate jewels – the innumerable creases of our hands, our chins, the long curve of our ribs.

An image: the cross formed by the vertical line between her mouth and sex and the horizontal line of her breasts, as the bells of an ancient church rang outside.

Another image, this one outside of time: Marina's breathing as she sleeps, the belly button that rises and falls, her tranquil chest, the outline of her collarbone. I arrive and admire jealously the dreams she has, made visible through the little facial expressions that modify the look on her face. They are in the present, the future that is, and I observe from far away that part of her identity forever hidden from me, like a prisoner watching a miracle from behind the bars on her window.

I remember in Lucca how I watched her get ready to go out. Then, unable to contain myself, exultant, I threw her onto the bed and gave her sex the gift of my tongue, pushing away her miniskirt, her panties, and I tried to adjust the beating of my heart to the beating of her cunt, and all it took for me to come was one look at her legs and those brown heels at their far end, the curved border, the birth of her toes, the smooth legs I held in my hands, the fragile offertory of her vagina from which I extracted the nectar of her ecstasy, in perfect rhythm with my heart.

I remember looking at those shoes and masturbating as she murmured rough words in my ear. Another day we mastur-bated together, in front of each other just like in the recurring dreams of my loneliness, in our hotel room in Siena, whose walls were lined with mirrors. I brought her hand down to her sex and she repeated the movement with me, and we were two twin figures, multiplied by the thousands in those walls, basking in every single reflection and figure.

And I also remember that time we went to the movies. We decided it had to become an event, and we put on our fanciest clothes. When I began to put on my makeup, Marina offered to help me, and I helped her with hers. And from making each other up we went straight into making love on the floor, our faces smeared with useless lipsticks and powders, smudged with colorful, impetuous kisses and black mascara tears. And it did turn out to be quite an event, even though we never made it to the movies.

Another image: during the hot nights of that summer, Marina would go to the bathroom, and when she returned, she would touch me with her wet hands. I would wake up; in the penumbral dreamscape her body sometimes seemed to be mine. The chill of her fingers against my skin didn't bother me, because it was the external signal that simply meant I was with another person.

With her I understood the enjoyment of searching out the pleasure of the person by your side. I once heard someone say that all love is selfish. Maybe that's true, but how beautiful selfishness can be when it emerges from itself to satisfy its vanity through the happiness of its beloved! And how complete it becomes when the gesture is reciprocated! How can you say Narcissus loves himself when he only wishes to satisfy his double?

I remember how long it took me to get used to our resemblance; that was natural. There were times I would turn to her, distracted – I would get confused at finding myself two paces in front of me. And we also worked to refine the resemblance, on purpose. We reached perfection with respect to haircuts, clothing, and bodily gestures.

Very naturally – not forced or contrived at all – we began to create a third person, equidistant between her and me, whose image we deemed to be the only true image and not a mask. But that wasn't enough for us; we aspired to more profound levels of communion. We had been born on different days, in different years – we weren't the same sign, nor were we from the same country. Nevertheless, something had to have united us, even before we met. Almost jokingly, we began to wonder aloud about the possibility that we really were sisters. It wasn't such a crazy idea. She was from Uruguay, sure, but her father had left her mother a few months before she was born. Wasn't it possible that her father and my father could be the same man? We invented his biography, which, once we finished, seemed like the most obvious thing in the world. After leaving her mother, he had gone to Spain, where he met my mother. They fell in love, she got pregnant, and from that union I was born, Marina's sister. With respect to our age difference, we had to admit that our father had acted fast. Only three weeks could have passed between the moment he escaped Uruguay and the moment he got my mother pregnant. Any other way you sliced it the story didn't work. And he was very good at hiding his Uruguayan origins, I added; in fact, his accent was that of a man whose ancestors had lived in Spain for centuries.

We saw many cities on that trip; some we visited only for a few hours and others a few days. Naturally, we stayed in many hotels, and in all of them we would put our legend into use. Everyone who saw us thought we were sisters, but there was the question of our documents, our last names. So sometimes – not for money reasons, but to challenge the world to distinguish between us – instead of pretending we were sisters, we wouldn't register two people at all, and would just register one of us. The other one would remain outside, waiting, and would later walk in, her head held high. 'I thought you were in your room,' the doormen would say, excusing themselves. 'No, no, excuse me,' we would say. 'I forgot to give you the key when I left.' And then we would find each other in a pre-arranged spot – the staircase, the elevator, the second floor. They never found us out.

To know what to say in the event they interrogated us, and to have a good alibi, we invented yet another biography: ours. That is, the biography of that third person we were when we weren't Marina or Sofía. We called her Clara.

But even that wasn't enough for us.

We ended up making a kind of pact, in Naples. A pact that has sealed the trajectory of our lives since then. A pact that I wouldn't ever dare break, even if I wanted to, though I don't want to, for fear of dissolving into the air like an ephemeral puff of smoke, for fear of disappearing like water amid flames.

We went to Naples because, after a month of vacation just wandering around, we found ourselves in Rome. Marina telephoned the owner of the apartment. As she had predicted, the apartment wasn't ready. Two days, in two days it will be ready, said the owner, and then he'd give it to us.

We drove the Marbella as fast as we could. We stayed in the Royal Hotel, on the waterfront, and checked in under one name. We lay down on the canopy bed, beneath the scrutinizing gaze of the pheasants in the wallpaper and the brilliant gleam of the golden furniture, and almost without noticing it, we undressed. We felt it, though, because we felt it together. Clara felt it, felt how our skins were united far beyond any objective physical separation. We wanted to be inside each other like those Russian dolls we remembered, to breathe with the same lungs, drive the same blood through our veins, digest with the same bowels.

We tried to express how much we loved each other, how deeply we had come to love each other in those few days we shared together, but we didn't have words for it. It was frustrating not to be able to communicate love, but it was a new kind of love and couldn't be described using old words. Marina

suggested that we each make a tiny hole in the pad of a fingertip as a blood oath. We did it, but we both knew that such an
overused ritual was as meaningless as any conventional collo-
quial expression.

So we made the pact.

After the pact I asked Marina to crouch over my stomach.
Night was falling through the blinds, and the grooves of sunlight
made identical furrows in our skin.

'Shit on me,' I said. 'Give me your shit. I want all of you.'

Her face contracted from the effort, and then I felt it. First
the tepid drop that shook me the instant it touched down on my
body, and then the light rumble of the rectum that I had kissed
so many times, and the slow release, the gradual parabola of her
feces around my belly button; and I caressed her buttocks as she
did it. She gave me everything, saving nothing for herself – we
were sharing even the castoffs of our bodies. And I touched it;
I felt the consistency of what Marina's infinite love had given
me, that love that went so far beyond what was usual, or what
was repugnant. So far beyond itself.

That night I ate her excrement and she ate mine.

I fell asleep kissing my neck of yours and I tasted that most
bitter, intimate taste of my entrails on your palate, I drank us,
down to our feces, and from then on my dreams were your
dreams, Marina, our Marina, we loved me, you loved yourself
more than ever, we dreamed that you saw yourself and I was
you, was Clara, because she multiplied our dreams and we
kissed you on my cunt, you slid my tongue over it and I put your
fingers next to our burning lips, you opened my abyss, we spun
around, you penetrated yourself again, with that careless, happy

smile, Marina, we came in me, we were me, we loved me, Sofía, forever.

The apartment in Rome was worth the wait. It was pretty: on the third floor of a decrepit old rat-infested building with no elevator, but pretty. Almost all the rooms got sunlight for much of the day, especially in the morning. We decorated it with things we found at the Porta Portese flea market. It had a window that looked out onto a piazza with a fountain in the middle; the fountain was flanked by four turtles that looked as if they had been the afterthought of some lunatic sculptor. That piazza is probably one of the few luminous spots in a neighborhood of narrow, twisting streets, built in the shade of Roman ruins. At a certain time, it had been the city's ghetto, and lots of Jews still live in the area; their synagogue is just a few steps away, right on the shores of the Tiber. Over the centuries, the ancient Roman structures gradually transformed, most of all during the Middle Ages and the Renaissance. These layers – of schools, styles, ages – are what I love most about Rome. They seem to symbolize the love between Marina and me, the thousands of people necessary for my tongue to play inside her sex, for her breasts to press against mine. They were like Clara, that new, perfect reality that was born above the ruins of two solitudes.

The ghetto was close to the Campidoglio, the Capitolio, the hill that the ancient Romans took to be the center of the world and that overlooks the remains of the Forum. At the top is the piazza Michelangelo designed, where I would walk alone after Marina started her job. I would walk her to the FAO building. We would walk along the Circus Maximus to the Palatine Hill and stop at a prudent distance. With a rapid, furtive kiss on the mouth, sheltered behind a tree, we said good-bye until twilight. On my way back, I walked with my head held down, engrossed in my thoughts, slowly, with that mixture of depression and happiness that I always felt when Marina and I separated. I missed her and it hurt not to be near her, but at the same time my heart would begin to prepare itself for our vespertine reunion. Solitude wasn't really solitude, because it was inhabited by the knowledge of seeing her again.

Then I would stop in the Campidoglio, and sit on a bench or on the steps, and that was how I spent my mornings. I would read, watch the tourists, or simply listen to the sound from the fountain, smell the perfume of the nearby orange groves, contemplate the plaza and the geometric lines of its ground. When it rained, I felt like I was missing something. Then I would get in the Marbella and run around Rome, the Aventino, the aqueducts and the walls, Bernini, Caravaggio, the baroque churches and the catacombs. I went alone and later would bring Marina to see the places I had liked best. In general I tended to pick places where cars were allowed, which were few. I got tons of tickets in Rome, more than I ever got in my life, mainly for parking in no-parking zones.

On my tourist itineraries I followed the exhortations of Astrologo, a Jewish man from the second floor who we quickly befriended. He was the person who revealed Rome's secrets to me.

In Italy, they don't put floor numbers on the downstairs intercom; instead they put the occupants' last names. So, the first time we saw our neighbor's name downstairs, we thought he must be an individual who practices astrology, and not just any astrologer: he had to be *Astrologo*, as his name indicated.

Only after we met him did we realize that L'Astrologo was his odd last name. And he was no less strange than his name. He wasn't stupid or crazy, but he looked like a real hermit, with a long white beard, myopic eyes without glasses, a hunched back, disheveled, mismatched clothing, and eternally dirty hair. He spent his life running away from people, but he had a special feeling for us, and came around once or twice a week.

The friendship began one afternoon as we were climbing the stairs, shouting to each other. When Astrologo heard us speaking Spanish, he abruptly opened the door to his apartment. We were sure he'd gone nuts, but in reality he was simply overjoyed to find people with whom he could speak Spanish. He invited us in for coffee. After a brief moment of hesitation, we went in. The place was filled with old books, dirty plates that had been tossed against peeling walls, and broken furniture. The only thing missing were the flasks, the tools, and the retorts of an alchemist. First he brushed off a couple of chairs heaving with papers. Then, moving his face closer to the various objects in the apartment because of his near-blinding myopia, he looked for his coffee cups, but couldn't find them. Then he realized he had no coffee. So the three of us went up to our apartment, and Astrologo stayed until well past midnight. A few days later, he came by, begging us to lend him a book by Borges; he wanted to read it in the original. He came back to return it to me and then asked for another book, I don't remember which. And that's how we got to know each other.

He spoke Spanish with a bizarre, delicious accent, and his archaically constructed sentences were always finished off with an anachronism. It seemed as though we were listening to an *hidalgo* from Spain's Golden Age. His specialty – the subject to

which he had devoted his life — was Sephardic literature and
Jewish-Arabic culture during the age of Moorish rule in Spain.
The mere mention to him of the word 'reconquest' was like
telling a Mexican about the 'discovery' of the Americas, or a
Spaniard about the 'victory' at Trafalgar. But it wasn't the only
thing he talked about, and our conversations were impassioned.
It seemed as though he knew everything. He told us all the
secrets, the history, the mysteries — of our neighborhood, of
Spain, of the Jewish cabala, of the American Independence, of
the Koran, of Ovid. He told us about the different methods
used to build staircases and to cultivate olives, and coca.

One of the few times we managed to get him out of the
house — by assuring him we were only walking to the car — he
took us to the Protestant cemetery so we could see Keats's
grave, situated near a Roman pyramid. The inscription on the
tombstone is so poignant: *This grave contains all that was mortal of*
*a young English poet. Here lies one whose name was writ in wate*r. We
used to repeat that, over and over: 'This grave contains all that
was mortal of a young English poet. Here lies one whose name
was writ in water.'

Astrologo, whether because of indifference, myopia, or discretion, never tried to figure out what kind of relationship
united Marina and me. He must have realized that we only had
one bedroom and one bed, so we didn't bother telling him we
were sisters as we did with everyone else. We simply didn't
talk about it. Often he would mix up our names, but we didn't
bother correcting him, because we liked it when people got
confused. And as for him, we didn't know of any other rela-
tionships he might have had outside of the one he shared with us.
We never asked him if he was married, single, gay, virgin, or

just uninterested. We suspected he was a cabalistic onanist, and we joked that maybe the rabbi had gone a little too far when circumcising him. In general, though, only women who didn't pay much attention to external appearances could ever have found him attractive. He was kind of ugly, and he smelled pretty decrepit, like old playing cards.

Over a period of weeks, he tried desperately to give me Italian lessons in exchange for Spanish classes. But he knew both languages better than I did, and tended to lose himself among all the etymologies, derivations, and abstractions. He would search for the most imperceptible nuances, he would compare words in the fourteen foreign tongues he assured us he spoke, he would recite in Ladino (the Sephardic dialect), and he taught me things I never could have used in conversation. I had a ball with him, but of real Italian I learned precious little. As far as my instruction, I only was able to teach him to say 'usted,' the formal 'you,' instead of the archaic 'vuestra merced' – 'your grace' – when he spoke. He grew tired of such a one-sided exchange, and I didn't insist on continuing.

The one tongue I did finally learn about was Marina's. Like her cold hands on summer nights, her picturesque expressions and her idiosyncratic accent were the external reminder that we were different, that our present was really the convergence of two separate pasts, built up by the sediments of all the cities we had both lived in as children. To tell the truth, I knew practically nothing about Argentina and Uruguay; as she always said, the old colonies were obviously not my forte. I couldn't have even picked them out on a map, and I was totally incapable of distinguishing between the different nationalities among South Americans, much less the way they all spoke Spanish in those

remote lands. Love was love and tits were tits, all right, but we
still had a lot to learn.

'And what do you call this, *che*?' I asked once, pointing to her
cunt, stroking it as we lay naked in bed, like a teacher and a student in a libertine novel.

'The *concha*,' Marina said.

Then she began questioning me, and that day we began to
compile a dictionary of private, personal vocabulary, in both
European and South American Spanish: 'fuck' — *follar, joder,
coger, garchar*; 'you're pretty' — *eres guapa, sos linda*; cock — *polla,
picha, pija, poronga*; 'motherfucker' — *gilipollas, forro*; 'skirt' —
falda, pollera; 'climax' — *correrse, acabar*; 'you want' — *tú quieres,
vos querés*, Marina-Clara-Sofía.

I hoped that when we got around to the clitoris, we would
find another, prettier way of saying it. Clitoris is too awful a
word to allude to something so delicate, so fragile. Clitoris — it
sounds like it has something to do with sickness, not pleasure.
But no, in Río de la Plata they say it the same way: clitoris. We
had so much fun — we used to parody the South American and
Spanish pronunciations in absurd dialogues.

'*Sho creo que la shuvia fue una beshesa y no entiendo cómo vos tuvi-
jte ajco de algo tan lindo*,' I imitated. '*Desime si tengo rasón y dejpués
ponete un dijquito bárbaro, che*.'

'*Que sí, hombre, que no se estrañe. La he dicho a su madre de ustez
que el Atlético Madriz ha estao perfeto*,' Marina answered. '*Ahí es
nada, que le he vishto iorar ese penalti que no vea*.'

After a while, we ended up speaking a sort of in-between
language which was neither hers nor mine, contaminated with
the Roman and Italian expressions we heard every day. It was a
dialect that only we understood.

We became so accustomed to that intimate language that
when I began to work at the Rioja Pou gallery, I had to concen-
trate very hard whenever I wrote a letter in Spanish. I got the
job thanks to the owner of the gallery I had worked for in
Madrid. One of the recommendation letters she had written
served as an introduction to a Catalan man whose gallery was
dedicated exclusively to promoting Spanish artists in Rome. He
gave me the job out of pity – the salary was miserable and my
tasks included helping him with correspondence, making coffee
for him, writing blurbs for his exhibition catalogues, and keeping the place clean. Even though he paid me so little, Rioja Pou
at least drew up a contract for me, which would make things
easier for me when it came time to apply for residence in Italy.
It was really the ideal job for me. It wasn't far from the apartment, walking distance, really. I'd go there two or three
afternoons a week, after having a salad or some fruit for lunch.
And there was never very much to do. When I returned home,
Marina would be back already making dinner, which she loved
to do. We would eat at the table in the kitchen, with no table-
cloth and only paper napkins, and behind the walls we could
hear the rats scratching as they dug their dark little holes. Then
she would read to me or we would listen to music as I washed
the dishes. Glasses would slip from my hands and shatter just
from the thought that we would soon be in bed fucking.

That was why we went out so little, and why our social life
was limited pretty much to visits from Astrologo. Like most
scatterbrained people, he was very meticulous and routine-
oriented about certain things, so we slid into a tradition of
having dinner together every Wednesday.

As time went by, we looked around for a man who could

initiate Marina sexually, but we were in no rush, so we rejected lots of people: two FAO delegates from some African country I can't recall – Burkina Faso, or Tanzania, or Senegal. They were two black fags, with bodies like hundred-meter Olympic runners. They were cousins and, thinking that we were sisters, they offered us the chance to have a really quality orgy on diplomatic grounds. Through the FAO we got to know some other people, mainly Marina's colleagues, to whom I was presented as her younger sister. This gave us a certain immunity to touch each other freely, during a conversation or a meal. These touches gave the impression of being simple fraternal gestures, their true meaning being evident only to us, accomplices of a clandestine love.

But with them, we never had as good a time as we did with Astrologo, and on those nights out all we ever wanted to do was come back home, take our clothes off, and tangle ourselves up in the bedsheets. I would lie down with my face against her thighs, and my mouth would feel its way around her panties. My hands held on to the sides of her hips, and her warm feet played in my cunt, or she would grab my fingers and masturbate with them. The bed was large, but we slept snuggled up in a corner on one side. So many times, I would wake up in the middle of the night in the purest, fullest feeling of happiness, free from nightmares. And then I would see her eyes open for a moment, go wide open in the dark clarity of the moon and the piazza. The incessant coo of the fountain, the squealing of the rats, the silence of the sleeping city, and then, just as it was with Francisca and her friend, all it took was the slightest, most groping movement and our flesh would begin to whisper like two silk sheaths rubbing against one another. We would place ourselves one

against the other, hugging, looking for that pre-established harmony, the renewed wonder of knowing that her mouth was
kissing mine, while her feet were level with my feet – the meas-
urement of our equality, the perfect size, the extension of Clara
in the mirror and the continuity of all our intermediate points:
shoulders, breasts pressed against each other, bellies, knees;
everything fit where it was supposed to, molding without violence like water in water, like the water of our united mouths,
and in the fusion of her pubis against mine, of my cunt against
her concha. And from there the most intimate bond began to
form, the hottest link, in the middle of the night of the desire of
the dream of love, as we caressed, touched, pawed at each other
from the back of the ear to the little hairs on the nape of the
neck, the crescent-shaped shoulder blades, smooth and curved,
and that wide abyss, long and soft and welcoming, of the back,
the middle line that runs from the neck to the buttocks, the eye,
the center, the tender canals of the spine, stopping at each and
every vertebra, islands in a transparent sea. At the same time,
our tongues played as our hands did, as happy as we were, inde-
cent and pure like our sexes, and then nothing more could be
heard except the sound of our agitated hairs rushing up against
each other, the sexes that fucked and screwed and pushed and
pushed their way to the leap that would transport us from one
body into the other, and fuse them, and transform them into two
other mouths kissing each other, whispering words of love, and
it seems hard to believe we could reach orgasm like that, but we
did. It came closer and closer and closer to us, and I came and
you came and we kept going, screaming, my toes against your
toes, *vos*, me, you, me, and we came, we came and came and
yet, somehow that was when everything seemed to begin.

We woke up countless times in the heart of the night like that, sometimes twice in the same night. Overwhelmed by desire, our bodies still exhausted from so much love, we nonetheless couldn't control ourselves. And that was when I understood the incurable exhaustion that had plagued poor Francisca, who was drained of all energy from the pleasure she shared with her lover.

Never in my life had I enjoyed sex so much, and Marina said the same was true for her. I guess every woman knows the things that will bring her the most pleasure – that's something as individual as temperament, or fingerprints even. Between the two of us, we had hundreds of ways to climax. We experimented with all different kinds of orgasms: extended and brief, slow and fast; interminable storms and sudden gusts, long detours and rapid shortcuts; the serene progression of someone climbing a mountain and the frenetic ascent of someone caught underwater. With a tongue gently resting upon the subtle equilibrium of a clitoris, through the tenuous lips of the vagina, in them, on the edges and in the intimate recesses of the anus, against the breasts; with the tip of the index finger against the upper, internal wall of the vagina, and the entire finger, or two, or three traveling around any part at all of our burning bodies, inside, outside, near, above, below, all around them. I swear we sometimes came just from looking at each other. All we had to do was want it. And we did it on the bus, on line to pay our bills, in the movies, standing in front of the statues in the Campidoglio, in bed, in the kitchen, in the shower, interrupting sleep or dinner to respond to the call of our passion. Everything made us crave each other.

We had discovered that, more than anything, love is a state of lucidity, perception, the inclination – sometimes intentional, sometimes involuntary – of discovering pleasure in all the folds of existence, a third eye; an intuition and a certainty, a new sensibility, and the only one capable of perceiving absolute happiness.

Our life seemed to be unfolding magnificently.

But I was incorrigibly superstitious, a coward; fear seems to be eternally stamped upon my soul. I contemplated the secure serenity of our love, the beauty of the city in which we lived, the incredible wisdom of our friend Astrologo, the harmony that reigned in our apartment, and I thought we were too fortunate, too pretty, too perfect, too together, for the future not to hold something ominous.

I knew that Paradise's perfume lasts until the rains begin to fall, that many lives require many deaths. And I also knew that our love, ever since that day at the pool, from the remote age of the first Narcissus, was like clear water: it had the same color and the same unstable fragility.

In the Spanish bookstore at the Piazza Navona, stuck between the volumes of catechisms, the lives of saints, and the latest novelties, you found a book that had escaped the watchful eye of the elderly nuns who worked there. It was called *Narcissus*, and I think the author's name was something like Lilian or Vivian Darkbone, or Darkbloom, or Darkstone; I'll never remember it. We read almost all of it, turning the pages as we sat on one of the benches in the piazza under the Fountain of the Four Rivers, next to the African men selling sunglasses, the silly auteurs of silly caricatures, and the Peruvians who belted out songs from the Andes.

The book gave summaries of all the Narcissus-like myths that
exist throughout the world. The one we liked the best was an
Oscan legend, which stated that a person finds himself exactly
two times in life and that only the wisest souls are able to truly
see themselves in those moments. If that legend is true, then
maybe I shouldn't look for you in Montevideo, in Rome, in
Buenos Aires, in Naples, or in Madrid. Maybe your name isn't
Marina, Clara, or Sofía. Maybe you'll read these lines and show
up for the date we have.

Anyway, I'll soon go to find you and then we'll know the
truth.

Occasionally I imagine – and the book didn't mention this –
that there exists another person: unknown, perfect, as great as
a God, unique, and of whom you, I, and everyone like us
constitute temporary pieces, simple apparitions, imperfect
approximations. I know this idea has all the beauty and all
the desolation of empty dreams, but I was taken by it all the
same.

I remember how indignant you became when the author of
Narcissus would refer to certain psychoanalysts and the theories
they had with respect to our 'case' (to them we were a Case,
capital C, just like cases of incest among twins). You said that
when all is said and done, psychologists run around in circles
with all their reasoning and logic, because they explain narcissism as a form of homosexuality, and homosexuality as a form of
narcissism.

'Well,' I answered, cruelly joking, 'you're homosexual and I
used to masturbate in front of mirrors. Add it up, put our two
pasts together, and you get the life of one single person who
explains everything.'

'That doesn't explain anything. Love isn't a category that psychologists can understand.'

And with that, you threw the book into a trash can, and I never held it again in my hands. Then, through the labyrinth of baroque buildings hewn above the winding outline of the medieval streets, we walked home together holding hands, to the suspicion of some and the indifference of others.

Scarcely had we walked in the door than we began making love in broad daylight. Still standing, we were submerged in a clarity like that of our first encounter in the pool. We heard the echoes of the turtles in the fountain as we compared ourselves and the contours of our bodies like Narcissus in his watery mirror, navigating down the rapids that flowed from your sex to mine, crossing the narrow narrows of your breasts, and then my mouth flowed onto your belly through the sweet channel of your neck, while you remained on the margins of my back, skirting the shore so you could look at me, jumping out into the surf from the promontory of your damp lips, and there in the shallow pool of my shoulders you found the arms of my arms, which were yours as well, a silent cascade, a creek that you filled from bottom to top and top to bottom, which flowed and overflowed between your legs. It was a lake which became a torrent in your hands, a clear shower to wash away the past. It grew, and dulled my senses, and I set into the deepest sails of your sex and of mine, blown open by the wind. I wanted to inundate you, as if I were being baptized in you, and grab on to the rushing rapids of my desire, and make you roll through the narrow pass between my thighs. But you built a gentle dam to detain the vertiginous path of my coming orgasm so we could enjoy it together, and distill it drop by drop, contemplate

ourselves in it, and finally took me to the very last whirlpool,
the final, shared communion, and then we set sail for the open
sea, infinite toward the infinite Marina.

Baxí left last night. I'm alone again, and it's better that way.

I don't think she'll come back; I think he's gone for good,
after the few weeks we spent together. Ours wasn't a true love,
it was just a consolation, like animals that lick each other's
wounds. Too many painful ghosts, mainly yours, Marina, passed
through our separate hearts. How could I love Baxí after knowing happiness at your side? No, I don't have anything to give
now, not even desperation.

I don't even know why I spent time with him.

Maybe in order to try to understand what Santiago did, after
I returned to Rome following my absurd trip to Río de la Plata
on that KLM flight, I would look at them all; all of them,
making no distinctions, because I didn't know then that Baxí was
among them.

I'd always loved driving around the tree-lined street that runs
alongside the walls of the old city, from the Baths of Caracalla to
the entrance to St. Paul's, even though it's a bit longer, with lots
of twists and turns. But now, for the first time, I discovered its
clandestine and scandalous nocturnal life, those exaggeratedly
obscene figures that contort their bodies as they offer themselves up to the highest bidder, sometimes slinking between
two cars, like bats that don't dare leave the safety of the darkness, and sometimes preening themselves shamelessly in the
middle of the street.

This place had everything: hookers, transvestites, queers.
They were divided into territories, so the clientele could

distinguish the different products. But I only slowed down by the transvestites, those confused creatures that were a mix of sexual deviance and profound suffering.

At that time, I had been without Marina for a year and a half. It was summertime, and the majority of the transvestites weren't wearing much more than panties, stockings and garter, and platforms. The rest of their anatomies remained revealed: hefty buttocks, solid legs, powerful tits, all of which they brandished before the onlookers, with a cheekiness that even the most whorish whores wouldn't have the nerve to exhibit.

I didn't interest them. I wasn't more than a chick, a vulgar, fastidious woman, the thing they wanted to be but couldn't. Once they were out of the glare of my headlights, they saw me, and either ran away or made fun of me, blowing me sarcastic kisses.

That was when I parked the car by the curb in front, and with my lights off I watched them for hours and hours. I couldn't do anything else now that Marina was no longer with me, now that I was obligated to put into practice the secret pact we had made in Naples.

The police would occasionally come down and raid the area, and the four or five patrol cars with the luminous racket of their sirens were like foreign invaders on a mission to eradicate this scum from the face of the earth. And the street would become deserted for a few days, but soon one transvestite would appear, and another, and five, and ten, and then the street would be filled once again. The customers would also return — men of all shapes and sizes. They would park their cars, small and large, haggle prices, pick their candidates according to the cruel laws of supply and demand, hustle the captives into their cars, take off, and then, sometimes before ten minutes had gone by, return their specimens back to their lair of shadows and trees.

And the transvestites were there night after night, with their ambiguous, fascinatingly perverse air, beneath whose influence Santiago had fallen, and who now awakened in me a curiosity that I couldn't quite identify. Maybe it was because I, like them, belonged to that dark cadre of people who can't be categorized simply as men or women, was one of those with an affliction of the soul that opens from the very aperture of their sex, a race that is both proud of and tormented by their condition. At the same time I thought about how with Marina, I had crossed a border through which there was no possibility of return. I was unable to give myself to another woman without making the inevitable comparisons. Any other woman, like the KLM stewardess, was insignificant when compared with Marina. Transvestites, however, weren't on either side of the border, really. They were the borderline, the blade of the knife, that uncertain moment of the day when night is over but dawn still hasn't come. I didn't like them, though, and so I could only remain at the margin, and watch them from the curb. Most of them seemed pretty ridiculous deformed fetuses, hags, freaks — because I still hadn't come across my beautiful monster, my siren, my unicorn. And finally I found him.

I didn't see him much, because he was in pretty high demand. One car would drop him off and another would immediately swoop him up. At first, from my distant observation post, I didn't pay him much attention. But as I became familiar with the transvestites, I got to know which of their attitudes and gestures

reflected only momentary whims and which were real personality traits. And that was when I began to separate him out from
the others, and look for him to return, lament his absences, and,
perhaps, desire him.

He was so good-looking I had trouble believing he was a
man. He had a tall, thin body and his feet created a single imaginary line as he walked, like a model on a runway. Of all the
transvestites, he was the only one who displayed any elegance in
his scanty costumes. I mean, at least he wore white panties and
shoes that weren't leopard-print or patent leather, and he didn't
dress up like he was going to Carnival. Nor did he dye his brown
hair blond or red. His brown hair, long, limp, and greasy, hung
down to his waist. Around his neck, like an actress from the
thirties, he sometimes wore a blue silk scarf. Beneath the crook
of his arm he clutched a tiny pocketbook, just big enough for
makeup, cigarettes, and the money he made. His delicate tits
drew my attention; he hadn't made them huge, round, and
pointy as the other transvestites had. His were serious, light,
and just a bit imperfect. He was generous, too: if he had lots of
customers swarming around him, he would move away from the
street for a while, lean against the bricks in the wall, and smoke
a cigarette, to give his colleagues the chance to get some work.
Then he would touch up his lipstick and go back on the street.
He loved to lean against a tree or a car and toss his head backward in one brusque movement, to show off his long hair, just
like in the shampoo commercials.

He had sad eyes and a delicate nose.

Upon closer examination, however, he had an air of mystery
that regular women – even whores – didn't have. And the sense
it gave me didn't come from something physical, because unlike

the rest of them, he didn't suffer from overly muscular calves
and brutish hands, which would have given away his masculine
origins. No, he was more ambiguous than that, each of his characteristics only held the faintest trace of maleness. In retrospect,
I realized that he reminded me of the women at Emilia's party.
That was what characterized this particular transvestite, and
that was where that confusing temptation came from: he gave
the impression of being a woman, but a homosexual woman, a
lesbian. He's like me, I said to myself (like you, Marina, my darling), he's not like the others, so it's not crazy to think that he
might be interested in me. He's a woman, I repeated to myself,
almost deliriously, he has a cock, but he's a woman, a woman
with a cock, who loves women. He's no longer a man like
Santiago, but he isn't a woman, either. And he won't make me
miss Marina.

In October, the season's first chill swept through the air and
the transvestites began covering themselves with incongruous
capes or formal jackets, which they would open wide as the cars
cruised by. On one of these nights, one of the transvestites
crossed the street and walked over to me purposefully.

This one was pretty tacky. His athletic legs wobbled as he
walked, because he didn't quite know how to balance himself on
his spike heels. He wore a black leather corset, full of rivets and
tassels, and he imitated the movements of a chorus girl, but he
didn't do a very good job of it. A bit unsteady, he planted himself next to the driver's-side window of my car. His mouth was
wide, and he had the face of an Indian. He had done a spectac-
ular job of applying his lipstick: at least a centimeter beyond the
lip line, which, given the size of his mouth, made it look as
though his lips represented a good half of his face. He wore his

hair flame-red, almost orange. And I would be loath to call his belly anything close to sexy.

'What do you want?' he yelled at me, point blank.

'Nothing,' I said.

'Yeah . . . You're always spying on us. You're not police, are you?'

There had been a raid the previous week, so the transvestites were naturally somewhat cautious. This one spoke pretty bad Italian, and from his looks he was unquestionably South American. I had become skilled at discerning these things.

'I'm not a cop,' I said. 'I'm a foreigner like you. Do you speak Spanish?'

He didn't seem to have heard me, and even when I assured him I was Uruguayan, he continued berating me in Italian, ruthlessly. Maybe he was afraid to confess that he was a foreigner because he was illegal and afraid of being deported, I thought.

All of a sudden, the other transvestite appeared – out of nowhere, it seemed. He was the only one who concerned me, the focus of my many long nights of observation. That day he was wearing new clothes, or at least clothes I hadn't seen on him before, all toast-brown and totally extravagant: a micro-miniskirt, which barely covered half his ass, a lace brassiere, and a gauzy shawl slung around his forearms. He must have been freezing to death.

'Leave her alone, Rony,' my transvestite said to his colleague. 'She's a friend of mine.'

Seeing him close up made my heart beat in a disturbing way, as if I was being caught in the middle of some covert, illicit action. Those flashes that came over me were very revealing, actually: up until then, my reason had been insisting that things were a certain way, and now my body was telling me something else.

'Why didn't you tell me before?' said Rony. And in a flash, he turned toward me and said in Spanish, 'Hello there, darling!' in an effort to show how nice he was. He told me he was Peruvian and then lit a cigarette that was *extra*: extra long, extra fine, and extra, extra smooth. He must have thought that it made him look distinguished or something. 'Not everyone that comes around here is as nice as you,' he added.

Then he went on, fawning over me more and more. If there's anything that gets on my nerves, it's flattery from people whom I couldn't care less about.

A car pulled up next to us and honked its horn.

'*¿Chercas a mí, bello?*' It was Rony, being flirtatious, butchering two languages at once as she smiled at the driver and pointed suggestively to her tits to see if he was interested.

Horrified, the person in the car indicated no with a wag of his finger, and signaled toward the other transvestite, my transvestite. But I wasn't just going to let him go now that I finally had him by my side.

'Wait!' I called out. 'I can pay you, too.'

I didn't have much money, but I was willing to spend it on him. I didn't want to just keep watching, watching from behind the windows of the car. Now I wanted to know the smell of his skin, the texture of his hair, his cock, his tits.

'What do you want from me?' he asked. 'What can you and I do together?' He emphasized the 'you,' as if to imply that I was solely responsible for our probable incompatibility.

The man in the car honked his horn again.

'I don't know,' I responded. 'I don't know yet.'

'I like your honesty,' he said, laughing, perhaps to show off his hair, as I had seen him do so many times before. 'Let's see what you can do.'

He looked at the man in the car and motioned for him to go away. Rony saw his chance, and tried to chase down the client his colleague had been so disdainful of. But the man took off right away, his tires screeching against the asphalt as he left.

'Awww . . . what a fucking asshole, man,' Rony shouted. 'Son of a bitch.'

'How long are you thinking you'd like to entertain me?' my transvestite asked me.

'All night, if you can.'

'If you can, that is. It'll cost you.'

'Money isn't a problem.'

'Hey! Don't leave me out in the cold!'

It was the Peruvian. He had come back to us; I suppose he thought I was some kind of extravagant millionaire with piles of money to throw around, and that all I would want would be to chat or confess something or cry on someone's shoulder – meaning, he smelled easy money. The other one waited to see if I accepted Rony, without understanding very well the words we exchanged in Spanish.

'Don't lose this merchandise, honey,' said the Peruvian to me, flexing and massaging his thick muscles. 'This right here is the hottest ticket in Rome.'

'Really? I didn't get that impression,' I said. 'I don't think the man in the car did, either.'

'Well, this is a tough business, you know. Yeah, man, tough,' he said, and then he uttered several onomatopoeic noises to make up for his limited vocabulary. 'Now, you know, there's tons of Russians, Polish, Albanians, Yugoslavians. There's too much competition, man.' He touched my face then; his hand was cold, unfriendly, and the physical contact sent a wave of anxiety through my body. Who he was referring to by 'man,' I had no idea. Maybe himself. 'I'm not kidding, sugarplum,' he continued, pretentiously blowing out his cigarette smoke. 'Before this place filled up with Russians, I was the most popular one on the block.'

'They must be in pretty high demand around here,' I murmured, leaning away so as to avoid his manhandling.

'Aww . . . what a silly you are.' He opened the immense surface of his mouth and let out a high, false burst of laughter. I couldn't tell whether he was insulting me or flattering me again. I didn't really care.

I was hoping the other transvestite would stop observing and intervene, to get rid of Rony. The Peruvian insisted, though, proposing a rate, and then lowering it, exhorting me to make a decision. He threw out three 'final' offers; he begged me, saying that his wife (yes, *his wife*!) was ill and desperately needed help.

'Enough!' I said. 'Leave us alone. *Via*.'

'But . . .'

'Get out of here, Rony,' the other one finally said, in Italian. 'This isn't your night.'

We watched as Rony walked away, indignant, hurling insults and incomprehensible onomatopoeias.

'Get in,' I said to the other transvestite.

He walked around the car and I opened the door. Instead of sitting next to me, he climbed over the passenger seat to the back, maybe to make a distinction between the rest of his clients and me. As he got in I smelled his perfume. Armani. The same one that Marina and I used to wear. As his nylon stockings rubbed against each other, they made a sound that reminded me of her, and it turned me on. I started up the car and got out of there, but I didn't know where to go. The transvestite didn't say a word. We drove past the pyramid, and on Via Marmorata, in front of the walls of the Protestant Cemetery, I thought of Keats. (And of you, Marina, once again.) Without realizing it, I was driving toward the apartment.

'So, where do you go in these . . . situations?' I asked.

'To some dark place where we can park. But now we're going to your house,' he said, sensing my thoughts. He lit a cigarette, and the perfume disappeared amid the smoke.

'What's your name?' I wanted to hear his voice, which I hadn't really noticed before.

'Call me Baxí,' he said, pronouncing it Portuguese style: Bashí.

'What an odd name!'

'It's not a name.'

He had a low but feminine voice, no falsetto. Through the rearview mirror I saw that he was staring at me. I felt uneasy. His eyes, as the oncoming headlights shone, were colored honey, black, honey, black. He hadn't asked me my name.

'My name is Marina,' I said, to get his attention.

(Yes, Marina, I told him I was Uruguayan, that I was Marina.)

'Pretty name,' he commented, and I appreciated that small gesture, just as much as I had disliked Rony's excessive flattery.

As we approached the river, I noticed the reflection of the moon in its waters.

'Are you a man?' I suddenly blurted out.

'In what sense?'

'I mean . . . have you had an operation?'

'Oh, that,' he said, smiling. 'No. I haven't done it. I'm still intact.'

I searched for his face in the rearview mirror again. There it was, sad and firm, sending me a message that I couldn't decipher. Every chance I got I would stare at him – I couldn't help it.

'Why did you rescue me from Rony?' I asked.

'And why were you watching us?' he countered.

'I thought you hadn't noticed me until tonight.'

'Of course I noticed you!' he exclaimed. 'You spend hours in this car, examining us like we're rare insects.'

'I only come for you,' I confessed. 'I like you.'

'I don't get it.'

I took a breath and said:

'I'm homosexual.'

(That was the first time I'd ever said it to someone other than you, Marina, the first time I'd said it out loud.)

'Well, to me it's a great compliment that a lesbian would find me attractive,' he answered in a joking voice. 'It makes me feel like a real woman. But you're not a lesbian.'

'What makes you say that?'

'If you were, you wouldn't go looking for me.' He opened the window to toss his cigarette butt, and then closed it.

'Don't other women come to you?' I hadn't seen a single one since I had begun my nighttime vigil of the transvestites.

'Very few,' he said. 'But yes, they do come.'

'How perverse!' I couldn't help saying that. I guess the women all felt as I did: alienated from it, thinking they were just indulging a whim or satisfying a curiosity, not really feeling

affected by the experience. Like someone who goes to a Third
World country on vacation, or a sociological study. But the fact
was, they were still going to a transvestite. Like me. 'Are you
cold?' I asked after a while.

'No.'

He put both hands on the back of my neck, without caressing
me. I left the Tiber and headed into the ghetto. I managed to
find parking not far from the house. I'd stayed in the same apartment that Marina and I had lived in.

It wasn't late, but it was Thursday, and the streets were practically deserted, blanketed in fog. In the silence of the night,
Baxí's high heels clicked against the immense floor of the Mattei
Palace. I gave him my coat as a cover-up, and he let it hang
from his shoulders. I stopped so I could look at him from
behind, enveloped in that fog as if in a dream. He walked with
his arms folded to protect himself from the cold, and held his
head down, as if someone was making him do something he
really didn't want to do. When we walked past the fountain, he
exclaimed affectedly:

'I just love those turtles!'

I put the key in the door. Before going inside, I said,

'Don't make any noise.'

'You mean don't talk. You're ashamed of me.'

He was right, and I was ashamed that I was ashamed. My
command had been an involuntary reaction, almost a reflex. For
a second, I thought about what Santiago would have thought if
I'd ever walked into our apartment in Madrid with a transvestite: *Look what I've brought you, darling, a toy, the kind you love to
play with* . . . But I didn't want to think about Santiago at that
moment; I wanted to forget him, for good.

We walked slowly up the stairs. I stayed behind Baxí, watching the outline of his calves, which, close up, didn't seem like his. Only then did I notice his shoes: brown high heels. He stopped at a landing and looked me in the eyes. I looked back, uncomfortable. Then he turned away and I continued up. Now he followed me, a few steps behind. Suddenly I felt his hand on my behind. Just as when he'd touched my neck in the car, it wasn't a sensual gesture, but more like a friendly slap or a supportive hand intended to block a fall. I caressed his hand and he squeezed my fingers affectionately.

'You have a lovely butt,' he murmured. 'I have several friends who would be quite jealous.'

'But not you,' I said, not whispering at all, to show him that I was trying to fight my sense of shame.

'Well, I can't complain.'

Now we were in front of Astrologo's door. I hadn't seen him in a long time, he was in Israel researching some Bible-related thing. We went into the apartment. I turned on the light.

All it took was one look – in the room where Marina and I had shared so many hours – underneath the inhuman light: jarringly unfamiliar, dressed like a whore, ready to do whatever I wanted as long as I paid. I suddenly regretted pursuing him as I had. (I knew that I could never love him, that I could never love anyone who wasn't you, Marina, my ability to love has disappeared along with you.) I was a heartbeat away from asking him to leave, from giving him a handful of bills and saying I'm sorry, I made a mistake, go back to your street, I won't bother you again. (Marina, I thought again, what am I doing? Marina . . .) I turned off the light and we were left submerged in the pale clarity of the moon, which rose up in the sky, through the clouds, and entered through the window.

There, in the shadows, things fell back into place, reflecting the state of black confusion I was in. I was transported back to that feeling of shared loneliness, in which insatiable desire was the physical manifestation of my desolation and nostalgia.

'Are you Italian?' I asked him.

I realized that I was starting to talk to him as if he were a she, as if he could be whatever I needed at any given moment. I took my coat off his shoulders.

'No,' he said, laying himself down on the sofa. 'I'm Brazilian.' He was lying; obviously, he was lying. I fully believed it at first, though. Days later he told me that he pretended to be from Brazil because Italians seemed to love that tropical 'flair,' even though he was more Roman than Julius Caesar or the Coliseum. That would be the first of a series of lies.

I remained standing, unsure of what to do. My eyes were slowly adjusting to the shadows.

'What do you want from me?' he spat out.

I saw the sad face behind his question. I was right at the point of telling him that I wanted him because he was a woman, a woman who still had the possibility of fitting inside of me when fucking. Instead, I said:

'Would you like a drink?'

Before he could answer, I went to get two glasses and a bottle of whiskey. I placed them right in front of his nose on the living room table. He was sitting with his legs crossed, and had placed his shawl and pocketbook to the side. I served the drinks, my pulse trembling.

'Ice?'

He grabbed the glass without answering me. It vibrated for a moment as it met his long red nails.

'Come sit next to me,' he murmured.

I obeyed.

'Don't be afraid,' he continued. He took a sip and then set the glass down; it was now stained with the red crescent moon of his mouth. 'You should never be afraid of the things that excite you. Never.'

I was sure she had said that line hundreds of times before, but I liked hearing it. She turned toward me, and rested her small mouth against mine. (It wasn't a kiss like the man on the plane could have given me; no, this one you might have liked yourself, Marina.) My tongue traveled through Baxí's mouth, to taste the flavor of her lipstick (your flavor), something that a man's kiss could never give me, unless it were a man like him, of course.

'Tell me what things excite you,' he said. 'I want to give you pleasure.'

'Oh! You know what, I couldn't tell you. I've never been with a woman like you.'

'Come on, Marina, tell me everything.' He began to unbutton, one by one, the buttons of my blouse.

'It excites me when you touch me . . . and when you call me Marina . . .'

'You're pretty, Marina.' He smiled as he opened up my bra. 'Don't think I don't recognize a pretty woman when I see one.' He kept on lying.

'You excite me.'

'Yes, Marina, yes.'

He leaned into me, kissing my neck, my ear, the corner of my lips, which seemed to promise a full kiss, but it never came because he would retreat each time his lips brushed mine. He unhooked my skirt, and the little bracelets on his wrist tinkled against each other. Then he took off the rest of my clothing, my panties, and my shoes as well. I was now naked before him, like a helpless animal (I was ashamed of my impoverished body, my darling, as I mentally compared it with Baxí's, I saw he had everything I didn't).

'Marina,' he said.

I stroked his long brown hair. I had become accustomed to Marina's short haircut, to my own short haircut, and it felt alive and satisfying to run my hands through that soft, endless mane. I stroked it again and again, from forehead to waist, losing myself in her as if I were falling into the cascade of a river, the cascade of time. I closed my eyes so I could inundate myself in her perfume without the interference of vision.

'Marina,' said one of us.

'Marina,' repeated the other.

She kissed my closed eyelids, and I heard her move away. I opened my eyes.

She was leaning against the arm of an easy chair, in front of me. She unhooked her bra and showed me the tits underneath. They were marvelous, with hard, protruding nipples surrounded by perfectly symmetrical circles. She stretched her legs and wrapped them around my waist. My fingertips traveled over the tight, shiny, sheer surface of her nylons, which contrasted sharply with the unyielding leather of her shoes, the point, the heel. With her left hand, Baxí rubbed her legs, up and down, as if she were searching for mine. Her right hand cupped, circled, molded the shape of her breasts; she was proud, and admired them as much as I did. Her bracelets clinked against each other, making sounds with no particular rhythm, they just rang like foolish bells.

I saw the sole of her shoe, covered in the night's filth, but I didn't care. I pressed it against my cunt, and he, she, Baxí, pressed back; she knew that I liked holding her shoed foot against my cunt, rubbing it, feeling my sex get wet. And the dust from the streets, the dog pee, the dry leaves, the cigarette butts, blended into the wetness of my cunt, and her other leg, in its sheer nylon stocking, caressed my waist, stepped over my hips, and I saw everything like that – in little fragments. Fingernails, long and red on top of my nipples, the sheen of her stockings, the miniskirt underneath which something dark and disturbing lay concealed, the disturbing suspicion that a woman as lovely as Baxí (look at her legs, darling, her breasts) possessed something more than what mere women possess (neither you nor I were anything like her). The sole pushed harder against my cunt, *she had a cock under there*, and then I couldn't resist any longer. I took her foot and yanked it away from my sex, but not to end the contact. Not at all – I wanted to intensify it, I wanted to put that heel inside my cunt, and at the same time he would say to me *You want it, Marina, and that's how I want you, aroused*, and the heel could be the cock that was unattainable for me. The miniskirt, the hand which lifted a breast and brought it to her mouth to kiss, and my hand that mimicked hers, transforming me into a reflection of her, the heel, the heel in my cunt, the sole resting against my clitoris, the black hair falling all around her shoulders. I closed my eyes (your perfume, Marina, the shape of your shoes in my fingers and your shoes in my cunt), your smell, Baxí, what do you have there under your miniskirt, promise me you'll give it to me afterward. Yes, Marina, I promise, I'll give you my woman's cock, but now cling to my heel, go to the bottom of it, come, come, that's it, Marina, that's it, and right then I wished Marina could have been there with me, so she could see how I thought of her, I always thought of her, even when I was about to climax on a transvestite's spike heel, and I came, I came in long spasms, wetting myself, spilling rivers just like she taught me, but I was doing it on him now, begging him to feel at least a tiny part of my pleasure, Baxí, your sad eyes, your dirty shoes.

'Come here,' Baxí said.

He reached for my neck and pulled me closer to him. I kissed his breasts, stomach, the light muscles of his abdomen, and I took off his miniskirt. It was easy. I barely had to pull and the zipper went flying down. And I saw a garter belt and panties, huge, destined to contain what a man like him had to hide, and nevertheless there it was, beating, a cock, a cock that rose to the surface when I took off his panties, her penis. It wasn't entirely hard – it hovered right at the upper edge of his stockings – but it wasn't soft, or fallen, either. There was hope, and I had to arouse it, kiss it.

Let me, let me try, and I started to suck it, the tip, the sides, I ran my tongue over it, and clutched his testicles in the palms of my hands to warm them up. *What would you like me to call you, Baxí? Call me Baxí, Marina. See, Baxí, you're getting hard. Slowly, gradually you're getting hard . . .* Now I was talking to her half in Spanish and half in Italian. *You like that, Baxí, you're a woman, you're a lesbian, or don't you notice how your cock is getting bigger and bigger? I'm like you, Marina, we aren't anything, not one thing or another. Suck me off more, bite into it, your name isn't Marina, I know*

*that, and my name isn't Baxí either, but I like to touch your shaved neck,
your short hair. And I like yours, Baxí, long and brown. Don't talk,
Marina, suck me off. I want you to come. I won't come in your mouth,
don't worry.*

He grabbed the pocketbook, that tiny toast-colored pocketbook, and took out a condom. *I never thought I'd be the one using
it, he smiled, I keep them for my clients to use,* and he put it on and
grabbed me by the hips, raising me up to the level of his hard
cock, and then I felt him inside of me (you never could have
done that, darling), filling me, watching me from the sofa, from
the shadow of his colored eyelids, his tweezed eyebrows, and his
cock disappeared from my line of vision. But I had it inside me,
I had the body of a woman beneath me, a woman who was penetrating me, *Do you like it, Baxí? I like you, Marina, I like your
breasts. You have such sad eyes. You do too, Marina, but you're hot,* and
we held hands and I rose up and fell back down upon him, as he
thrust his pubis against mine. *I like your perfume, Baxí. It's the same
one you're wearing, Marina, I smelled it. Let me hold you, I still haven't
done that yet,* and his hug was so different from Marina's, I felt
that in an instant, his skin, his flesh was so much harder, as hard
as his cock inside of me. *Do you feel the fountain, Baxí? I feel the
sound of the water, Marina. It's foggy outside, Baxí. I know, Marina,
but move around a little more, don't stop in the middle. No, Baxí, that's
it, think of me as a man if you want. No, you're pretty, like a woman.
You're more of a woman than I am, Baxí, you're wonderful, you're a
turn-on, your tits are perfect. Wait, Marina, turn around,* and he
separated from me a little bit, guiding me, lowering me off his
body, and then the cock came back into sight. It was real (we
knew that already, my love, but we liked it that he had a cock).
He pushed me down onto all fours, and very gently kissed my

anus while he held his sex in his hand and caressed it. His tongue traveled around the rim of the same abyss in which Santiago had twice humiliated me. He wet me, preparing me for his cock by introducing his tongue a bit, and then he wet me, licking the rim again, as it slowly opened up. *You like that, Marina. With you, Baxí, yes, put it in, I want you to come*, but he kept on kissing me, moistening me (just like you did, you were always able to inundate me with pleasure, fill me with warmth all through my insides), and then he took me by the cunt: with all five fingers he seized it, his bracelets shaking. And then he pulled me toward him and penetrated me. He put it in slowly, waiting for my anus to open up in order to receive him, without hurting me, *No, it doesn't hurt, Baxí, keep going, don't stop*, and his penis became larger and larger in my rectum, I could feel it. He liked it, *You like it, Baxí. I like you, Marina*, and then he put his whole cock in, farther than anyone had ever gone, even Santiago (or you, my love), *I'm going to come, Baxí, I love it*, and my belly began to shake, and so did my buttocks against his thighs, and I could feel the straps from his garter belt, the lace edging of his stockings, the dividing line that separated hot flesh from the sheer fabric. *Push harder against my cunt, Baxí, as I look for your legs*, and I kneel down, sitting on his cock, *I can make out the shape of your shoes, your tits, your long black hair. And you, let me kiss your neck, your short hair, Marina, I'm going to come, Marina, your cunt. Tell me, Baxí, we're the same, nothing, let's come together. Yes, Marina, now, now you can come, now. Now, Baxí.*

I don't have to tell you these things, Marina. You know about them even though you weren't there. I don't have to tell you how Baxí stayed with me until yesterday evening. I didn't love him – he was so different from you, but for a few days he was able to fill the loneliness with memories of our pleasure. He gave me an avenue through which I could find you.

I loved him – it's true, in a way I loved him. I took him to work, but then I would leave right away, I didn't stay to look at all the customers who wanted him. I was jealous, Marina, like I never was with you, my only love. Then I would pick him up, just at the break of dawn, and he slept all day long. He was tired, dirty, he had sucked so many dicks, and so many of them had given it to him up the ass. But before leaving, after I had made him dinner and he had touched up his face with your makeup and dressed in your clothes, he was stunning, and immaculate once again. And he would let me masturbate while looking at him, or he would slowly sodomize me, or fuck me with your high heels. Then he took my money, as if my apartment, our apartment, Marina, were a hotel for transvestites – a backward hotel, where guests slept and ate and got paid on top of it. I then had to drive to the street that bordered the walls, and leave him among the men who would never see his sad eyes, never become aroused by the sight of his heels. They would go with him like Santiago did, either preferring Baxí the man or Baxí the woman but never Baxí the person, the whole person. It was never the same as our first night together, because we would see each other in the daytime, and my desire withered in the sunlight. Even though we would close the shutters, close the curtains, the sun was still there. All it took was the invisible presence of the male sun, the thing that made me see how Baxí was not a woman like you or me, and I would see him as a monster, a freak, and not the siren that I saw in the moonlight, the female moon in whose light you and I had loved each other so many times, the moon of the skies and of the mirror.

I felt bad for Baxí – you know that, Marina, I don't have to tell you that, either. Every single gesture of mine could be made by you just as easily, every single feeling I have is yours as well. You would have felt bad for him, too. Baxí's parents had wanted a girl, since they already had three boys, and so they raised him as if he had been born a girl. That's what he said, anyway, but who knows if it wasn't another one of his lies. He said they let his hair grow long and combed his long brown mane, dressed him in girls' clothing, gave him a female name . . . For years they raised him like that, he said. For a long time they hid it, until one of his brothers explained it to him. And he couldn't believe it – how could he? He was a girl, and that was why his body had so few clues of a masculine past, Marina. That was the way Baxí was, he had always been a woman; even if the whole story was a lie, he still didn't want to have an operation. He didn't know who to love, and his sad eyes couldn't find himself in the mirror like ours did. There was no way he could ever find anyone exactly like him in the same way you and I were identical. I gave him everything, Marina, and he didn't despise me, but he didn't love me, either. He took my money, and made me drive him everywhere – to work, to go shopping, to his apartment, which was a microscopic little room that he shared with Rony, and we would stop in just so he could pick some things up. Then he would give me his clothes to launder, the same clothing someone had paid him to stain with their semen. I was aware of this dark power he had over me, and if he spoke to me it was only to utter a lie or to make me go out for cigarettes. But he wasn't bad, Marina, he just thought he was incapable of feeling anything, and so everything he did and said was a way of

confirming that belief. Poor thing — to him my money sym-
bolized the fact that our love would never be a true, authentic
love, a contract. It could barely even be considered a mutual
consolation, but in his way he tried to make me happy during
these few weeks. He tried to help me withstand your absence,
and he refused to get me pregnant. I wanted him to be the
father of our child, Marina, I wanted him to give Laura back to
me, a little girl with three mothers. That would be funny —
you, me, him, but identical to four others: to you, to me, to
Laura, to Clara. But he wouldn't do it. He rejected the idea,
saying, What if it were a boy? Would you raise him as my parents raised me? He was adamantly opposed to it, maybe only
because he knew he couldn't come in my cunt. He didn't want
anything more than my asshole, and anyway, winter is here
again and Rome isn't the same without you. It's hard for me to
see the beauty without your love, and I've tried, in your
Montevideo, in your Buenos Aires. They were both hostile
places, as foreign as Madrid. Both of us had gone in search of a
city, and only Rome belonged to us. It will always belong to us;
that's why I have returned. My memories and my ghosts are all
here, it's so cold, and it reminds me of the winter I lost you.
Baxí is gone now. I ran out of money, and Baxí left me last
night. I didn't have to drive him to the street by the walls or to
his tiny room. He won't come to me anymore, to sodomize me
with his cock, the same cock that disturbed me so, the same
cock that he always covered with a condom. *Why do you do
that, Baxí? I asked him one afternoon. Are you afraid? I don't want to
infect you*, he said, and I was shocked, my mouth wide open, I
cried, I understood his sad eyes, they were the indication of
imminent death, and I had to lick that wound as well, as I went

in search of you, and so I didn't eat his excrement (no, love, only yours), I did something better. I lifted his skirt, the skirt of a woman, to search out the penis of a man, of a man condemned to death. I caressed it, I sucked it, and I bit it until it bled, *You're crazy, Marina*, he said to me, but no, no, I wasn't crazy, and I didn't stop sucking it, tasting his sweet, contaminated blood, until he came in my mouth and I ate all his semen, down to the last drop, the best way to find you, Marina, wherever you are, to once again feel the warmth of your embrace and not just these memories. To rediscover the happiness of being by your side, even if it must be in death, the happiness that was invaded in Rome. When you left, it was the only way to reassemble the pieces of this broken mirror, to visit your grave without tears, here, in our city, the only way to undo this life of mine, so sterile, useless, empty without your presence, a life with no meaning, and that is something worse than death, ever since the New Year's Eve that I saw you die on top of me.

'What should we do for New Year's Eve?'

'They say that whatever way you begin the New Year, you'll do the same thing for the next two months.'

'You mean at midnight?'

'Yes, when the clock strikes twelve. Whatever you're doing right at that moment will seal your fate for the coming year.'

'We'll start the New Year together.'

'Yes, Sofía, my love.'

'We'll start the New Year fucking. We must be naked by midnight.'

'In each other's arms.'

'Like right now.'

'With my mouth on yours.'

'And your legs inside of mine, Marina.'

'And a bottle of champagne next to the bed.'

'To get drunk together.'

'And make love.'

'Like now.'

'Like now, Clara.'

Winter had come. In the streets of Rome, the rain swept through the dead leaves, formless clouds cloaked the gray sky, the days ended before you even realized they had begun, and the branches of the leafless trees were decorated with colorful lights to celebrate Christmas. Every one of the six hundred Roman churches had its manger and nativity scene, with the baby Jesus missing; he would be placed on December 25. The prettiest one was in the Piazza di Spagna, arranged on the flight of steps that lead up to the Trinità dei Monti church, right near the house of Shelley and Keats, whose name was written on water.

The months had flown by. It seemed as if only a few days had passed since I'd first met Marina at El Tórrido Trópico, a place and a name ridiculous to even think of in the middle of that Roman winter. But at the same time I felt as if I had been living with her for years, for my entire life. We bought a Christmas tree, and decorated it with ornaments, lights, and artificial snow and filled the house with roses.

On Christmas Eve we had turkey, and we cooked it in advance, so we could just pop it in the oven for a couple of hours before dinnertime. But we made the mistake of leaving it on the kitchen table while we went out for a walk (remember how we held hands inside your coat pocket?). When we returned, we found the thing all picked at. The rats had eaten it.

'Well, after all,' I said, 'the poor rats have to celebrate Christmas, too.'

So on Christmas Eve, we ended up eating pizza. We had invited Astrologo for dinner, without telling him why, to surprise him.

'My God, I come to you in surprise!' he said in his cockeyed Spanish when he entered the apartment and saw the Christmas tree, all lit up. 'Inopportune is he who led me to this place, to which I thought I was welcom'd, but it wasn't to be, and now, oh, ladies, let us take rest of our cares and trivialities, give me food and send me on my way.'

He swore that for the New Year he wouldn't let us trick him like that. He would come by to say hello, but nothing of dinners and celebrations. We wouldn't have invited him for New Year's Eve anyway, because we had other plans – to start the year fucking, for one, and Astrologo wasn't the man to initiate Marina. Declaring that Christmas Day was a day like any other, he stated that he would leave our place before midnight, but we managed to hold on to him with *Tirant lo Blanc* in Catalan, a gift which made up for the offense we had committed by inviting him to celebrate a Christian holiday. He had been after that book for a long time but hadn't been able to find it, so we had ordered it from the nuns in the bookstore in the Piazza Navona. We gave each other so many gifts that even after we'd thought we were through there seemed to be more to open. Astrologo was incredulous, he was convinced that his myopic eyes were playing tricks on him, as usual.

During the week, a sudden storm caught us in the middle of the street, soaking us to the bone. Back in the apartment, we turned on the heat, took off our dripping clothes, and gave each other the heat from our bodies, rubbing our tight skin together, standing up on the rug. We had a few sips of grappa – only a few sips, though. It was very strong, and very few have a tolerance for it. I sat on the rug, holding the glass of liquor with both hands. Marina, still standing, massaged my shoulders and neck.

Under the pressure of her fingers, I felt my muscles relax, releasing all the contractions the freezing rains had brought on. They softened, receiving more heat from Marina's hands than from the old heater. Marina squatted down behind me, with her knees wide open, and I felt her sex against my back, extended to the widest possible angle, moist, warm, pressing up against the precise line of my spine, and Marina's breasts replaced her hands on my shoulders, and they circled my neck and brushed against my cheeks, because her arms were now wrapped around me, and she clung to my ribs to support herself as she rose and fell with her sex, moister and moister against my vertebrae, and in my ear she whispered sweet words, words I couldn't repeat, words that I want to silence. Then I fell into an orgasm without realizing it; it emanated from my spine, and then spread out through all my nerve endings, to the deepest parts of my body, and my most extreme appendages were submerged in an ecstasy that covered and sheltered everything, and the glass fell from my hands and spilled onto the rug, just as Marina came on my back, right into my marrow, transmitting her orgasm to my nervous system so that it could run through all its passageways and bifurcations. But I didn't have an orgasm, or maybe my first one hadn't ended, because I continued shaking, endlessly, I was tense and calm at the same time, sensitive, my nerves like a wide-open net to fish all that was before me. I could have stayed there for hours, with the satisfying warmth of Marina on my spine, her cunt on top of me, hours, hours. But I didn't. I came, with one long moan, a whispered scream. If I had known she was about to die, I never would have moved from there, I would have remained there, immobile, for all eternity, in that interminable strain, the indefinite anticipation of something imminent, the pure and happy expectation in my lower back and nerve endings, the desire that never ends and finds satisfaction in itself, and in the satisfaction of renewed desire, like an invisible circle, like the infinite cycle of seasons and days, like true love, the movement of Marina upon my spine.

December 31 arrived. It was supposed to be a holiday for us, a love date, an intimate celebration, the signing of a new contract that would confirm all previous contracts, and instead it became the date of our separation. The last day of the year would also be my last day of happiness. Midnight found us naked, in each other's arms, but nothing turned out the way we had planned.

The weather was inclement, and the steely sky contrasted against the ochre walls. A cold, wet wind whistled through the winding streets of our neighborhood. That morning, we woke up sad, inexplicably sad. The night before, I had dreamed that I had entered a cathedral that I had never seen but knew intimately. I didn't want to go inside, but they made me, they forced me all the way inside, and I passed through two rows of identical columns. It was very dark, but I could see everything. All of a sudden, one side of the cathedral disappeared, taking with it one row of columns. I escaped through the opening created by that strange disappearance – although I really saw myself escape from a distance, because I remained in the center of the church, thinking, My God, I have to get out of here, the roof is going to fall on me. And as I thought this thought, all sorts of things came crashing down around me: ceiling beams, images of saints, bricks. And I ran away but at the same time was buried underneath the ruins of that cathedral. At that moment I opened my eyes. It was a few minutes before eight in the morning and the doorbell was ringing.

I wrapped myself in a bathrobe and went to answer it, slowly. They were Jehovah's Witnesses, a man and a woman. I couldn't make them out very clearly, because I was still half-sleeping. They wanted to convert me to their faith, they said, in the face of an inexorable apocalypse. They also wanted to sell me some literature. I had a tough time getting away from them, because for every answer I gave, they found some way to keep talking to me.

I made some coffee, trying not to make any noise so as not to awaken Marina, and I drank it on the sofa, next to the closed window. I looked over at the portrait Manolo had given me, the one he had created using the method of Orbaneja, the painter from Ubeda. I missed him. How is he doing? I wondered. I looked at the clock: 8:10. He wouldn't be asleep yet, but I could never figure out the bizarre hours he kept. I grabbed the telephone. Zero-zero-three-four-one . . . It was my first contact with Spain, with Madrid, since June 25. Six months, I thought; it's been six months. I heard how Manolo, as always, picked up without saying anything, suspicious of whoever it was calling him.

'Manolo!' I shouted.

'Manolo who?' he said. He was awake; no doubt he'd just finished painting and was eating his dinner-breakfast before going to sleep.

'Manolo, you are incorrigible!'

'Sofía, it's so nice to hear your voice!' he exclaimed, no longer suspicious. He had recognized my voice. 'Where are you?'

'Well . . . not in Madrid.'

'Yes, yes, it's better you don't tell me. I'd rather not know.' His voice clouded over. 'Listen, you didn't hear it from me, but be careful.'

'Of what?' I asked.

'What do you think? Santiago. He's heard some strange things about you, and I don't know how he'd react if he were to see you. Try and avoid him. The last time I saw him he was furious, out of his mind. He really seemed insane.'

'Okay,' I said. I wanted to change the subject. 'Tell me about you.'

'Well, the truth is, my life is the same as usual. Nothing new. Painting, still, when I can. Listen, that guy that was following you around is a real pain in the ass, much worse than that reporter ever was. He comes around every day just to be a pest. Says you sent him to me.'

'I haven't sent anyone to you! Never! Who are you talking about?'

'Carranza.'

Carranza; that son of a bitch was still hovering around my life like a vulture. Thank God I was far away from Madrid. I said good-bye to Manolo. We wished each other a happy New

Year, and I reminded myself to try and get him an exhibition at
the Rioja Pou gallery. It was nice to hear his voice, to know that
painting was still the most important thing for him, even
though the other news he gave me was alarming.

I woke Marina up with breakfast in bed. Usually she was the
one to do this, but just this once I had woken up earlier. We
stayed there until about noon, reading shoulder to shoulder,
playing footsie under the sheets.

'What are you reading?' I asked her.

'One of your books. *The Garden of Caresses*.'

'Do you like it?'

'It makes me sad. Listen to how this poem starts: "*A woman's
love is like the shadow of a palm tree in the sand*."'

'Very pretty,' I said. 'Read the rest to me.'

'"*In the twilight of your grave, think of the lonely garden I once led
you to*."'

'How awful! What's next?'

'"*I remember the peaceful morning when you were blown over from
my love, like a palm tree in the wind. But the gale covers over with sand
the branch it tore off . . . Oh, my lovely palm tree, that the sand of the
cemetery blows light over your grave*."'

'You're right, it's very sad, it's—'

Marina didn't let me finish; instead she threw the book
aside, grabbed me, and filled my mouth with her tongue.

In the afternoon we cooked a chicken for our New Year's
Eve dinner. We wanted to eat early and then run to bed to ring
the New Year in there. Marina called her mother and her
brothers, and Emilia too, but there was no answer at her
friend's house.

By eight o'clock we were all dressed and made up, ready for

our big night. I was taking some potatoes off the stove when the doorbell rang again, for the second time that day.

'Can you get it?' I called out to Marina from the kitchen. 'It must be Astrologo!'

I heard the door open, and then insults, several blows, and a howl of pain from Marina's mouth. I turned off the flame and ran over to see what had happened. Santiago had found us.

Epilogue

*S*everal clues enabled him to locate us. He explained this to us little by little, after closing the door behind him, to keep us on edge. His sullen voice sounded as if it had come from the bowels of time. First: he discovered that I had gone away on that cursed Thursday that was supposed to have been our last date, which I had scheduled knowing I would no longer be in Madrid. He knew it the second he walked into the apartment: my dresses, some books, and, of course, the suitcases were all missing.

The second clue came from the Portuguese mechanic. Once again, his dream of going to Brazil had been thwarted, and Santiago found out through him that my trip was intended to be a long one.

Then there was Carranza. He found him hovering around the doorway of our apartment building. At that time, Santiago still thought that I was having an affair with him, and threw him a punch that would've killed a bull. But Carranza had been spying on us, and from the ground, as best he could, managed to convince Santiago that if in fact I had escaped, I had done so with a woman. Not with a man – much less with him. Santiago lost control when he heard that.

And the confirmation came from Francisca. As it turned out, on those summer days when Marina and I were running around Italy, Santiago visited every last person I knew in search of information as to my whereabouts. Manolo, the gallery owner, Francisca, even Pulga – they all had to suffer his interrogation. Nobody knew anything, except Francisca, who at first

pretended not to have seen me in years, but later on contra-
dicted herself, at which point Santiago tortured her – literally –
until she confessed.

Then there was the question of credit cards. The expenses
were drawn from our joint account at the bank, which allowed
him to reconstruct the various stages of our trip through Italy,
and in the end, he naturally saw that our money was always and
only being spent in Rome.

And then there were the traffic tickets. That tied up any
loose ends. I never thought that the Italian bureaucracy would
be efficient enough to send tickets all the way to Spain. But
they did, and on each ticket the precise day, time, and location
of the infraction was recorded. On a map of the city, Santiago
marked off the area with the highest frequency of tickets, and
was able to create a relatively small radius from which he could
begin his search: our neighborhood, our ghetto.

He arrived in Rome around the middle of December. For
days, he walked the streets of our neighborhood, until one night
he saw the car. Systematically, he went through all the buildings
in the area, reading the names by the intercom. On December
31, at seven, he finally found my last name, alongside another
which he had never seen before. That was all he needed. That
name, a Spanish name in the middle of all those Italian last
names, could only be mine.

He hid stealthily in the doorway until someone entered the
building, and here he was now, ready to do what he wanted.

He couldn't believe the spectacle before his eyes. He had
figured I would be with another woman, and instead he found
me divided in two. He thought he would find two women and
instead he found two Sofias. This, the only thing he didn't

already know, enraged him even more. Taken aback by the shock of seeing me appear in the doorway to the kitchen, he landed a punch in my mouth that threw me over the table. Marina tried to react but he knocked her down, lashing out at her with a violent, backhand slap.

'Which one of you is Sofía?' he screamed, furious. 'Which one?'

'Leave us alone!' I begged, trying to get up. 'What have we done to you?'

He was very thin, all skin and bones. But he hadn't lost his strength.

'Slut!' he howled, slamming me to the floor with a sharp blow. 'I don't know who you are but you're a whore!' and he kept after us, screaming, berating, telling us how he had found us, abusing us, kicking us with every last ounce of his hatred.

I realized that this story was repeating itself: first he had taken Laura away from me, and now he wanted to take from me the thing I loved most, my reflection, Marina, you. I had never been hit as much as I was that night. I passed out, and when I woke up, I was in bed. I heard Santiago saying:

'I never should have trusted you, whore!'

But I couldn't see him. My eyes were swollen shut from the beating I had received. On top of my body, I felt a uniform weight that covered me entirely. It was Marina. He had tied us to the bed, wrist to wrist, ankle to ankle, with our legs and arms loose.

He had two women all to himself now, Marina and me, tied to each other, face-to-face, naked, at his service. How could he not take advantage of the opportunity?

'Clara,' Marina whispered, to comfort me.

'So you're Sofía, huh?' Santiago asked.

'No!' I said. 'I'm Sofía!'

'I'm Sofía!' Marina shouted, but her South American pronunciation was enough to belie her affirmation.

'All right, now I know who's who,' Santiago interrupted with a crooked smile. 'But I don't care. What I'm about to do, I'm going to do to the both of you.'

I tried to beg for help, thinking that maybe one of the neighbors would hear us and call the police, but my voice came out suffocated, weak, useless. Santiago shut me up with a slap. Then Marina began shouting: she screamed for the Astrologer as if it were a secret key, a friendly image in which we could seek refuge.

'Silence!' Santiago bellowed. He grabbed her by the hair and threw her backward.

Holding Marina up by a handful of her hair, he tore savagely into her face with his free hand. Her head flew to the side and fell on my shoulder. Santiago stood there with a tuft of hair in his hand. And he continued to beat us.

Then he crossed the room, in big, wide strides, and I lost sight of him.

We didn't know what would happen.

Marina and I kissed each other to prove that nothing could separate us. But he came back and gagged us; he didn't like us doing that.

Then he went from my vagina to Marina's anus, and from my anus to Marina's vagina, which was receiving a man's penis for the first time.

He enjoyed the final spasms of his orgasm, extinguishing it ever so slowly, and from the humid smile sitting on his satisfied mouth he hurtled an insult at us and cursed us.

He spit on Marina's back and lifted her up. He looked around, dazed and unsure of what to do. He fell down in a corner of the room and rested his forehead against his naked knees. He remained there for a long while. My teeth were clenched together, and saliva was building up in my throat, unable to slide down to my stomach. Marina's tears hesitated a moment on her lashes and finally fell onto my eyes, onto my own tears. I think he was crying, too, over in his corner, but his weakness didn't last very long.

He got up and began to masturbate while staring at our bruised bodies. He had a very weak erection, and he tried to fuck us again but couldn't. I pleaded silently for him to leave us, praying that his male ego wouldn't be wounded by this failure. But my prayers went unheard.

'I told you that I was capable of doing anything,' he said to me, 'to keep you from being with anyone but me.'

With that, he got up to leave the room. I thought he was going to continue drinking. I tried to scream again, but my voice died in the gag before I could make a sound. I heard the rats scratching behind the wall, the drop of blood that fell onto the sheet, Marina's breathing. He came back. He hadn't gone for alcohol. He was chewing on a piece of chicken, which he held in his left hand. And in his right hand he held a kitchen knife.

'How do you turn each other on?' he asked. 'What do you put in your cunts?'

He slid the knife over our skin, slowly, making sure not to cut us with the blade, as he continued chewing on the chicken. The same path he had drawn with his hand he now traveled down with the knife: a long sweep, slow and ecstatic, down the length of Marina's back. Then her buttocks, the outside of her thighs, the backs of her knees, her calves. Then he turned around and made his way back up, touching the two of us at the same time, calves, knees, he kept going, he wasn't going to stop now, the insides of our thighs, and then, of course, our vaginas, mine and Marina's, just as he finished eating.

'Let's see how you like this.'

At first all I felt was the cold. Then I recognized the contours of the knife, the blade that he inserted into my vagina. I didn't realize he was slicing me. It felt like a very light brush, a scratch, a chilly caress. But he didn't stick it all the way in me. He extracted it from my vagina and then put it in Marina's, slowly. Marina, whom I could never have hurt – her fragile skin, her sweet flesh were being reviled with blood and pain. It lasted a long time, although he sped things up afterward. He pulled the knife from Marina's anus and then put it back inside of me, and then in Marina, and then me. Each time he did it just a little bit faster, and it seemed as if the cold steel was what aroused him now, and he was just about ready to come on Marina's blood, on me. From outside, we could hear the hilarity of the celebration: it was midnight. I screamed then, shrieked like an animal that came from behind the gag, from behind my mouth and my vocal cords, from behind my lungs, from the deepest part of me, from my love in agony.

When he heard my screams, he became more enraged than ever.

'Shut your mouth! Shut your mouth already!'

He rammed the knife as far up the vagina as it would go. But it wasn't my vagina, my God, no, no, it wasn't mine, it was Marina's. He shoved it in up to the handle, twisted it from side to side, and pulled it out, full of blood, of life, of Marina's life that must have left her through her legs. And I screamed, and screamed more, and even though he could have stabbed me to death I kept on screaming. He didn't know how to shut me up. He started to slice Marina's back, trying to cut through her to get to me. I saw the last glimmer in his eyes, I felt in my chest how his heart stopped. In my hands I felt how his fingers couldn't reach me any longer, how the knife didn't do anything more than scrape me with its tip. Sadly, it didn't reach any farther than Marina, Marina, who, already dead, had protected me from Santiago, saving my life with her death. She received the stabs, innumerable times as they sliced through her desecrated skin, ferocious, and no more would you ever have pleasure in my arms, Marina. It would be impossible to turn the clock back now, it was irreversible, they were smashing the mirror of your skin, *You left me!* I screamed, Marina, *Why couldn't I have died with you?* I screamed, the stabs, Marina.

Someone pushed the door open then. The sound of men running through the house, finally finding Santiago. They tied him up, wrenched the knife from his hands, and immobilized him.

I looked at the bloody blade, now in the hands of the police. Was that where Marina's soul had gone? I looked in her eyes; they hadn't closed entirely, but they didn't look at me any longer. When they took my gag off, I kissed her face, her wounds, I drank her tears, her dead lips, her blood, and in the flow of her blood I saw the inexorable retreat of my reflection, my perfect twin, me myself, Narcissus in that red-colored river of death that has forever left its mark on these hands, that blood which has been replaced with someone else's, the blood I drank from Baxi's penis to condemn myself, to relieve me of this body that prevents me from embracing Marina.

They took me to Tiberius. And I spent the first few days of
the New Year, without you, in those antiseptic hospital rooms.
Astrologo came to visit me, carrying a bouquet of flowers. He
had been the one who called the police. He had come upstairs to
say hello, and on the other side of the door he heard strange
noises, slaps, a man's voice, and then, the policemen hadn't
known what to do until my screams told them to break in. He
told me that Santiago was in jail now, and that it would be years
and years before they let him out. I wanted to believe him.

The Astrologer came to visit me several times while I was in
the hospital, and those visits seemed to me to be a sign of
unconditional friendship. I knew how much he hated to leave
the building, to lose precious research time. Thanks to him I
managed to get Marina buried in the Protestant Cemetery – far
from Keats's grave, but at least within the same walls. That's
where I can find your grave, upon which I can cry, Marina.
Next to it will be my own, because I want to die in Rome. I have
Baxi's sickness in my veins now and soon I will leave in search of
you, so we can be together again, and I will love you in your
grave as I loved you before in your bed, as only dead people can
love each other. It will be a love without time, without screams,
without end, and without blood. It will be the love we always
wanted but could barely see, barely even touch with the tips of
our loving fingers, and we will be worthy of that love. We will
see each other again, face-to-face, just like the night they killed
you. I hope that the earth is light atop your open eyes, Marina.

After a few weeks, I returned to the apartment in the ghetto,
and at first I couldn't bear to see the scene of our love without
our love anymore. So afterward, once I was completely recovered, without thinking twice, I decided to travel to Montevideo,

the city where a part of me was born. And on that KLM plane, I knew that the exercise was useless. Then I went to Buenos Aires, and saw the tree-lined streets. I saw the Paradises but I didn't see the flowers – the rains had already done away with them and their perfume. For a while I felt the temptation to go and see Marina's mother, to see if it was true that her husband was also my mother's husband, that Marina's father was my father. But in the end I gave up the idea, just because it was so absurd, and I returned to the apartment in the ghetto, where at least I had some tangible memories of Marina.

Back in Rome, I got Rioja Pou to organize an exhibition of Manolo's artwork; it will go up at the end of the year. If Manolo comes to visit, I don't know where I'll be able to keep him.

I don't have any more money. My bank account is empty, and they took away my credit card. It's been months since I've paid the rent. And today, the owner of the building came by with court officers to evict me. Thank God they didn't find Baxí. If they had seen him, they wouldn't have taken such pity on me. They let me stay a few more days, and later I'll have to go back for a few things – the yellow hat that Emilia gave us at El Tórrido Trópico, the portrait Manolo had given me, those Christmas gifts, like relics from a lost civilization.

Maybe I won't come back to see Astrohyulogo. I'd like to give him our books. He's the only person who knows which one of us died and which one survived. Nobody else does, and I want to keep it that way. When I went to South America, I used Marina's passport and nobody realized it. I tried to speak the way she spoke. I write in this uncertain language, which isn't Spanish, isn't the tongue of the Río de la Plata, or Italian, although it has a bit of all of them, because it's Clara's language.

I only write for her; it's possible that she hears me, wherever she is, and knows that I haven't forgotten anything. My memory reconstructs every moment of our love as a way of protecting myself from forgetting, which is like death. I remember you, Marina. I remember you as you are now, not as you were when you died, because all I have to do is walk the streets and catch my reflection in a shop window and there I see you, and I see the signs of illness and desolation in your eyes.

Our love was like a dream, a mirrored game, a splendor among shadows that no longer exists.

That is why nobody knows who I am.

That was the pact we made in Naples. 'If one of us dies, the other one will have to be Sofía and Marina.' I would rather be Clara, not me, if I can be anyone at all. Marina whispers in my ear the words that I don't have. I don't know which of us writes this page. Nobody could ever know that I am Sofía, or Marina pretending to be Sofía, or Sofía pretending to be Marina, and on until infinity, just like the mirrors that faced each other in our hotel room in Siena, like the identical faces of Narcissus in the reflection of his desire.

And on our graves, the epitaph will contain one name only, the same one, which will disappear when you and I finally reunite, Marina, because all names are writ in water, in the current that passes by, never to return.

THE TASTE OF A MAN

Slavenka Drakulić

One autumn in New York, Tereza, a young Polish poet studying literature, and José, a Brazilian anthropologist researching a new book, meet, fall in love and move into a tiny apartment together.

As Tereza recounts the extraordinary substance of their lives together, there emerges the mesmerizingly explicit portrait of a relationship conducted at the extreme edge of sensuality, defying conventional definition. Breathtakingly erotic, intensely physical, profoundly intelligent, *The Taste of a Man* pursues the path traced by a love based on pure appetite with shameless and unflinching candour, to its ecstatic, terrible conclusion.

'A disturbingly insightful novel of love gone wrong . . .
gruesome and highly accomplished'
Time Out

'Ghastly in its purist sense;
read it in the kitchen if you dare'
Daily Telegraph

'Celebratory in tone, *The Taste of a Man* is also a heartfelt, if unrepentant confession . . . Drakulić does not disappoint'
New Statesman

Abacus
0 349 10866 8

HEAT

Sally Emerson

All your loves come back in the end, in dreams or reality. When you look at each other, you see the old selves. Choose lovers carefully, because you'll have them for ever . . .

'A story of obsession and love
and the difference between the two . . . Emerson writes
superbly about the dark side of love'
Sunday Times

'In this tense, sensuous novel, Emerson leads her characters
away from everything safe and dependable'
Helen Dunmore, *The Times*

'Sally Emerson writes like a dangerous angel'
Douglas Adams

'Quivering with subtle erotic tension and sparkling
observatoir . . . hypnotically menacing, emotional thriller'
Celia Brayfield, *Mail on Sunday*

'It takes courage and nerve to put passion at the centre of a
novel, and to take it and its companion, obsession, as seriously as
Emily Brontë did. Compelling.'
Allan Massie, *Scotsman*

Abacus
0 349 11342 4

Now you can order superb titles directly from Abacus

☐ The Taste of a Man   Slavenka Drakulić   £6.99
☐ Heat   Sally Emerson   £7.99

─────────── ⬭ABACUS⬭ ───────────

Please allow for postage and packing: Free UK delivery.
Europe: add 25% of retail price; Rest of World: 45% of retail price.

To order any of the above or any other Abacus titles, please call our
credit card orderline or fill in this coupon and send/fax it to:

Abacus, PO Box 121, Kettering, Northants NN14 4ZQ.
Fax 01832 733 076   Telephone 01832 737527

☐ I enclose a UK bank cheque made payable to Abacus for £ . . . .
☐ Please charge £ . . . . . . to my Access, Visa, Delta, Switch Card No.

Expiry Date ☐☐☐☐   Switch Issue No. ☐☐

NAME (Block letters please) . . . .
ADDRESS . . . .
. . . .
. . . .
Postcode . . . . Telephone . . . .
Signature . . . .

Please allow 28 days for delivery within the UK. Offer subject to price and availability.

Please do not send any further mailings from companies carefully selected by Abacus ☐